COBRA FLIGHT

A HIGH ARCTIC THRILLER

RICK GRANT

CONTENTS

AUTHOR'S NOTE

The Arctic is a land of strange tales, legends, and mysteries. Parts of *Cobra Flight* draw on these strange events to form the background of the action.

It is odd to think that such a seemingly barren waste as the High Arctic could be home to so many curious tales, but let me assure you that one could compile an Arctic version of Grimm's Fairy Tales quite easily in the Circumpolar Arctic.

ISBN: 978-0-9939317-10

THE SNOW TRENCH

I crawled into my snow shelter and eased the flat roof slabs over the top. I couldn't help feeling that I was sealing myself into a coffin.

Tommy slashed the trench shelter out of the wind-hardened beach snow while I scrounged around the burned tents looking for food and extra clothing.

There wasn't much left.

The sun went. The air turned a damp cold that cut through the parka I'd pulled from a hut. I had no idea what I was going to do once I reached Jenness Island. I could hardly knock at the front door and ask myself in. I also didn't care for the idea at all of going back. That made me shiver even more violently.

I fell asleep while running vague plans and sharper fears through my mind.

Those fears turned to screaming terror when the hell-demons stabbed through the earth to rip me from my coffin. For long, horrifying moments as my mind changed from sleep to consciousness I was gripped by a demon fear born of old legends from the middle ages.

The terror moved back slightly from the edge of insanity when I recognized that it was Teller who had smashed through the roof slabs. He hauled me out of the trench by my throat.

* * *

MUCH EARLIER

he starboard engine cut out with a sharp shuddering jerk. I'd been waiting for it, but its suddenness still caught me by surprise. I snapped forward in the shoulder harness. My left foot rode the rudder pedals as I reached down and flipped the tank selector.

I gave a thought to the six passengers, three oilmen off an Arctic Islands Ltd oil rig at Melville Island and the three territorial government types finishing a swing through the Central Arctic communities. I half heartedly debated whether I should have donned the air of a professional pilot for a moment and warned them.

I let the idea pass with the thought that they would appreciate having a climax to their flight after 3.3 hours in a tired Dakota making its way over the Arctic Ocean to Resolute.

It's good practice in the Arctic to run the tanks dry before switching. This far north the type of aviation gasoline a Dakota needs is hard to come by as no modern aircraft need it. The whole thing about deliberately allowing an engine to start running out of fuel is a procedure argued about in the south, but not by me.

The airport beacon was in sight ten miles ahead through the near dark of the early winter afternoon. The sun wouldn't be clearing the horizon for about another three weeks, but already there was a heated gold look to the horizon where the sun was skimming just under the Arctic Circle.

The Resolute airport sits on Cornwallis Island at the center of those hundreds of islands that go to make up the Canadian Arctic Archipelago.

As an airport, it is only fair. There's just one runway north and south, and it's in a near perpetual crosswind. It's long enough, however, to handle a B-52 bomber loaded for war over Siberia. That I knew because I had seen them here at Resolute on military exercises, snuffling along that two-mile strip of ice caked concrete, rolling faster and faster without the least sign that they were capable of leaving the ground. The slow acceleration and seeming reluctance to leave the ground always made me think they would end by plowing through the pressure ice ridges in the bay. Then, like Augustine leaping from the ballet stage to hang for an impossible instant, they float up into the ice fog and head home to Charleston and grapefruit, or perhaps off over the pole to listen to Russian generals talking on mobile phones to their mistresses. Behind on the ground the rolling crack of their eight engines would shake the rolled aluminum sides of the hangars and cargo sheds.

I wasn't thinking of bombers that night. The Trans Northern Airlines 737 was up on its thrice weekly sched. A Hercules from some California outfit landed right after the airliner in a great show of radio procedure that confused Andre, the duty radio operator at the tower. Andre's english is not good. He is much more comfortable with the cryptic slang of the northern pilot than the polished and formal routine airline pilots used.

There was something familiar about the Hercules pilot's voice. I almost had it, but just then my right engine picked up and ran smoothly. I went to to the mixture controls for both and made slight adjustments as the engines warmed and smoothed out.

I ran my right hand, then my left hand around the cockpit in the pre-landing check. There is a printed checklist for this, but it was in the copilot's pouch at the far right of the cockpit, and since I wasn't flying with a copilot there was no one to either pass it to me or read it. I wasn't about to unstrap and lean across for it. I relied on my hours in DC-3 Dakotas for the memory of what should be where and how. It wasn't out of any concern for the safety of the aircraft that I spent time doing it correctly. I just didn't want to have to spend the next forty-eight hours filling out accident/incident forms then explaining over a satellite telephone link to the Air Safety Office in Edmonton why I had landed wheels up, or with the brakes full on, or some other screw-up and closed the airport while the tractors pulled the bird off her nose. I don't worry about accidents more severe than that because the forms for major foul-ups are filled out by the people who are alive. Anything more serious wouldn't leave me around to fill out the forms. I'd be busy getting flight training on feather wings instead.

The needles weren't where they would have been in 1939 when the plane rolled out of the Douglas plant. Then again, my eyesight, blood pressure, reflexes and nerves weren't up to specifications either. Jack Standish and Douglas DC-3 serial number whatever, were in the same sort of state; functional, safe, but no longer frontline material.

The flaps went down to 15 degrees with the power back and the wheels dragging through the light ice fog. I lined up nicely on the lights at the end of the runway.

Then I saw the landing lights of the Erebus Airways sched from Grise Fiord.

I shouldn't have been able to see them at all, but he was at my altitude, with the same amount of dirt hanging out on final, and we were coming in on the same airstrip from different ends.

We'd hit the numbers at opposite ends of the runway at the same time and roll to a stop with about a mile of strip between us. That kind of stuff even I don't approve and of course the paper shufflers in Ottawa would have strokes if they ever heard about it. If anything went wrong, and either of us had to make a go-around, we'd be chancing a midair collision.

I picked up the microphone and went direct to the aircraft straight ahead of me. "Uh, Erebus Three on final. I flipped a coin and it says I land first."

"Ack, Uranus Air. You buy."

I could tell from the steepness of the turn he threw it into that his aircraft had little or no load on board.

Clearly, the co-operative at Grise Fiord still didn't have its spring collection of Inuit stone carvings ready for the Toronto and New York shows. Nor could he have the usual, two kids, aging grandmother, and sick infant on board. Medical evacuations were about the only ready business Erebus got out of the settlement and there didn't seem to be one tonight otherwise he wouldn't have turned off final.

By the time he finished his turn, dirtied up the plane again with flaps, wheels and cowl vents, I'd be making the first runway turnoff for the collection of ex-USAF warehouses that Uranus Air used as an office and laughably called a terminal.

Resolute is a good airstrip for bombers because that's what it was built for. When the cold war settled in during the early fifties a fleet of U-S ships plowed their way west into the Northwest Passage on the hunt for a little spot for a northern airbase. They pushed as far as Cornwallis Island before the freeze-up started and at Resolute Bay they stopped. The valley they anchored off wasn't what the planners wanted but waiting for the next summer was an intolerable idea while the Soviet Union supposedly built its fleet of pole spanning bombers. So they unloaded and built the strip. It turned out that a more unsuitable location for an air force base couldn't have been chosen by any size army of planners. The runway could go only one way, right across the prevailing wind. The weather is almost always bad, and it's hard to resupply by ship during summer.

I eased back on the wheel column and felt for the float. Out of the sides of my eyes I watched the horizon and waited for the sudden enveloping feeling that lets a pilot know the ground is close. One of the hardest things to teach a new pilot is how to feel for the ground, and when to sense that the plane wants to stop flying. It's a skill that takes some people a long time to to pick up but it sticks once learned. There are other ways to land airplanes including simply driving them down until the wheels slam to the ground and holding them there with brute muscle power to the flight controls and then reducing power, but there's no art to that.

A good landing should be, float, float, float, ground rush, control column back into the chest, shallow breaths, then crump, thump, rumble.

Well, mine was more like, crump, thrump, thump, rattle. It didn't matter. The flight was over. I wouldn't remember it any more than I could remember more than a handful of thousands of others I'd put in.

The six men in the back might, depending on how nervous they were. The territorial government officials might shy away from Uranus Air the next time, but the oil rig contract was written in stone. The poor buggers, stuck on those rigs for fifteen days straight, 12 hours on and 12 off, would count themselves going first-class even if the only way out to the South was to be towed out on a hang glider. They hated the rigs and hated every moment away from the bars of Edmonton, Winnipeg and Montreal.

I taxied up to the office. For once, the lights were on. That meant the place was warm. Instead of arriving from the cold and dark, into the cold and dark, we could head straight for the instant coffee and synthetic milk substitute in foam cups. Billy would hump the bags and boxes from the Dakota. Too often these flights seemed to end with me swearing at a padlocked door in a 26 knot wind bent on moving all of the snow out of Siberia into the Eastern Arctic while the passengers grumbled and moaned until I gave up and started them shuffling off across the two hundred yards of concrete to the main airlines terminal. But this time the Ford extended pickup truck was there with its motor running to take the six to the Arctic Hotel and its bar where they could buy me a beer and lie about the glorious flight they'd had.

I was looking forward more to a few scotch than just one beer, but that would have to come after the paperwork and the plane had been looked after. I swear I spend more of my life behind a fuel loading report form than behind the controls.

Sometimes, I thought about what it would be like to fly for one of the major airlines, but I never thought for long. Part of that came from serious doubts that an airline would even look at my resume. And, I knew, just knew that I would only last half a day in that hypercontrolled world before wishing I could barrel roll a 767 to prove I was alive.

Instead of life on a gigantic salary and the time to spend it in, I pass my life getting up at hours that a Roman Catholic priest, saying three early morning masses, would shudder at. I gnash and freeze my hands preflighting planes built when passenger ships were the only serious method of getting across oceans. I drive aircraft across terrain that looks like the Moon, if only the Moon had snow, and through weather that puts permanent fear lines across the mind. All of it for a weekly sum that a bus driver would go out on strike over.

I had just scrambled up the wing to make sure that Billy had locked down the wing root caps on the fuel tanks when the California Hercules fired up with a scream of turbines. The pilots were going through the start faster than what I remembered was normal for a C-130, but then the crew might have done some preliminary checking before turning the props to save going through the much longer individual start checks. Still, whoever was driving started to roll before the flaps had been cycled and did no brake check. A quick press on the brakes right after starting to taxi is a universal check common to all aircraft. It was such a basic omission that I tightened my jaw in surprise. Whether the manufacturer's procedure or not, it always makes sense to test those things that can be tested before moving an inch away from ground mechanics in case they have to haul out their screwdrivers. Ground crew are notorious for slipping away to unknown realms the minute a plane starts to move.

CAL-AIR. A rather obvious and uninspired name for an outfit, I thought. That was wistfulness, just me pining for the merry old days of competent co-pilots, watchful flight engineers, a cockpit of gauges and instrument lights that worked, and the salary that goes with getting a couple of dozen tons of load hauler into the air and back down safely while turning a tidy profit for the shareholders.

He was loaded too, I could tell from the way the high cocked tail swayed as the Hercules turned onto the runway. The 130 waddled, its belly almost scraping through the light drifts left by the clearing crews. Even in the intense cold the heat exhaust from the turbines made the blue taxi-lights waver as if they were underwater. The stink of burned jet fuel drifted to me.

I would have stayed to watch the takeoff although I was turning into solid frozen brass as I perched on the top curve of the wing. Spilled aviation fuel soaked into my jeans.

Above the rising roar of turbines and propellers I heard Billy.

"Jack...sereeee.. you in off....sssrreee."

I slid down to the trailing edge through small rivers of spilled fuel and landed flatfooted on the ice and snowpack with a jar that hurt my feet as the Herc went to full throttle. The noise hurt my ears even though they were deadened by the hours in the Dakota.

That morning I had asked Stanley for two days leave so I

could have a bit of a weekend in Montreal and I was expecting the go-ahead. The Trans Northern 737 was still on the ramp readying for the run back to Edmonton. If I left on it I would have an even longer weekend there instead of in Montreal. The First Air flight wasn't due for six hours.

I ran to the office and went through the double doors without knocking the snow from my boots. The spilled gasoline that I had picked up on my jeans in sliding down the wing was burning my skin. There's nothing colder than gasoline in the Arctic because it doesn't freeze, and burns the skin as it leaches out the heat. Water freezes and then doesn't conduct very much heat, unlike avgas that just goes on sucking heat from skin until well below the freezing point.

The musty smell of dust and old paper was fresh in the air. The furnace hadn't been on long. The room seemed full of sleeping bags rolled and stuffed into nylon carrying cases, cardboard boxes taped on all edges with shiny green plastic tape, aluminum equipment boxes, and people. The place was full of men and women. The only comfortable place for me was behind the counter with Stanley.

I squeezed past him thinking I wasn't going to get that Trans Northern flight. I had a feeling that I was going flying again and probably it would be somewhere that I would hate getting to, and love leaving.

There's no security in bush flying; no severance pay, and no union. There are so many pilots coming out of the training schools, all so eager for flight time so they can meet the entrance requirements for the airlines, that they work for next to nothing. It means that the least sign of unwillingness to work will find you out of work and someone younger and cheaper taking the flight. Unless a pilot is grounded by a doctor, there's never an excuse good enough to turn down a flight and still be sure the job will remain.

Here in the High Arctic, at the end of the road as far as flying jobs go, the pressure is always sitting there. It is always reminding me that another DC-3, Twin Otter, or whatever driver, is only as far away as the next scheduled airline flight.

Stanley is a tough nasty base manager. He only comes up to my shoulder but he has so much bulk, not fat, but bulk, that he seems bigger than me. His face is in a set scowl all of the time as if the whole world operates just to mess up his private life. He flies infrequently and when he does he treats the aircraft with a lack of grace and care that admits no art to his flying. He's a technical pilot, and while he may never get killed, there will never be any hangar stories told about his flying.

He laid his yellow and white striped ballpoint down on the loading manifest clipboard quickly with enough care that it sat in the middle, lined up with the broad black line dividing the aircraft entries from the cargo and passenger sections. It snapped hard against the paper as he pressed down in the middle with his forefinger and held the end of the pen off slightly with his ring finger and thumb. It is a trick he uses whenever he wants to give orders. The first time I heard him do it I thought the pen had broken.

"Jack. Willy wasn't on the sched. I've booked charter." He nodded to take in the room. Willy was supposed to have been my relief pilot.

I didn't say anything. I shook my ski mitts off and slapped them together against my right thigh while I glanced around. More government men, or perhaps executives, touring the rigs. But that didn't fit.

The two standing in front of us stood three feet apart in complete stillness. It was the direct and dead look that police officers, or intelligence officers, carry with them. The look that seems to say they know something about you which you don't want known. The six others, three men and three women, behind them also stood. That struck me as odd because the place was piled with boxes that made inviting seats. Bureaucrats and executives always head for chairs, their normal environment, the only place they feel in control and at ease. These were neither government officials, nor business executives.

I knew about the charter. It had popped up on the board that morning before I had left for Melville Island. Stanley had slugged it "Bio-Jenness Surv," which let me know it was something to do with biology, on Jenness Island, and likely a routine research survey. We get dozens of charters like it during the summer. This one was just earlier than the rest of the pack. I also knew that I would be taking the trip. It was the work of perhaps two seconds to eyeball the pile of litter in the office before I was sure I could take the Twin Otter instead of the DC-3.

The strip at Jenness had been built by the USAF in the Cold War to take the C-47, or DC-3, and not much else that was any larger. No one had done any maintenance work on the airstrip's surface in decades. I didn't care for the idea of trying to get a Dakota down on who knew what pile of rubble had been left by the freezing and thawing. The de Havilland Twin Otter could land in a fraction of the space of the DC-3, and if it had to it could land anywhere on the island where it was flat, although from what I remembered of the island there wasn't much of that.

"Tonight?"

"Yuh. PZO is ready. Weather's fine, and Pond Inlet has the rooms."

I nodded. There are supposed to be laws about the amount of flying a person can do in one day, but somehow they never seemed to apply in this part of the world and just as certainly never to me.

"OK, let me get something to eat while Billy loads and we'll go to Pond." The extra mileage for the flight added to the minimum salary Jack was paying, would help.

"Deadhead back here?" I said, thinking of making the flight out the next day.

He shook his head. "Iqaluit has a trip waiting. Book off there and take that time off you wanted."

Better and better, I thought. The Montreal flight stops at Iqaluit on its way back down from Resolute. The three hour margin I'd gain by picking it up in Iqaluit meant less chance of missing it because of foul weather and that was all too likely if I had to fly the length of Baffin Island to return the empty Otter to Resolute Bay.

I walked around the end of the counter and spent a couple of minutes shifting boxes and cases trying to get an accurate idea of the weights involved so the cargo could be stowed with some intelligence in the Twin Otter. There was one, seven foot long and five foot wide monster of a box made of pine. In the center of the sides, top, ends and probably the bottom were black enamel rectangles the size of a telephone book. White lettering was stenciled over them, "Goletta Marine Station." I tugged on one of the twelve-strand cables banding it to get an idea of weight. The box didn't shift.

Before I could try again a hard hand fell on mine.

The shock of the grip startled me, "Hey! Watch it!" The hand didn't move. I was stuck, doubled over the box.

"Teller!" The word snapped across the room. A dark haired woman half a head taller than anyone else in the room had half turned from Stanley to look at us. She had clearly been settling the final details at the counter.

"Leave it." She said in a normal sounding voice that somehow still seemed to get into every corner of the room.

The hand left mine and I straightened. There wasn't a sound from the others. None of them had said a word since I had come in. Stanley glared at me. I didn't know why. But then, he always seemed to need to glare at people.

"Jack," he started to say, but the woman at the counter waved a hand.

"Captain," she said.

I straightened some more because it was the first time in many years that anyone had called me that. It took a moment to realize that she meant it as a functional title and not a rank. "Mr. Teller is my equipment manager and very protective about our instruments."

She walked the ten feet over to us, the sound of Gore-Tex sliding on Gore-Tex and Nylon loud in the office. Her parka was like all the others in his team, a shiny orange quilted affair, the type that look like they've been stuffed with party balloons.

She shook my hand. "My name is Aeva Horst, Captain. I'm sorry, but the case contains a deep water sampling tube and it is every fragile."

Bloody heavy sampling tube, I thought, and if it got this far north it would survive any two-inch drop I'd be lucky to subject it to, assuming I could even get it off the ground. "Jack Standish ma'am. It's all right. I was trying to get some idea of the weight so it doesn't get into the wrong spot in the plane."

Teller still didn't say anything. He pointed to the black rectangle on the top. Under the two-inch high letters was a line of half-inch script, "257 Kilograms." No wonder I hadn't been able to move it. I couldn't see how they had even dragged it into the office. The air-freight from wherever the Goletta Marine Station was must have cost them a huge amount of money.

Stanley," I called. "You'd better tell Billy about this so he can get some help. If he puts this in the tail we won't get off the ground. It has got to be 600 pounds at least."

Stanley snorted to let me know I was telling him his job again. "He got it in here, so he knows."

"Not quite Mr.Davids," Horst said. "My men brought it in. They know best how to handle it and if they can be shown where to put it in the airplane they can carry it on." She turned back to me. "How long do you need for your meal Captain?"

I felt like saying we'd leave when I felt we should leave, but there was something about the woman that wouldn't allow it.

"Oh about 45 minutes I suppose, if the plane is ready." I wanted time to get to my room and change my jeans which were filling the overheated office with the reek of aviation gasoline. It was mixing oddly with the smell of instant coffee, dirty engine oil from the back workroom, and the oddly twitching smell that preservative grease gives off.

The bar had one empty table, so I sat there while I waited for what passes as a super burger in Resolute Bay. I was taking my first swallow of cold beer when Charles Edward sat down at the table.

Charles flies for Franklin Charters, the biggest outfit operating in the islands and was like me, ending a professional career at the poor end of the business in the High Arctic. We would get old together while the younger, less experienced, went on to tourist charters in the Caribbean sitting in the front office of a wide body jet and getting paid fat salaries to match.

"Jack you bastard. How's Rae Point and the girls these days?"

Every time for past six months when we had met, Charles had said the same thing. It was likely the only smart comment he had ever come up with.

The oil base on Melville had me do a crew change one week and it just so happened that everyone on the flight was a female oil or exploration worker. Unusual, a bit, but women are far from rare in the High Arctic exploration camps. Times have changed.

When I landed Charles had been at the airstrip and had instantly come up with his stupid gibe about me and my flying harem.

I didn't give him a chance to go on. "Any news on the search?" A C-130 was missing over the Old Crow Flats in the Northern Yukon. A once close friend was on board, although I hadn't known that he was even in the country until the crew list had been made public. The plane at that point was eight days overdue and there wasn't much hope. The Northern Yukon is home to minus fifty degree weather even in the late winter.

"No. SAR Edmonton says tomorrow is the last day unless they get something."

"It just doesn't seem right. A Herc like that must have three different kinds of ELT. One of them should have gone off."

"Maybe. But they could have had the wrong batteries," he said.

Emergency Locator Transmitters are supposed to send out an electronic howl when a plane crashes but they've been dogged by technical problems since they were invented. The Canadian government practically banned the devices altogether at one time when it discovered the lithium batteries powering them had a habit of exploding. Explosions of any kind aren't liked on aircraft. They could be run off ordinary batteries, but ordinary batteries don't last for any time at all in the cold.

"But," I said, "if they got it down on a lake the crew could have used, I don't know how many, radios to call for help. That thing should be sticking out of the radar screens like an igloo in Dublin."

"If they made it down," he said it quietly because he knew I had a friend on board.

The super-burger arrived, only a shade larger than a normal hamburger anywhere else. The fries were microwaved to the last trace element of their nutritional value. A piece of lettuce that looked like a sheet of wet green toilet paper hung like a skirt around the bun. "Anybody see anything?" I mumbled past a mouthful.

"Nope. I talked to Inuvik." He meant the Frontier office in Inuvik, which holds down the company's business in the Western Arctic. Inuvik was only a few hundred miles from the search area. "They say we're going broke flying the search on gas costs alone. Well anyway we're not the only ones with a missing plane."

I hadn't heard of another, but it was some time since I caught up on the gossip. "Where, here?"

"No, the Americans lost an F-104 ten minutes out of the Kennedy Space Center"

"A Lockheed 104 Starfighter? Nobody has been flying them for a couple of decades. Are you sure?"

He nodded. "NASA bought some ex-Canadian 104s from the Turkish air force and others from Norway and Greece. They've overhauled them for some sort of high-altitude research. I think the 104's are to launch small orbital rockets from the top of an extreme altitude zoom climb.

And there are several more in private hands, most working for hi-tech companies into private space research"

"Surely they could have used something a lot more modern." As impressive a fighter as the 104 was it had been designed in the early 1950's after all.

"I would have though so but apparently NASA thought it had a bargain on its hands. A couple of million dollars in overhaul costs for a plane that can do twice the speed of sound at altitudes that even today other fighters can't handle well. And NASA has at least half a dozen in the sky."

I nodded, remembering what that dagger in the sky could do. "What do you mean lost ten minutes out of KSC? How far can you go in ten minutes in an 104? I mean they have that whole region so lousy with radar you can cook hotdogs right in the cockpit."

"I know but there was a story this morning on the radio that said the U-S Air Force and just about everyone else in Florida has been turning the place upside down and can't find a trace of the guy."

Odd, but more common than most believe. In a few months some hunting party, or hiker, would cut through a ravine on the side of a hill, or wade through an Everglade swamp and find a pile of shredded aluminum and steel wrapped around a body so badly burned that it would take the pathologist two days to piece the teeth and jaw together to identify the pilot. It would turn out the crash site was under the flight path of the search missions and been searched a couple of dozen times. I've seen intact aircraft lost in the bush that could not be seen from the air even when they have been pointed out. Trees, rocks, brush, anything that breaks the regular shape of a plane, can do an remarkable job of hiding a wreck.

There was a Beaver that went down in the Western Arctic a few years back that was only found by chance on the ground months after it went missing. The plane had gone down in rolling country near the treeline. Trees only grew in the shallow valleys and they were stunted, no more than the height of a man. To look at the ground from the air you'd think a plane with a wingspan as long as a house would stand out as though it was in a city parking lot. But when that one went in it hit between two sharply crested hills twenty feet apart. The ground between was choked with trees. The wings had come off, folded back along the fuselage, and closed like a grasshopper's wings to form a tent. It went missing in the winter and the snow on the bare aluminum hid everything. Even after it was found, the rescue helicopters needed a man on the ground to guide them to it.

"I hear you're off to Jenness." There weren't too many secrets about which outfit had what charter.

"Yeah, Pond tonight then the island about noon if the winds are right."

"That's the high powered scientific crowd from Geneva," he said.

"You mean the Goletta Marine Station don't you. I thought they were American." Aeva Horst was not American and neither was the silent Teller, but that doesn't mean anything in the world of science. Their equipment had tags on it from Edmonton and Seattle, so I assumed they were a U-S outfit.

He shook his head as he drank from my beer can. "No. This is some other bunch. Biologists studying the strait or something for the oil companies. There's a bunch of them already there."

"Ah well I suppose my crowd is joining them." Why anyone

would pick late winter to sit on that pile of rock is just beyond me."

"Who cares what time of year they want to do their rock tapping? Count yourself lucky it's not summer."

He was right. Summer time in the Eastern Arctic carries a special madness. Just about every university in North America, and just as many from the rest of the world, sends teams to the region to tap rocks, scrape lichens, tag geese, and generally take inventory. They all want flights out to their research camps at the same time. They all have mountains of equipment and they all are in so much of a rush to get out onto the land after a winter of dreaming up their projects that the fun goes out of the flying.

The research business really took off when the major oil companies thought they could find oil. It got worse, much worse, when diamonds were discovered and a full blown mineral rush started. But to get permission for test drilling they had to prove to the Canadian government that the ecology wasn't going to suffer so millions in research grants became available. Overnight, it was the in-thing in American and Canadian universities to have a Northern Studies program. It is a gold mine for the academics, the last unpublished area of the world. Even undergraduates score doctoral theses out of a summer's work.

I still hadn't finished my hamburger when old iron grip Teller walked in. He threaded himself through the round-topped tables directly to me without a glance around to find me. It was as though he knew before he walked in where I was sitting. His bulk and height made his progress through the tables more graceful. I would have expected a muscled giant like that to stride through the room making the drinkers get out of his way but he swung his hips and twisted his shoulders like a dancer.

"Madam Horst says it is getting late." He stood over the table and spoke to me in a low bass with an authority that made the statement the order that Horst wanted delivered. I rolled my eyes at Charles to let him know I didn't care for the insult to the lordly independence of pilots we all tried to carry with us. Pilots are never supposed to take orders and advice from the passengers but of course we all did, although we are careful to try to maintain the fiction.

"When we work we work, I suppose." I got up from the table. Charles swallowed the last of my beer. I pulled my parka off the hook on the wall behind me and ran to catch up with Teller as he fishtailed out of the bar.

FIRST DAY AND NIGHT

*S*omebody, likely Stanley, had the Twin fired up and the lights going. I got a little irritated. If there's one thing, and it is about the only thing, that I have kept from that stringent military training is a religious adherence to a proper walk-around and preflight. Stanley was pushing things. He had done the preflight himself, probably overawed by whatever he thought Horst was, and would now insist on me leaving right away.

He tried, and he failed. I slipped through the pilot's door and slammed the throttles to cut-off.

"Jack, what the hell are you doing!" He screamed against the lowering whine of the props.

"Screw-off. I'm flying this truck. I do the preflight." He was about to argue with me, but Horst appeared behind him. He thought better of arguing in front of a paying customer and turned away.

I probably could have lifted wheels without doing the checks myself. There had been hundreds of flights in the military like that when the ground-crew had done them for me, yet there is always the nagging doubt in the back of the mind that they might not have been done well. One of my first instructors, when I had learned to fly on a cadet scholarship, gave me a chilling little lesson about it at the end of a runway one of the first mornings on the course.

"Standish," he said as I finished waggling the stick around to prove the controls were free and just before I pushed on a bit of power in the Aeronca Champ. "How do you know the elevators are coming up when you pull back on the stick?"

I thought it was an unanswerable question. What else could happen when the stick is pulled back? "Uh sir? Well they come up with the stick sir."

"How do you know?" McWhirter said. The other two Aeroncas on the course were sitting behind us waiting for me to roll out onto the active and get off the ground.

"Well sir, I checked the controls and they were free."

"I had a friend who did that one day and he got fifty feet off the ground, pulled the stick into his right thigh for a fighter-jock turn, and rolled left into the ground. Somebody had messed up the controls while doing maintenance. He would have lived if he had had the sense to look out of the cockpit when he tested the controls on the ground."

"Yes sir," I said, not sure what he was on about.

"If you are sure, really sure, that you aren't going to roll over, or nose dive into the runway when you pullback on takeoff, you can roll out."

Well of course I wasn't sure at all so I deliberately rocked the stick forward, back, and side to side, damn near breaking my neck as I craned to see whether everything was going in the right direction.

Ever since, I've approached aircraft as if some insane saboteur has been sawing away with a hacksaw at the main spar while I had my back turned.

McWhirter ended up getting killed by something he couldn't have checked for himself. He ran into a flock of Canada Geese at 400 knots and ejected. The seat rails were cracked. He came out spinning and broke his neck on the side of the canopy. The thing you don't check is the thing that will kill you, that's true. But sometimes its stuff you can't check that get you. Which is why pilots who are deeply paranoid, convinced that their aircraft will try to kill them, are the safest.

The Twin Otter's wings seemed to be in the right places, and the wheels were full of air. I climbed up the air step door to check the cargo. That huge coffin seemed to be in the right place, but the straps on the six steel boxes at the tail were loose, so I went to work on them.

This group puzzled me. They had flown from I didn't know where to Resolute, as far north as one can get and still buy beer, then chartered a slow turboprop bush plane for a 900 nautical mile flight south-east again. It made more sense to have shipped the stuff to Iqaluit through Montreal and charter from there for the two hundred mile trip to the island. I couldn't begin to guess what they must have paid already for airfreight, but the Otter was going to cost them a far bigger pile of dollars.

As I strapped the boxes down tight. I couldn't help noticing that as rich as this team appeared to be, they saved money in odd ways. They were using surplus USAF ammunition boxes for equipment. Cheap they might be, I thought, but they're made from steel and far tougher than anyone would need. Aluminum boxes might cost more, but they're lighter and strong enough for anything. Besides, ammunition boxes don't look nearly as impressive on a scientist as brushed aluminum wrapped with leather straps.

I waved to the office from the cockpit to let them know it was time to go and settled into the left seat. By the time I finished checking the route headings and radio frequencies for Pond Inlet, Billy had loaded everyone on board and made them buckle in.

Aeva Horst sat on the right side in the seat behind the partition, leaning forward so she could look closely at the instrument panel. "Feel like sitting in the right seat?" I said, gesturing to the co-pilot's seat.

She didn't answer, just moved forward and into the seat. I helped her with the straps, but she didn't need much help. "Spent some time in planes?" I grinned. Most scientists, or wildlife biologists anyway, have. They spend their summers in the back of beyond scouting for new things to publish and fresh stories for the seminars.

"Some, Captain, but not in this type of plane."

I nodded and started the port engine, ran it for 15 seconds and turned over the starboard. We were wheels-off Resolute at 1800 on the nose, and I had the plane trimmed for hands-off flight twelve minutes later.

A de Havilland Twin Otter is made to be flown by two pilots like most other twin engine aircraft. But de Havilland spent a long time talking to bush pilots before this design even got to the blueprint stage. As a result, it is made for ease of operation, dependability and single pilot operation. Unlike the Dakota I had been flying just a few hours earlier, there were few switches and levers that demanded more than a mild stretch of the arm. And unlike the Dak, which probably had seen four instrument panels in its life, each one just a little more confusing than the last, this panel was a dream. For one thing, the fuel gauges weren't buried in some impossible place. In the Dakota they had been down on the right hand side near the floor. They were meant to be read by the co-pilot which is fine, except when you fly solo and then they're unreadable. In the Twin they sat in the middle of the panel at waist height.

The ice fog was thicker than during the afternoon and the ground was lost in the dark. The islands around Resolute have some nasty hills so the radar was painting merrily away. Horst spent several minutes studying the coastline on the screen.

I didn't need the radar because PZO was equipped with a machine that will do away with people like me in my lifetime.

GPS uses a chain of satellites around the world and a thumbnail sized computer brain to constantly figure an aircraft's location. The thing makes it impossible to get lost unless a circuit board breaks, a fuse blows, or you do a lousy job of programming it before leaving the ground. It was worth as much as the plane for the savings it made in allowing a pilot to fly direct to a destination rather than doglegging around the countryside following airways and navigational beacons. Someday soon they'll start thinking for themselves and then we won't need pilots.

I didn't trust it, more out of sheer reactionary conservatism than any real distrust in the worth of the electronics. I'm sure that had I learned to fly in biplanes I'd mistrust anything with only one wing. So I kept the radar going and my map out and the mental mathematics needed to plot a rough position every fifteen minutes.

"When will we reach Pond Inlet?"

I'd forgotten she was there and didn't hear her the first time.

"Uh, oh should be about nine o'clock, depending."

"Weather?" It sounded like a command.

I shook my head. "Oh about like this," I said waving my right hand across the windshield to indicate the clear stars and the washed out gray of the ice fog. "Shouldn't be any problem."

"Is there no one you can reach by radio to find out?" She made me feel as though I wasn't doing my job.

"Oh sure, but I'll leave it for a while. I got the latest Pond before we left. No point in asking again for it." I busied myself with the sectional, folding it so the line of track was aligned with the fore and aft line of the plane. Although it meant that on this flight all the place names were upside down it made it easier to identify the island coastlines as they showed through the murk.

The altimeter was showing a slight climb. I rolled in some down trim. "Your guys are moving around a bit back there."

She shrugged and didn't look at me. I turned and peered

around the cabin partition to see Teller and one of the others in the tail going through one of the ammunition boxes.

"You guys planning on getting a lot of work done at Jenness?" I asked Horst.

"Oh yes. We have a full sampling schedule worked out. There's a lot to be learned about the strait."

"I was at Jenness a few weeks ago," I said, "there was no one there. I'd have thought your boat would have been at the dock."

"Boat?"

"Well sure. How else you getting your samples done? The ice will soon start getting pretty broken up off the island this time of year. I wouldn't care to try much from a snowmobile, at least not on the strait side of the island."

She gave a snort and a sort of half chuckle the way people do when they are talking to a child and see something funny but don't want to offend. "We're not sampling the strait, just near the island."

The faint glow of the sun was still lurking behind the horizon as the turbines droned on across the southwest cliffs of Devon Island. They showed as a black slash across the dirty gray of the ice fog and gloom.

She stared down at the sea ice from the right window for several moments without moving. I thought the conversation was dead. "How well do you know the island, Mr. Standish? Will we be able to get a snowmobile near the floe edge?"

I shrugged while I finished my mental calculations to see whether the panel of electronic chips was leading me astray, then pondered the question that lay behind the question. "Oh, I suppose the Inuit hunt the area all the time. I suppose the rest of your party must have found all that sort of thing out for you already." I was fishing then because it struck me this was a different research team from any of the ones I had ever handled before.

Usually scientists working in the North had spent half a year studying large scale maps and going through all of the published literature as well as talking to fellow scientists who had already made the trip. Sometimes, indeed most times, their knowledge of local conditions issues and concerns exceeded mine. They carried a mental baggage of information that gave them a wide base from which to greet the north. Some of the Inuit land-claim details I had only the haziest feel for, yet I worked in the region year round. The summer-wonders though would know chapter and verse of the situation and could expound at length. Where they all fall down is in the area of practical experience. They're careless with their clothing. They forget to brush the snow dust from their boots and leggings when they enter a heated building and allow the fabric to get damp. That freezes when they go back out, and frozen clothing sucks up body heat. They think nothing of jumping onto a snowmobile and racing off a dozen miles into the hills to check a weather installation, not realizing that if the machine breaks down they will have to walk. And twelve miles at minus thirty degrees without a tent can become a last journey. It takes experience and time in the High Arctic to instinctively follow the rules that let a person live. You can't remember them; they have to be trained into place so they are automatic.

The Otter dipped again. Teller was dragging one of the ammunition cases forward. I turned back to the controls, retrimmed, then half leaned back to tell them to stop shifting cargo, Horst beat me to it. She called to the back, "Make sure the arming switch is off."

"A bomb," I thought, "for sure it's a bomb." My wide eyes caught Horst's.

"Deep water sampling tube," she shouted against the shrilling turbines. "They're designed to shoot themselves into the bottom sediment. It's unlocked now but it is like cleaning a gun, you never know whether it is loaded or not. Never assume."

I nodded.

Before turning back to the controls I looked over the rest of the group. One was asleep on the rear bench, another was helping Teller open the box. Asleep or awake they looked like extremely hard men. They had that well exercised firmness to their skin you see in mountaineers or skiers. They moved with a control that comes from frequent and sternuous exercise, certainly not the kind of grace to be found in laboratory researchers who walk about cloaked in a chalky white cloud of skin baked under fluorescent lights.

I settled down to the flight. We passed into full night as the Twin Otter droned on.

"What are the lights Mr. Standish?"

A sprinkle of small lights clustered together in the dark below the hills on the horizon directly in front of us. "Pond Inlet Ms Horst. We'll be down in twenty minutes."

"The hotel knows we are coming?"

"Yeah should do, in any case they should have plenty of room. You know of course that they are communal rooms."

"Oh yes Captain. I don't mind sharing rooms. We are rather used to it." She said that in the distracted way of a person thinking of something else.

Pond Inlet is the second nicest place in the Eastern Arctic. Grise Fiord is the nicest because it is so isolated and picturesque. It sits below the mountains where they cascade off the southern end of Ellesmere Island. Its isolation reminds me of a South Pacific island, pretty, tranquil, and far enough away from everything to be a real retreat. Pond Inlet is on the regular flight route around Baffin and sees a lot of transient traffic, so it doesn't have the isolation that makes Grise Fiord so captivating. Pond makes up for it with physical beauty.

The community overlooks a strait that separates Baffin Island from one of the most spectacular islands in the Arctic, Bylot Island. The island is all mountain. It is as though something had carved out a chunk of the Rocky Mountains of the west and plunked it down in one tidy heap. The island rises from the strait, one stupendous mountain after another. There are so many peaks it resembles a child's drawing of a mountain range, one triangle piled on another.

Thousands, perhaps millions of birds, spend the summer there on the crags and ice shattered slopes. The Eiders and Brants are a prime source of food for the Inuit despite the island being an international bird sanctuary. The Inuit struggled for years to win the right in treaty to harvest the eggs claiming their forefathers had been doing it thousands of years before the idea of bird sanctuaries was ever thought of.

The Pond Inlet hotel sits on a low hill.

Its front picture windows look out over the strait at Bylot. There had been many nights when I had sat there telling stories with biologists, a soil scientist, a tourist couple from Miami, assorted project team leaders from the federal government, drinking their booze and staring at that incredible sight. The view is at its best in the spring when the sun is returning. The contrast of the hard sunlight on the black rock and the blue of the far off ice shocks the senses with its vibrancy. Somehow those discussions always started with the Arctic and ended about four in the morning, revolving around the universe and its origins. There's something about the effect of moonlight over the ice of Bylot Strait that does that to conversation.

It wasn't happening tonight. We were all in the front room, sitting at different tables, staring at the ice. Horst and Teller muttered together in the corner farthest from the door. Between me and them were the other six and they hadn't spoken since I entered the room. I felt lost by myself in the other corner, glass window in front of me and plywood to my right covering the hole made in the side window by some rock throwing kid. It had been like that for all the months I had flown into Pond. The cost of shipping new plate glass up from Montreal would keep it there until it could be delivered by ship in the summer sealift.

"Hi Jack." Johnny, the manager of the hotel, came in with a

tray of instant coffee, instant milk, and a coffee urn of hot water. He was supposed to be sixty, but he looked ninety. A lifetime of seal and caribou hunting, first behind a dog sled, then on snowmobile, had creased his face into deep wrinkles and crevasses. The months and years he'd spent on the ice, hunting in the dark and the winds, had turned the skin into a mass of leather like creases. He'd been manager for the past year.

"How would you like french fries for breakfast?"

I'd brought him ten pounds of potatoes. It's almost the standard gift so far north. With Arctic airfreight running what it does, a sack of potatoes soon becomes a luxury rarely afforded. Food costs up to four or five times more in the High Arctic than anywhere else.

"A nice caribou steak for me would be fine Johnny, with a couple of goose eggs eh."

"Wrong time of year, you know that Jack. Beside we can't get to the island."

"How come?"

He shrugged and poured boiling water into a foam plastic cup for me. I watched as the powdered coffee and lightener turned into a greasy brown ball and floated about in the swirl. "What's the trouble. Is the ice bad?"

"Nope. Game officers. They won't let us across. The council says it is discrimination but the government won't listen."

It was the first time I'd ever heard of the game officers stopping someone from going to the island. Occasionally an Inuk would be charged with taking eggs or hunting birds illegally but only occasionally because it was such a touchy subject among the Inuit who took it as their right to use the island as they saw fit. To actually stop people from crossing the strait was asking for trouble. It didn't make sense. "How many are there?'

"Five or six I think. They've been on the island..."

"Wait a second. There aren't five game officers on the whole of Baffin Island. Where'd they come from?"

"I don't know. One man said they are from Ottawa but no one know for sure. They've been there all week. Every day they drive around the strait telling people to stay away. We can't even go fishing Tommycod without them telling us to move away. Some of the young guys are getting very angry."

I looked at the curving snowmobile tracks left in the snow over the ice and followed them as they swept away to the west and the east from the community. There were none that ran straight north to the island.

He took one of my cigarettes. "There's army there too."

That took me off guard. "Heh. You mean uh..." I really didn't know what I meant. Horst was staring across the room at Johnny's back. The room was silent except for the rushing noise of the furnace fans.

"Yes army soldiers. Some hunters saw their camp before the same officers got them off the island. The council thinks they're there for exercises but Ipellee is a Ranger and he says they don't know anything about it."

The Rangers comprise a sort of Inuit militia. The idea was formed back in the Second World War and grew during the long years of the Cold war until these few dozen Inuit, armed with ancient Lee Enfield rifles, would be the first line of warning if troops marched over the pole. They were also used as spotters for the submarines that regularly use Canadian Arctic waters, but their main use is as guides for Canadian Army exercises in the north. They were always involved in the exercises because their advice about how to travel and live in conditions that killed people within minutes was invaluable. I thought that if Ipellee hadn't been informed then something was quite wrong.

"How'd they get there? Did they use the strip?"

"No. They must have come straight down from Resolute."

I shook my head. "No way. There hasn't been any military through Resolute in months. Been no talk of any exercises either. And pilots are usually told ."

I wasn't a diligent reader of NOTAMs, but I was sure I would have noticed any warning about restricted flying space or special air corridors. And aside from the lack of official notification of an exercise there wasn't any talk about one either. Arctic pilots, indeed pilots everywhere, carry a highly mobile grapevine around with them.

"Last week there was also a lot of jets around too. Some of them flew right over the school and the teachers couldn't get the kids back inside after they ran out to watch." Horst was still watching Johnny's back. "Tom Columbus, the new guy with First-Flight, says there was a search."

"I don't know about a search. No one is missing except for that Herc out west. There wouldn't be any search around here because there are no planes missing. Probably just an exercise from Thule. They were American planes were they?" No Canadian jets could get as far north without staging at Resolute and Alert. Thule was just a few hundred miles east of Alert on the Greenland coast. It's a major USAF base.

But that bothered me. If they were flying supersonic aircraft about the Eastern Arctic I wanted to know when and where. It's one thing not to know about a ground exercise but military aircraft exercises are something else again. The minute you send something that flies at twice the speed of sound into the air you have to keep it away from everything that flies slower, such as migrating geese, airliners, and plodding Twin Otters flying bush routes. The only way to avoid the danger of a midair with a fighter is to make sure no civilian aircraft ever gets close to its flight path. In this case, it looked like no one had bothered to send out the NOTAM, and that was criminal.

BROUGHTON ISLAND

*F*ive hours later I rubbed the last of the sleep from my face as I shambled into the front room again. Johnny was there. He looked as if he'd been there since I went to bed. The sun was coming back after months below the horizon. Sleep cycles get smashed around in the spring time. The sun rises earlier and earlier, sets later, and the natural tendency is to stay with it as long as possible, to glory in the light, and that seems to throw the circadian rhythm out. Once the sun is fully back, however, sleep returns to normal and although it is bright and full daylight in summer there's little trouble getting back to the normal cycle. Except for the children that is. They seem to spend the entire Arctic summer awake and running around the roads raising hell, while their elders sleep.

"Your people are already at the plane," he said as he handed me a coffee. "They seem in a big hurry."

"Scientists. They're all like that, work all day and can't wait to get started the next." This was more like it. I've yet to meet any researchers who ever slept in late while in the field. It must be their attitude to their life's work; as if they really were fast on the trail of the grand secret of the universe and a little bit of hustle and push might catch the elusive secret in its lair.

The boxes had been pushed around in the cabin again. Not much, just enough to let me know that all the straps had been undone, and each box in turn opened, then replaced. Some of the boxes, the heavy metal ones, were moved too far to the tail, so I went to work rearranging the center of gravity.

"Everything OK," I said to Horst in an attempt to justify why I had spent ten minutes grunting and sweating as I dragged things around on the cabin floor by myself. One of the silent six had stood on the ground looking through the cargo door during the whole time and hadn't offered a hand or a comment. I would have asked, but after the first few moments it almost seemed as if she was guarding me. She the jailer, and me the hard sweating roadganger, plotting escape and hoping I'd get away with it.

There was no cabin chatter this time as we flew south directly into the sun. The wind was kicking up snowdust and flinging it up to us at five thousand feet. That made the sunsights difficult in the glare, and I had to spend fuel and time climbing on up to fourteen thousand feet to get clear shots. The GPS was having small fits and couldn't be relied on. The increased altitude made the passengers dozy from lack of oxygen.

Normally I didn't need the sunsights with the GPS and other electronics on board, but doing them was a useful exercise and insurance for times like this when the GPS acted up as it sometimes did so far north. I also didn't need any radio fixes, but I spent a lot of time trying to raise the North Warning System station at Broughton Island without luck. There was too much noise on the HF frequencies, and we were too far for VHF to work. The trouble seemed to be at the Broughton end because both of my radios gave the same results and conditions were right for reception.

I did hear some guttural talk between an unidentified transport and Broughton, so I knew their radios were working to some extent. The reception wasn't clear enough to let me hear the conversation and all I could get out of the exchange was an impression that the pilot's accent sounded German, or perhaps somewhere east of Germany. The transmissions also sounded like there was an argument going on and I listened closer out of curiosity because an argument in the air is rare. You don't argue with a ground controller who has the power to route your flight through the nastiest parts of the sky, heavy cloud, thunderstorms, turbulence, or other traffic.

After a while, the transmissions stopped and I tried again to raise Broughton. This time there was hard purpose behind my attempt. I wanted to tell them that, no I was not a Badger bomber, no I wasn't a drug smuggler, and please don't scramble a fighter after me. We were flying in the ADIZ, a belt of airspace around North America that aircraft are not supposed to cross without identifying themselves. The North Warning System stations take the role seriously and are quick to report airspace violations to the Canadian and American air forces.

It had happened to me the year before.

I was flying a DC-3 from Grise Fiord to Qanak, just north of Thule. The transmitting antenna of the Three had failed, and I wasn't aware of it. I couldn't raise the station to identify myself and put it down to the hail of solar particles that were screwing up radio transmissions that week. I thought no more about it. Although I wasn't concerned about it, the Thule controller certainly was nervous about not being able to identify the blob on his radar and called for an intercept.

I was in that half awake state pilots settle into on a long flight, not dozing, but powered down. The slightest change in the flight, a burp from an engine, or a harder rock of turbulence than normal or an instrument needle jumping an eighth of an inch too much and I would shoot alert. But as I say I was letting the plane fly me for a while as I stared at the Greenland icecap coming up on the nose.

I damn near had a heart attack when the interceptor, an F-15E Strike Eagle, blasted over the top of the cockpit and showed me twin fiery afterburners, not ten feet from my face. The turbulence of an aircraft accelerating through MACH point eight or nine is a rapid series of snapping shocks of savagely disturbed air. The old Dakota rattled like a rusted out car on a washboarded gravel road. The blast of turbulence threw me out of the sky and by the time I had the thing straightened out again and level, my heart under control, and before I could start to think of profanity, the F-15 had finished its turn and shot back, nose on. He knew what he was doing. I had enough experience to know not to touch the controls. I didn't want to jink when he decided to zag and have us make one pile of wreckage out of two planes. He flashed overtop, and a few seconds later I saw the black radar nacelle of the F-15 creep past the port wingtip and the cockpit came into view. The pilot had his airbrakes out and flaps down to slow as much as possible to my speed.

He couldn't talk to me on the radio, but his hand gestures passed the message, "Wake up sleepy truck driver."

I swallowed the insult, waved him on, and watched as the square yards of flaps pulled themselves back into the supercritical wing. The speed brakes snapped back, the nose dropped slightly, and with a blast of twin afterburners he was accelerating in a rising curve across my nose and south to Thule. For a few seconds I tracked him in an imaginary gunsight and pretended I was a better pilot. I would never have turned across the nose of any aircraft, unarmed or not, but my face burned for days afterward every time I remembered the shock of getting bounced and the split second of tightness in my chest as my reflexes warned I was under attack. Fighter pilot instincts never quite leave, no matter how many trucks one flies. Since then I have approached Air Defence Zones with care. This time the Broughton operator returned my call and logged me through.

Horst put her left hand on my shoulder. "Broughton Island?"

"Yeah, that's it," I said as I picked out the radar dish on the mountain. She had good eyes. "The settlement is on the other side. Won't see it until we're right there." I eased more to the south and pulled back some power in a slow descent. The change in prop noise roused Teller in the seat behind the cockpit partition and he leaned forward to look at Horst, then reassured that nothing was wrong, leaned back in his seat.

I heard the click in the earphones and the slight burst of noise as Horst's lip mike picked up the engine noise before she spoke. "Jack," It sounded so formal. "How long?"

"Lunchtime I suppose, depends of course on how long it takes the truck to get out to the strip and refuel us. I'll circle around the settlement to let them know I'm landing." I could have told her more exactly by punching the numbers into the nav computer and allowing an extra twenty minutes for refuelling. I didn't because there was something about the woman that didn't make me want to go to the effort. I didn't like her, and I didn't know why. There was a coldness to the woman that put the back up on that part of my mind I use for politeness. She was too formal, too correct, and carried herself with such an air of power that I constantly felt I was her subordinate. Which I was in fact since she was the one paying for the charter and therefore my boss.

But my ego was clashing against her very presence and I didn't know why.

I kept saying to myself that there wasn't much more left of the flight. A refuelling at Broughton, then the hop down over the peninsula to the old North Warning System station at Jenness Island and I'd be rid of her and her team. In charter work you learn to put up with all sorts of people who decide to hire an airplane and a pilot.

"Are your people going to be expecting us at Jenness?" I didn't want to hang around while someone walked up the mountain to get a truck to unload the cargo. I wanted to make the Montreal flight from Iqaluit.

There was a long pause as she continued to stare ahead at the waves of hills and mountains stretching south along the coast; a sea of whites and abstract splashes of black where rock lay uncovered by the wind. "Don't worry about that Captain. All is prepared."

She wasn't a native english speaker. The "r"s came from the chest and the "p"s had a bite to the end of them, but it was only because the headsets took so many of the overlying sound frequencies out of her voice that I was able to detect the foreignness.

She scanned the instruments when I pulled back more power. She'd done it frequently on the flight.

She was a pilot of some type, but I was afraid to make any comment. One of the hazards of professional flying is having to put up with the aviation enthusiast, seasoned air traveller, private pilot or ex-combat flier from the some old war. They all want a hand at the controls, and they all pretend they know more about the plane and how to fly it than they actually do. What they really want is to join for just a few minutes what they see as a glamorous secret profession packed with adventure and excitement. At times I've tried to explain to these people just how much like truck driving, charter flying really is. There's the same boredom of the route, the same time pressure to get the job finished and started on another one. I tell them how poorly paid it is for the risks and about the crummy hours. They don't listen.

Of course, I must confess I act the same way they do whenever I get a chance to get on the flight deck of an airliner, and I don't listen to those pilots anymore than my passengers listen to me.

I swung in over the settlement and on toward the strip. I didn't bother with overflying it because I could see someone had been out with the plow, so I dumped out the flaps and slapped back on the throttles and the Otter plunged nose down and hung in mid air.

That caught her. Her eyes flashed across the panel, through the airspeed, the altimeter, VSI, engine instruments and then to the throttle quadrant overhead. She wasn't just a weekend pilot. This woman had flown twin turbines before. She tightened her shoulder harness as I pulled the green plastic coated checklist from the map pocket, gave it a quick glance, and chucked it back.

I flicked the cabin lights to warn the passengers, although only someone who has never flown before would have been ignorant of the impending landing. I waited for the end of the strip to come under the nose.

Within twenty minutes of landing we had refuelled and we were off and climbing. Eventually the hump of Jenness crept out of the maze of headlands, islets and fiords that splintered the coast.

THE OLD STATION

I came over the top of the old station. It was wrapped in wind blown snow. Parts of the complex of narrow barracks, mess hall and the command center seemed to grow out of the snow dome on the summit. The twin radar meshes were white with ice and snow. I made out the abandoned trucks buried to their cabs and saw that the road to the top had been plowed clear. I let down on the other side of the hill with the power right off. "I'll be goddamned!"

The sight was so unexpected I let the airspeed fall off to within five knots of stall before I recovered. The CAL-AIR Hercules that had been at Resolute the night before sat mid-way down the strip to the side and turned nose on. It was a bit like finding a horse in a parking lot. Aircraft of that size never hang about abandoned airstrips that haven't been used by heavy transport in a couple of dozen years. I couldn't understand what it was doing there and assumed quickly the crew must have suffered engine failure, possibly a fuel shortage, or maybe they were lost. There didn't seem to be a quick answer, so I pushed on the power and circled around for another attempt at landing. I chuckled and grinned as if I thought it was perfectly natural to see a multiton aircraft in the middle of nothing, "Well, we have a traffic jam."

Horst didn't respond. She pressed her head against the co-pilot's window and looked at the Herc as we flew past. "Can you put it on the numbers and stop before him?" she said. I almost offered to let her do it since she seemed so familiar with flying.

"Sure I can. This thing won't get halfway down the strip before it comes to a stop. But I'm not going to do it."

That shook her.

"This place hasn't seen a grader since the fifties. There's no telling what the surface is like. I don't want to hit a lump of ice and go skidding around only to have that pig sitting in front of me. I'll use the road."

She didn't say anything and watched the road surface carefully as we floated down. I watched it too, but it was clearer than the strip and more importantly there was fly out room if I had to do a go-around. It was an uphill landing of course. There's no flat ground on Jenness and even the strip ran up, a factor that helped the old Globemasters and DC-6's get in during the old days but sheer hell when the weather was bad and the poor bloody pilots had to fly a back course then a let down through low cloud to a runway that ran straight into a mountain.

The main wheels smashed through a foot deep drift on touch-down. The inch thick sheets of sun hardened snow plated off and slammed against the tail section. The fuselage bucked and dropped as we bounced and the shoulder harness came up tight with the impacts but it was no worse an off-strip landing than most. The DHC-6 was designed for exactly this kind of landing, and it would take some pretty rough terrain to smash it up.

"Very impressive Mr. Standish," she said as the Otter bounced to a stop on its nose wheel shocks and I pulled the props back from reverse pitch. "I will admit you are a better pilot than I expected to find in these environs."

I raised my eyebrows at her as if to say, "Who the hell are you to judge?" but didn't open my mouth. I had seen her hands during the landing. They had hovered half an inch over her thighs, ready to snatch the controls if I botched the landing. She was a command pilot of some type for sure.

Teller and two of the men were out of the door before the blades had stopped on the port engine. I kept the starboard turbine going so restarting would be painless.

They hauled all the bags and ammunition boxes out first before tackling the wooden crate. An ancient U-S Army five tonner was backed as close as it could get to the door. The three men who had been in it were helping Teller. Horst stood by the nose with me and watched. I made sure I was upwind of the Otter and lit a cigarette then turned to look at the Hercules thirty feet away. I was parked in the same cleared stretch of ground the 130 was sitting on.

Horst moved forward to supervise the unloading of the sampling tube crate. I wandered over to the Hercules.

It was the same one, only I had known it before CAL-Air had been splashed along the side. The markings were different, but the three foot streak of blackened aluminum along the cheeks at the rear cargo ramp were still there. A JATO bottle sprung loose from its rack had done that. The undersized collision light at the top of the thirty eight foot tail was still there although I remember it was supposed to have been just a temporary replacement. Somehow all through the many years since I had last seen it, the damage to the Hercules had survived all of the maintenance overhauls.

The thump and scrape of the unloading, overlaid with the whine of the PT-6 and the rushing of the air as the props turned flat in the still air faded when I walked around the far side of the fat fuselage.

I shivered. There was a slight waft of supercooled air from the sea ice, and while I felt it, there was also a different type of cold gripping me.

I wandered back to the Otter kicking pads of lichen on the way, acting bored. I was refusing to react, but the hindbrain was dominating and there was a flutter in my stomach and groin. I walked up to Horst and threw the cigarette end into the snow. "All finished huh?" I said as Teller latched the doors. "Well no point in sitting around here freezing. I've got a flight to Montreal to catch."

She shook my hand and offhandedly thanked me for the flight while she signed my flight manifest. I didn't wait for the truck to pull away from the plane before I had the port prop turning and the Otter heading out onto the strip. I didn't bother with any kind of pre-flight and I got off the ground and away from the Hercules and Horst as quickly as possible.

I was frightened.

I put the nose down, pushed the throttles forward and used the drop to the sea ice to pick up as much airspeed as possible then headed for the mainland at fifty feet without bothering to set up for best cruise. All I wanted was to get within radio range of Pangnirtung, Broughton or Iqaluit.

OLD SCARS

*I*t was the same Hercules that everyone in the western Arctic and Alaska had been looking for during the past three weeks. It was the same one that was carrying my air force classmate as command pilot and it was the same one that I had lived with for two months.

Somehow, Horst and Teller and the crew on the island were connected with its disappearance. I could see that, but beyond was a mystery. Ordinary aircraft theft was out. There are easier ways of getting a plane than having to hijack it out of the Western Arctic.

I was trying to work out where I'd be before it was worth trying to raise Iqaluit on the VHF when the reptilian holdover in the back of my brain took over and the pictures started forming.

Johnny and I had talked about the search on the hotel porch. Horst would soon remember that. She'd also remember me telling Johnny about the summer in Norway with Transport Command and how we nearly crashed the Hercules on takeoff; the same Hercules now sitting on Jenness. The scars from the JATO bottles marked the beast for life and I had told Johnny about those scars. They were dark enough to see but not so bad that they were worth replacing several square feet of fuselage skin.

The bottles had been loaded in the clamshell doors as we brought on board a platoon of Dutch soldiers, a 105 Howitzer and with it, steel crates of ammunition. We were going to airlift them out of one mountain meadow and into another on the other side of the mountains to play some more in the NATO wargame. The soldiers had already been knocked out in one pretend firefight and were going back to play as Soviet reinforcements for the other team.

Our loadmaster was not yet twenty but the trade is taught well and I didn't worry about the distribution of the total weight. I was flying co-pilot and finding it all pretty dull. I was a fighter jock seconded to transport for the games to see how the other side lived. The theory was that it would give me an insight into the troubles of the heavies in combat. I really didn't care. All I wanted was a 104 Starfighter back. The taste of aerial truck driving had long since lost its initial allure.

Bob Matthews was flying in the left seat and seemed as bored as I felt, but I knew him to be a different breed of pilot than me. For one thing, he actually cared about transport flying. The man was pushing fifty and ready to take on the airlines if he could find one that would hire past the age limit. He was trying hard to stay in flying but at that age and with the rank of major he was in danger of a desk job. I wished him luck because he was a nice guy, patient to a feisty fighter pilot, and patient as he explained and explored the realm of heavy transport pilotage to me.

He sat in the left seat chewing the end of a long dead cigar. I never saw him light it outside of the mess and then it was always at the end of the day with the first scotch. He said that chewing the cigar helped to kill his nicotine craving. I had a different technique. I just smoked cigarettes whenever we weren't refueling.

Tony came on the intercom as I felt the thump of the rear

ramp closing and checked that the lights went out. Bob ran us up on power were we stood. This was to be a rocket assisted take off. The JATO bottles would give us a kick like the afterburner in the Starfighter so we could get off the meadow and into a steep climb soon enough to make it over the moraine that sprawled across the end of the airstrip. I'd sat through two assisted takeoffs already. Matthews wanted me to take this one and I didn't feel good about it. Two were not enough to make me feel confident about hauling that monster safely out of the meadow and besides, the night before I had overdone it in the mess. It was my twenty fifth birthday and we drank to within twelve hours of the first morning flight in defiance of the rules and basic common sense.

Those repeated gin and waters saved our lives. Without a hangover, I would have made the takeoff and there wouldn't have been time for us to survive. Instead, I insisted that he do the take-off. The accident investigation later found that a weld on the bottle mounts had weakened over the years of JATO takeoffs.

I followed through on the controls and when Matthews let go on the brakes I reached over and tapped the back of his throttle hand to let him know I was there and that he could use both hands on the control wheel.

Bob hit the JATO stud and hauled back on the column. There was a sharp slam in the small of the back as the rockets went off and we left the ground in a fair imitation of a punted football.

Then we lurched. The Herc skewed sideways in the sky while still going up. The skid threw me against the side console and the shoulder straps bit hard into my right shoulder. I later remembered a colossal bang but at the time it didn't register. We were fighting the controls for our lives, trying to stop the 130 from cartwheeling back into the grass and boulders.

We were both using all of our strength on the right rudder pedals to stop the skewing. I remember the strange clarity and how time slowed down during those few seconds. I've felt that clarity since in other dangerous situations.

The mind goes into top speed. Thought stops and automatic pathways open between the hindbrain and the reflexes. It's a kind of mental afterburner. Time slows because the reflexes have sped up so much and emotion is stripped out of the brain while the real work of keeping the organism alive goes on. It's as though the controlling circuits of the brain decide that being scared, amazed, terrified, or shocked is too much of a luxury to afford when everything must be devoted to life. I can clearly recall looking at one particular clump of mountain flowers, yellow and blue and white sitting fixed in the left center of the windshield. They were a wingspan away and I was concerned that perhaps we might damage them when we hit.

I also remember a scrape of paint on the glare shield that looked like a white outline of New Zealand. Bob told me afterwards that he could smell the shoe polish I used and was surprised it wasn't the KIWI brand most military used.

The two of us pulling and straining, the airframe shuddering and slamming on the point of a stall, the scream of the turbines and props as they went against the limits and we lifted the left wing-tip a fraction. The Hercules chopped through the top of the pine trees at the base of the moraine and all but scraped its aluminum belly up the slope. It was the closest I'd ever been to burning to death.

We flew on, not well, but we flew. The prop tips were twisted and bent from the trees. A tree had smashed the radome open and the engines vibrated so much from the imbalance they threatened to jump from their mounts. We flew that bugger all the way to the main base at the lowest power settings we could manage to ease the strain. We put it down very carefully on the concrete.

I couldn't get out of the cockpit for twenty minutes after we shut things down. I trembled from the after effects of massive adrenalin doses. My nerves and muscles paid for the system overloads and weakness smothered me. As I sat there, staring with unfocused eyes, I marveled at how the simple decision of refusing to do the takeoff because of a few too many drinks saved our lives. Instead, Bob Matthews, with his 15 thousand hours of flight time was on the controls at takeoff, in charge of a plane he knew better than any other. If it had been me at the wheel when the overstressed weld on the JATO mounting bracket had let go, Bob wouldn't have had time to react and that clump of flowers would have been incinerated, along with us.

Oddly the damage didn't take more than a week to repair. But the mechanics, while able to replace the props, tweak the engines back to specs, and replace the radome, weren't able to do anything about the blackened aluminum along the rear fuselage without sending the plane back to Lockheed in the states, so it stayed blackened and scarred. They also didn't have a collision light of the right size for the tail. The old one must have been smashed off by a chunk of pine tree. They replaced it with one from a different type of plane and the little light sat up on the tail as a pimply blemish instead of nestling into the top of the fin as part of a custom fitting.

Horst would remember me telling Johnny of the flight. She'd look at the Herc on Jenness and see the scars as well as the tail light.

THE BULLETS CAME

I kept the Twin Otter close to the ice. Occasionally I lost the far shore in blowing snow and had to rise to fifty feet to avoid clipping the top of any hidden pressure ridges. The scattered islets and islands of eastern Baffin Island needed dodging and that was fine because it hid me from Jenness. Gradually the critical side of my mind started clicking in and I stopped the panic reflexes. I relaxed enough to pull the power off a bit and let the plane fly easily. I wished I hadn't made such a dramatic take-off. It could only have started Horst thinking.

Second thoughts put a different color on the world. "There's nothing Horst can do," I said to myself, "she couldn't run after me and beat me up, there are no local Mafia types to hunt me down. She's stuck on a wind blasted island in the Davis Strait with no one within a day's snowmobile ride of her." I relaxed more and actually chuckled thinking how absurd I was being. I laughed out loud at the thought of her leaping into the Hercules and chasing me down, old fashioned Maxim guns blazing as she peeled out of the sun into me. Jack Standish versus the deadly foe in the Arctic skies. "Kid's stuff." I laughed.

I stopped laughing when the wheel twisted hard in my hands

and the fuselage buffeted in the roil of wing tip vortices as the CAL-AIR Hercules showed over the top of the cockpit five feet from my head. Only the fact that the Twin Otter was still riding at near max-cruise and empty saved me from plowing nose down into the ice. My long rusty fighter pilot reflexes burned their way through the synapses and I kept the plane off the ice.

The rear cargo ramp of the Hercules was down halfway, forming a flat and level gun-platform. Three men with heads and shoulders pushed past the end of the ramp so they hung half free in the air, fired endless bursts of automatic fire at me.

Glass exploded; the right half of the throttle quadrant fell to pieces, but the engine kept going. A bullet smashed into the back of the right rudder pedal slamming my foot back against the seat base.

The GPS flight computer exploded in a spray of silicon dust and copper shards. The thick smell of fuel swirled in the cabin. Acid rushed into the back of my throat as vomit tried to surge up.

I had the Otter pulling up now and over to the left. Very soon I'd be inverted on top of a skewed loop without enough altitude or speed to avoid the ice.

Still the bullets came; through the floor as I arced vertical, then through the side as the plane rolled.

I couldn't see for the haze of glass particles in front of my eyes and the terrific blast of subzero wind screaming through the broken windshield straight at me. I didn't feel the cold. I couldn't see beyond the bright glow of the sun. I blinked desperately trying to free my eyes from the glass and it was all I could do because I needed both hands to fight the roll of the control column. Something was wrong with the ailerons and the plane was not responding quickly enough. I was going to hit the pressure ice inverted and probably go right through into the seabed. I wouldn't have to worry about drowning because the shock of hitting the ice would telescope the fuselage and me in it to half of its length.

A PLACE TO DROWN

*CW*hen I was nine and a few days old I went to a park one afternoon with some school chums. We'd been given the day off while carpenters did their best to sand away odd knife gouges and compass point holes whittled into the desktops by class after class of bored nine year olds away from home in a private school. I don't know why the work was done during a school day, but I suppose the problems of getting tradesmen were just as chronic then as they are today.

There was stream that wound around an ash tree on its way to a lake in the main park. The hillside was formed of large round boulders, moss covered and wreathed in ferns. The easiest way up the hill was along the stream bed. Where it swept around the tree a dark pool had formed. It was the only spot where the water got more than knee deep. How deep it was we didn't know, nor as I recall did we even care. It was just a nice place to go for a swim on a late May morning. The pool was also reputed to hold thousands of coins tossed in the legend had it, by lovers who believed the pool had some magical quality to bring them permanent happiness. None of us knew for sure whether there was any money in the pool but as kids do we weren't going to question what appeared to be conventional wisdom.

I was terrified of water and couldn't swim, but I wasn't going to show that to my chums. The schooling we were going through was devoted to the long faded and ridiculed principles that made the British empire a world affair. We were not going to be allowed to let old traditions die although to the rest of the world they were all but fossils of dead animals.

As a result of that kind of ancient nonsense I was more than willing to chance drowning, or having a water creature of some hideous lineage leap up and pull me under, than admit I feared something.

That determination not to show fear saved my life. Instead of being the last one into the pool, as you would expect of the timid, I was the first.

The water was shockingly cold. The stream had been cold but as the water crept up to my thighs it got colder as if the bottom of the pool was a slab of ice. I slithered down the sloping rock shelf that seemed to lead toward the center of the pool. It was slick with algae and my feet started to slip. I couldn't stop moving deeper and deeper into the water as though some force was propelling me into the very center of the pool. Soon I was dancing on my toes and thrashing with my arms as I tried to maintain a vertical posture but it was a losing game and I had that clear feeling one gets during moments of great danger when all is certainly lost that I was about to die. I was drowning even with my head still above water.

I had the curious feeling that something had gone very wrong with the way the universe was supposed to be running my life and somebody should be doing something about the injustice of it all. And that all of this would be corrected if I could just slip back in time a few seconds and redo it all. It was a feeling of great confidence that there was such an ability to set the world right. It was like writing a letter and knowing that it was just the first draft and the clumsy phrases could be taken out the second time through.

All the same, panic was building. I was losing control of my own control over life in that pool.

In the Twin Otter the same feeling wrapped itself around me. There was nothing I could do.

In the pool, one of the boys had grabbed a hand and pulled me back to safety

There wasn't any one to help in the Otter's cockpit. As the horizon spun and debris shot around me and the plane bucked on the edge of a stall, I got the insane urge to light a cigarette and wait for it all to end.

There is a lot of hard psychology and physiology behind the Zen principle of action without thought; the archer doesn't feel the bow or the string and has mentally put the arrow into the target before he releases the string. A woodcarver feels for the shape wanted from the chisel before the edge cuts and when it has, the shape is there, as it always was.

A large part of flying training, especially in the military, is devoted to developing that autonomic reaction in a pilot. The hours of practicing what to do in a forced landing, what to do when an engine shuts down on takeoff, what to do when the de-icing boots don't work, how to avoid and outrun the beast of death before he has caught your scent, is to make the pilot react without thinking because action without thought will always be cleaner and better than if it all has to be thought out in advance. More time is spent preparing for disaster than learning the simpler tasks of navigation, weather lore, and the job of straight and level flying.

My feet moved on the rudder pedals by themselves and my hands pushed, pulled and twisted the yoke, all while my conscious mind was far away in long gone childhood and a swimming hole. There didn't seem to be any point to what my body was doing but then the body is a terribly hard thing to kill.

The mind will give up far sooner than the body and that body will bring the mind back from death if it is given the chance.

The hummocks of pressure ice couldn't have been more than forty feet directly in front of me as the Twin plunged down. Then I did something that is never intended for any of its aircraft to do — ever. With what twisted and snapped stumps of metal that remained of the throttle quadrant I could grab I shoved the props into reverse pitch. The blades turned flat to the airstream until they acted like solid disks.

The plane slammed into a pillow of air that wasn't much softer than the ice I was trying to avoid. There was no doubt that the airframe went far beyond the limits of its design. There was a shredding scream of metal from behind as the main spar shifted in its mounts and the yoke came right back into my lap as something snapped in the tail. The nose reared though and kept climbing as the ground leaped toward me. The horizon came down from the top of the cockpit, then through the middle, and finally below the nose and I was there and so was the ice. The ice hills rose around the cockpit and the engines screamed more. Then the air separated from the wings and the Otter stopped dead and slammed its belly onto the sea ice.

THE ICEFIELD

*T*he Hercules was in a forty five degree bank a mile ahead of me turning to sweep back and spray the wreck with bullets. The smell of fuel oil finally did make me vomit and the mind came back to life and thanked the body. I smashed my way out of the cockpit and fell to the snow dragging an Arctic sleeping bag and the survival kit with me.

I slithered into the lee of a ten foot slab of sea ice. It stood like a twelve foot dagger stabbed into the pressure ridge. It was as good a lean-to I could find. All around there were dozens of crazily leaning ice-slabs. Two vast sheets of first year ice had slid one over the other, like continents colliding to form the jumbled mass.

The Hercules went overhead without seeing me. It was so low that the downdraft from the wings and the props kicked up a swirl of dry powder that cut into my face and blinded me for a few moments. The blast of air shot under my unbuttoned parka bottom and sucked the warmth from my chest so quickly that I gasped. The sound of the propeller blades thrummed into the ice and my head.

I didn't think the Hercules could land on the ice at this time of year. Perhaps if it were carrying skis it might have but the weight on that huge body on high pressure tires would have made it a dangerous experiment. They would be after me any way they could and that would have to mean a ground trip from Jenness by snowmobile. I knew she had them because she had asked about the types the Inuit used. She had also talked briefly about the Arctic Cats her so-called expedition was using.

I hoped that by the time she was able to organize a hunt from Jenness, the signals from the locator beacon in my Otter would have been picked up and a plane sent to look for me. Its electronic howl would now be screaming up and down the frequencies and automatic location equipment would be locking on.

The Hercules came back again, more to my right this time and just as low. I squeezed back into the base of the ice slab and tried to stay as flat and as motionless as possible. It's always easier to spot movement from the air than shape. Many animals have the sense to freeze when they see a predator. The predator's eye is adapted to catching movement. If the prey can stand the stress of not moving while some fanged monster hunts for its dinner then it simply disappears from the hunter's eye.

The C-130 quartered over that pressure ridge for an hour before piling on the power and climbing out and back to the island. The rolling grind of its four engines dropped and finally the only sound left to me was the hiss of the snow blowing on the tops of the ice slabs. I could hear my breathing, rapid and shallow. My hands shook and I couldn't stop them.

I was in deathly trouble. No one is safe alone on the sea ice in the Eastern Arctic. Unless I could find or build some adequate shelter from the wind, I would start losing body heat. Despite the rations in my survival kit, and the small pressure stove, that heat loss would be irreversible. I didn't want to bet too heavily on the search planes arriving right away. Anything could delay my rescue. The weather in Iqaluit could be bad, or the location receivers might not be able to lock on to my position. Whatever, I couldn't afford to waste time and body heat standing around doing nothing to help myself.

The sun was trickling down behind the mountains of the Hall Peninsula when I caught the faint snarl of a snowmobile engine coming from the west. It wasn't too far off. The range of ice slabs I was in would be cutting down the distance the sound could travel. I pushed my gear into a crevice and kicked snow over it, then crawled up the edge of an ice sheet using the jagged edges as a ladder. Carefully, without getting my head any further into the skyline than necessary, I eased my eyes over the top and scanned the ice field.

The glare from the setting sun bounced straight into the nerve endings; it was like someone stabbing a fine steel needle into each eye socket. Gradually and slowly I rotated my head in an attempt fix the direction of the sound. The snow crystals flicked into my eyes. As well my ears went hard with the cold as the wind got to them. The tips took on the hot squeezing sensation that precedes tissue damage but I had to keep them exposed to hunt for the sound. I was willing to suffer some slight frostbite if it gave me warning of where the machine was coming from. The sound bounced around the ice mounds and although getting louder didn't seem to come from any direction at all other than somewhere in the general direction of the setting sun. The engine noise rose and fell as the driver threaded his way through the pressure ridges. The noise would rise to a shrill snarl then down to a burbling idle and back up as the machine worked through the hillocks of ice. It was coming fast.

I was getting desperate in my efforts to figure out where it would appear. I wanted a chance to slide around the ice slab and let him pass by without seeing me. But I couldn't decide which way to go because the sound boomed off the ice in all directions at once.

And then, he was there, directly in front of me.

The battered machine rose and twisted around the base of the slab in front and slid into the valley with its engine idling. He was standing up on the running boards, his head lifted sharply to look at me against the sky, surprise opening his eyes.

He wasn't part of Horst's party. He was an Inuk, about 18 years old and headed for a long journey by the look of his loaded komatik. The snowmobile might have been just a couple of years old, but it was so battered it looked like one of the first models ever built. The engine cowling was missing and with it the head-light. A slight haze of blue smoke drifted from the engine as the machine slid to a stop below me. The long seat cushion was broken open where sled dogs had got at it and the yellow foam spilled out in tattered chunks. He was dressed in a caribou parka and nylon windpants. A yellow and red Greenlandic hat was all the protection from the cold that he gave his ears. Yet no matter how used he was to the climate he had to be deeply cold. The windshield of the snowmobile was gone. Just a row of two inch triangular plastic teeth were left across the top of the dash. His face must have felt like it was being whipped by steel wires in that wind blast.

I let the air from my lungs in a long whoosh of relief and condensing vapor and slid down the slab to him.

The smell of burned oil was sharp in the clear air. The rattle of the idling engine filled the world as I walked slowly up. He gave a quick grin and flicked the kill switch and as the noise slipped away he let me know that he was over his surprise.

"Tea?"

It might be coffee, or just a cigarette or just the time to pass some banter, but it all came under the expression, tea. The Inuit will stop every few hours when travelling on the land to boil some snow and make tea.

I nodded. He swung off the machine to walk back to the komatik and unlash a wooden box a foot on a side. There were black streaks and the odd charring on the top where the stove had from time to time flared too high. The box contained all the tea makings.

"You've been here a long time?" he said as he pulled his seal-skin mitts off and then the foam filled ski gloves. Both looked like they had been run over a few dozen times by the snowmobile. They were dirty, cracked, and split along both outside edges at the heels of the palms.

"Since noon. How did you know where I was? Iqaluit radio, the camp?"

The only place he could have come from, travelling alone without protection and running the risk of slow death if he had a breakdown, was Iron Island. It was a camp of five families who had given up on the alcohol and the wage economy of Iqaluit to return to the harder, yet to them, more satisfying life of hunting. They didn't shun the benefits of southern life. They still had their flour, gasoline and ammunition flown in regularly and their furs and skins out. They just didn't like the effects of the white man's society on their own lives.

"Radio doesn't have batteries. Was going home and saw the plane. Do you want to go to Iron Island?"

I would have replied that I would prefer to walk for the next two weeks to get to Iqaluit, but sarcasm does not go over in a culture that is genuinely polite. "Yes I would like to go the camp, if you don't mind."

He nodded.

We drained some fuel from the wrecked plane to fill a ten gallon drum on the komatik. The fuel could be used at the camp for warmth and cooking. I loaded some scraps of metal along with the engine covers and the spare blankets. No one would want them back and the camp could use the extra supplies.

"You get this trouble at Jenness Island eh?" he said running his glove along a jagged bullet tear under the wing. "They shot at Simonee two days ago when he went to the old buildings for wood."

"Was he hurt?"

He shook his head. "All what we wanted was the wood. There are no seals there to hunt. We weren't hunting their seals."

"Did you report it?"

"No. No batteries. The radio doesn't work."

I pulled an extra set of batteries from the rear fuselage and stowed them in my pocket to keep them warm and charged. With a little bit of wiring, I might get the spare batteries to drive the camp's satellite phone and raise Iqaluit. I wanted to get the word out that something very wrong was going on at Jenness Island. I was about to take the Emergency Locator Transmitter with me as well, then thought better of it. The wreckage would be far easier for the planes to spot than tiny me lost in the peninsula hills. I left a note instead and impaled it on the stump of the control yoke where it would be found quickly.

Tommy Ipuluk might not have had the latest word in snow-mobiles, and he certainly didn't have the best maintained, but he could have shown the makers of snowmobile television commercials a few tricks. He drove that machine through the jungle of ice with a grace and fluidity that kept us moving without wild surges of engine power and frantic braking.

He had the grace that racing car drivers get; the grace of a carpenter putting up a wall without the need for a level, the grace of the top aerobatic pilots. He was a master. And it wasn't surprising. They say that the marauding Mongols of the Asian steppes were the world's best horsemen because they had been born on horseback. Well, Tommy was the same way only he had been born on a snowmobile, not a horse.

I had my hands clamped as tight as I could make them to the tie-down ropes on the komatik, thirty feet behind Tommy. It leaped and twisted violently as the snowmobile rocketed through the ice field, enveloped in blue acrid smoke.

It was going to be a race between freezing to death, or dying of carbon monoxide poisoning. The komatik lurched and slammed at the end of its yellow plastic tether, skewing and twisting as it followed Tommy. I don't think the sled ran its entire length in a straight line for the first half hour of the trip. I gave up trying to sit on the thing and sprawled face down over the boxes and packs and hung on with all my strength. The beating the komatik was taking would have torn apart anything built with nails and screws. But for thousands of years the Inuit have built their sleds with lashings so that the structure can flex and twist without breaking. They still make them that way now because there're no fasteners, nails, screws or glue strong enough to withstand the terrain of the Eastern Arctic.

Every once and a while some well meaning southerner builds a komatik with a box of screws, five ply, and a good buttering of epoxy glue. He ends up with a sled that is rock steady and inflexible. The Inuit have seen it before and are always too polite to say anything. That marvellous komatik usually falls apart halfway through the first winter and often miles out on the land during the coldest day of the year.

Tommy's best trick on that ride was one that left me gasping with fright. We had been running inshore to the hills and had to cross from the sea ice to the landfast ice. There was open water in the gap. The ice was losing its grip because of the growing hours of thaw during the early spring days. The gap we were heading for must have been fifty feet across. From where I was, stretched down over the komatik trying to see through the haze and wind blast, it was all black clear water only God knew how deep. He didn't slow. My hands tightened on the ropes while part of me tried to decide whether to jump or hang on.

He opened the throttle all the way. The sled leaped violently, the track snapped viciously at the underside of the chassis, and the runners crashed and vibrated through the ice and snow.

We hit the water doing about fifty miles an hour. The lead was filled with broken chunks and slabs of ice forming a lumpy black carpet of ice all the way across. Even the lightest of cats would have sunk trying to cross from one to another, but then a cat doesn't have its weight spread out the way a snowmobile does. The long and broad track and twin runners as wide as water skis, let snow machines slide easily over the softest of surfaces.

The water shot back out and up from the track and landed on me in a welter of slush and solid ice and quickly freezing water. I couldn't see and the shock of the cold, as well as the difficulty in breathing, left me face down as Tommy shot across the lead. His machine reached solid ice just as the momentum started to go from the komatik and its nose started slowly down toward the water. He kept the throttle open. The tip of the komotik's runners hit the far side with a slam and we bounced free of the water. He braked and we stopped on firm ice.

"Tea?" he said.

I shivered an answer.

The packs I had taken from the Otter held dry clothing. Despite the wind blowing against my bare skin it was a huge delight to strip naked and change. My parka was drenched and already starting to crust with ice.

"Put this on," he said taking off his parka.

"What about you?"

It's not far and it's not that cold."

The water we had charged through had refrozen in less than two minutes. The water in the pot on the stove had been there ten minutes without a sign of the little heat bubbles that show a boil is coming. I was far too cold to argue with him about the temperature and took his coat. "How far are we?"

"About an hour maybe." He didn't seem very confident about it although I supposed he should know since it was his backyard.

"It's getting pretty dark, are you sure you can find your way?"

There was shake of his head as he bent over the stove. I had insulted him in some way.

I added, "Oh I suppose you're right, but I've never been out on the land this far. I've never been so damn cold before either."

"Just over that hill," he pointed to a young mountain that shot up out of the bay, all black rock and scarred with packed snow in the twilight. "We'll be there before the moon gets up."

At one end of the sky, the red slash of the falling sun painted a dark streak, At the other, a silver gleam from the rising moon just below the horizon showed beyond the ice in the Davis Strait.

I drank most of the tea without waiting for it to cool from the pot. The air was so cold that the water lost its fire hardly before it was in the cup. When we started out again I sat behind him on the snowmobile. "Why didn't we do this before?"

"Might have gone through the ice eh. Too much weight."

The climb was slow. I had a bad tendency of leaning away from the hill when the machine started to rock instead of into it. That bad habit risked sending both of us tumbling down the slopes. Tommy would go one way, me the other, and the machine would teeter on the brink of flipping over and down to the sea ice. I think he regretted putting me on the back although I couldn't begin to imagine what the ride would have been like on the sled as it slithered crablike along the slopes. Perhaps with me on it I would have finished the trip upside down.

The moon was well up and to our left when we came over the top. Its light filled the valley in front. An inlet of water from the strait slanted across our path. On the other side were the hills and mountains of Baffin Island proper. At the base of the hill, directly below us, the rocks flattened out and formed a wide plateau before slipping easily into the inlet. It was the only area of the coast I had seen all day where the rocks didn't plunge directly down into the water. I suppose in the summer it would have been a gravel bed, a sort of wide rude beach left by a twist in one of the last great glaciers.

But Iron Island Camp was no longer there.

SNOW DRIFTS AND TRENCHES

*W*here the wood and canvas huts had stood were black smears on the snow. The five huts that had been buried to their roofs in snow the last time I had seen them in early winter, as well as the boats that had been beached for the winter, all were black smears.

Tommy flicked the kill switch. The silence wrapped us.

I cleared my throat before saying anything. "Where is it Tommy? Where's the camp." I wanted him to say they had moved and burned everything they left behind, yet I knew that would not be the answer. "Where are they? What has happened?"

He pulled the rope starter. The engine didn't catch. A shadow drifted across the scene and then I realized that it wasn't a shadow but the smoke from the charred remnants of the camp. I thought I could smell it but it was too far away. The engine started. Tommy opened the throttle and we plunged down that slope under acceleration until the engine screamed at full power. I couldn't think for the terror of the ride.

"For Christ sakes slow down," I screamed against the motor and the crash of the skis against the rocks, the roar of the wind mounting as we sped. I thought I heard the komatik smashing against the rocks behind us. The slope was a good forty-five degrees. He wouldn't listen. "For God's sake I'm going to fall off."

I couldn't hold onto his waist hard enough to stop being thrown around the rear of the machine. My feet kept flying out of the running boards. I feared flipping off the rear of the Arctic Cat to be run over by the five hundred pound komatik charging behind.

Tommy charged straight ahead without trying to find the snow path. He went straight over boulders, over small drops of three and four feet, charged up hillocks without worrying what was behind them and kept going straight down. I don't know how fast we were going, but I have never had such a ride in any vehicle even during supersonic low level combat sorties.

The last hundred yards were under full braking as the hill flattened out. It became a question of whether we would stop before charging into the still red and flickering ruins of a hut. The snowmobile slewed and bucked and shuddered and stopped finally ten feet from the ruins. The engine stopped and the cessation of its noise and the wind roar, together with and the fright of the ride made me feel like my heart had stopped with the engine.

There was nothing left of the camp. We had seen it all from the top of the hill.

"My father, my brothers...."

I shook my head. I didn't know whether it was because of the scene or whether I was still recovering from the ride. "I don't know kid. It was one hell of a fire that did this." I walked into the black, kicking bits of wood and canvas out of the way. He hung back.

"Are there any people there?" his voice was weak and young.

"I don't know kid, let me look around a bit." I sniffed the air. All I could smell was the charring and the faint smell of gasoline. There was no smell of meat.

I waded through the wreckage of the hut then another ten

feet away. The huts had been fired separately. There was too much space between them for a flash fire to have jumped across the gap. While it might have happened to two, it couldn't have happened to all five. It also could not account for the destroyed warehouse hut and the boats which were fifty yards away.

There were no bodies.

"Tommy, it looks like they all got away. There's nothing here."

He was now kicking through the ruins himself. "Maybe they got medevaced to Iqaluit?"

I grunted. I couldn't see how that might have happened without a working satellite phone to call for help and it didn't answer the question of who had burned down the camp. As for why, it was beyond me. Jenness Island though seemed to have the answers.

A shout from Tommy brought me quickly down to the boats. "Mr. Standish, here are some dead things."

I shuffled over in no real hurry. They were bodies but until I was sure I didn't say anything. "Dogs Tommy. The sled dogs were shot." One of the corpses had an unburned head and the bullet wound was clear. Without that head, I might have thought they were children. "Someone really piled on the gasoline here."

"Look there," his arm raised out to the inlet white in the moonlight. "A plane was here, they were rescued, everyone went in a medevac plane."

A long furrow of churned snow down the inlet showed dark gray in the light. The blast of the props had fanned out at the far end where the pilot had turned for his takeoff. The prop blast and turbine exhaust had sprayed the snow straight off the ice to leave a black teardrop. Between it and the shore was a trampled mess of snow where people had marched back and forth.

I didn't say anything while he went on. "They got them out to Iqaluit after the fire. Someone must have seen the smoke. How are we going to get out too?"

"Can you ride your machine to Iqaluit?"

"Don't think so no, the machine won't last. Could try maybe."

I didn't care for the idea either. Still, there wasn't much choice. It was either head out into the bay and make a run for Iqaluit on his cranky and near collapse snowmobile, or hang about at Iron Island waiting for the ELT to be picked up.

"They'll be back though. My father will tell them I was hunting and they'll be back in the morning. Sure you bet," He grinned and laughed. I laughed too, but I thought that we should have seen the plane that picked them up. The pilot wouldn't have left behind anybody, even for a night, without trying to make even a quick search by air. I also didn't think that Iqaluit had a Hercules to send out on an evacuation flight. It could only have been a Hercules that had churned up the snow on the inlet that badly.

I was talking to myself more than to him. "I have a feeling that there won't be any search planes looking for me." He stared.

"I have a feeling that something is stopping the ELT from getting through." I had no basis for that other than a deep paranoia about a group of people who would hijack a four engine transport, fly it three thousand miles, possibly kill its crew, shoot down an aircraft, then either murder or kidnap a hamlet of thirty people to keep their activities secret. "I was getting a lot of radio interference on the flight to Broughton. I'll bet it was the same thing that stopped your satellite phone from working, not batteries. Something is blacking out the region."

He didn't follow me although he caught enough of my emotion to look stunned. I gave him a cigarette.

"Would they kill them?"

I searched through my trouser pockets for the lighter. I stared blankly at the mountain ranges to the west before speaking. "I don't know Tommy. Probably not. If they were going to kill them, they wouldn't have bothered to fly them out." There was no conviction in my voice and he felt it. "Look," I said, "we can't stay here. They'll be looking for me and they might just decide to come back. I'm going to need your machine."

"What are you going to do. Where are you going?"

"I think I'm going to have to go back to Jenness." I didn't know why I had to do such a thing. It just seemed to make more sense to attack the enemy than to keep trying to run away. "You can't stay here by yourself and if you come with me it will be dangerous. Can you get me to walking distance of the island and then maybe go to Iqaluit?"

"Maybe can. I dunno. I need gas though." He was looking around the camp and feeling the loneliness. "Maybe I can get help."

"Sure kid. You go to Iqaluit and tell the Mounties where I've gone and what's happened and it'll all work out." I've never felt such a lack of conviction in my life. By the time he got to the settlement I would have been in the hands of Horst and her friends for quite a while. Either I would've found a way out of the mess by then or Horst would have killed me.

"We go and see if the gas is still there." He ran off down the beach and started kicking at a snowdrift. It was the camp's gasoline cache and untouched.

We dug snow trench shelters into the drifts so we could survive the night cold.

JENNESS ISLAND

*A*nd then, Teller smashed down through the roof of my snow trench and hauled me out by the throat.

He tossed me out on the ice.

All I could do was lie on the snow and shiver.

Tommy lay nearby, dead.

I couldn't take my eyes off the kid's spread-eagled body, blood splashing down with an obscene plopping noise onto the running board of his snowmobile.

Teller reached down to me and slammed his fist against the side of my head. I saw it coming, knew what the pain would be and felt the waves build for a second before I tumbled out of the world.

I came to in the rear seat of a Bell 412. They'd landed it behind a twenty foot pressure ridge out of sight of the camp. I wondered whether it had been Horst who had landed the gunship under autorotation to avoid noise; instead it was Teller who swung himself into the pilot's seat and buckled in.

Teller had the turbines spooled up and the blades biting in one quick series of movements that betrayed his abandonment of any checklist. A window vibrated beside my left ear as the turbines spooled up. Waves of pain shot through my banged head. I stopped paying attention until the helicopter dipped and half turned to the left a few seconds after takeoff. Then I saw the wreck of my Otter. It was an odd sight. The tail was cocked high because of the broken back, the wings were buckled just past the struts and drooped onto the ice. Both turbine nacelles were broken loose from the mounts so they hung down and splayed out. The impact forces must have been enormous. Some freak of luck had somehow resulted in the cockpit hitting the ice slower than the rest otherwise I would have been smashed dead.

A sharp stab of white yellow appeared in the wreck to be joined by another. My eyes were watering from the pain in my head and I was having trouble seeing what was happening on the ice in the dark. The shadows in the wreck were impenetrable until the helicopter circled and came around on the down-moon side. I saw four orange parkas studded in the metal. They were cutting up the Otter. A pile of cabin insulation, seats and landing gear struts sat near the tail where a flame was working on the stabilizer. Horst, it seemed, didn't want any trace left of the plane. They were going to have to helicopter those loads out. It would have been pointless to try blasting a hole through the ice and pushing the Twin through. Explosives have little effect on ice unless planted deep within and in vast quantities and this sea ice must have been five feet thick. There'd been attempts in the second world war to blast icebergs out of the way of the North Atlantic convoys using naval guns. It turned out to be a pointless gunnery exercise on an impervious target.

The Bell 412 stopped over the Otter, pivoted on its nose and settled on a course to the northeast for Jenness where the sun was just starting its rise. Soon the sun began to shaft through the acrylic windshield between Horst and Teller, and into my eyes. The pain caused by the shrill of the turbine blades slashing at the edge of supersonic, and the thrashing of the rotors as we vibrated toward the sun climbed over me. I slipped back into blackness.

"We'll be there soon Standish." The half shout from Horst toward me in the back pulled my eyes open. I hadn't been out more than a few minutes. I watched a flight of ducks skimming a floe edge. I couldn't tell their species or whether they were pushing the season. A ring seal plopped off a floe and disappeared from the rush of the helicopter. I wished I was that seal with only the occasional Inuk hunter to fear.

The island showed as a black splotch in the glare splashing across the plastic screen. To the right and left the ice flared white silver. The sky ranged from dusty black through purple to bright grey blue, except where the horizon met the sky. There it shone with a flickering blue white from the sea ice in the Davis Strait. The helicopter slipped sideways toward the rocks where the pressure ice rafted against the shore. There wasn't the slightest sign of turbulence. That was rare. Normally in any flight, aircraft, helicopters included, shuddered and bounced through the changing density of the air, or the buffeting from air tumbling over rough ground. There was always the faintest tremble, but not this time. We slid smoothly through the air. The sea ice lay flat and smooth, except for dark irregular streaks where the wind had blown the snow free to expose the bare ice. The rocks came closer with a rush and Jenness stood before us filling the windshield. It went up vertically but oddly seemed to hang over us like a wave about to break as we flew nose down the way helicopters do at high speed. It was an approach you'd never make in an aircraft because you would never be sure that the plane could pull up sharply enough.

A spur of rock curves out of the west side of the island to form a channel about sixty feet wide and perhaps three hundred long. It's a natural boat shelter and the rocks are high enough that the rafting ice and pressure ridges cannot make it over. There was something black and tall sitting behind the rocks as we moved in toward the cliff face. I couldn't make it out at first and then its straight lines and blackness hardened. It looked like an oil company storage tank that had been squashed and sat in the water.

The helicopter shot straight at it. About the moment when I started to get really worried about the cliffside the steel tower dropped below the level of the instrument dash and Teller pulled the craft up. The G forces pushed me down into the seat and we popped over the shore cliff to the steeply rising hills of the island, following the line of the gravel road on up. The road went to the old North Warning System station built into the crest of the hill above the dock constructed in the fifties.

More than half a century later the road still looked serviceable. The years had made little difference to its surface. The occasional runoff channel had eaten across the road, and some patches or road were hummocks of rock and dirt where buried ice had erupted through. But it was passable. There were tracks and ruts on it. The deep cut tire treads of heavy trucks were sharp and clear and could only have been hours old at most.

GALETTA

The Hercules wasn't on the airstrip when we flew around the last hill-shoulder before the North Warning System station. I supposed it was off dropping bodies into the Atlantic or something just as horrible. Horst seemed to read my mind. "Those people at the camp. We took them to Helliwel Island. They'll be all right, but it will be a long time before anyone finds them."

They knew their ground, I had to give them that. Helliwel is a community on Radio Tower Island at the north tip of Labrador in the Hudson Strait, just where the borders of Quebec and Labrador meet. It was there in the mid 18 hundreds as a whaling post and a doorway into both the Davis and Hudson Straits for the British Navy expeditions of the century. It's a pretty hard place to live in because Helliwel gets the worst weather in the Arctic. If it's not snowing, then it's raining or perhaps fog. It's a depressing place and when the last government nurse pulled out a few years ago the 20 Inuit families left behind packed up and moved into Northern Quebec settlements. They left behind the houses, the Hudson Bay Store, the grocery and general store, and a working power plant. The entire community was left intact with everything but people.

"They could be found tomorrow you know," I said.

Horst answered. "Not likely Captain, but then it doesn't much matter anyway."

I thought of the spreading waves of seal hunters who set out each spring from the communities when the sun is warm on the backs of the ring and harp seals and lulls them into dozing sleep along the floe edge, easy prey for the Inuit hunter. Port Helliwel was an attractive hunting base. An empty house with fuel oil still in the tanks would be a hell of a lot more inviting than a tent no matter how warm the spring sun got.

It wasn't surprising that Horst's operation would know about Jenness, but its knowledge of an abandoned settlement several hundred miles away did. It's not the kind of thing that the tourism department makes mention of when you write for information and the maps no longer show Helliwel as a community. Horst was right. It wasn't likely that they would be found quickly, if ever, because this crowd that was flying me around seemed a little too quick with a gun to have left potential witnesses alive. "How did you get them there? Not with the Herc?."

"Oh, but yes." She was grinning hard enough to show me her gums.

"You didn't land that monster on the ice." I didn't know whether she could or not, but I was more amazed that anyone might have tried. There's a forty foot tide at Helliwel. I'd have to be pretty blasted sure the ice was holding before I'd try to put a four engine transport down on spring sea ice, skis or not.

Her grin turned to a chuckle.

Teller swung the helicopter around the scoop antennas of the radar base and set up a hover close to the base of a long dirty black stretch of one story building partially covered in drifted snow.

"Yes we used the Hercules but I was not the pilot. My man put it down on the landfast ice. Besides this is not Trans Northern or First Air." She turned away to watch the ground coming up.

She had a point. Charter outfits with Hercs running halfway around the world operated to pretty strict rules. They'd no more put a Herc down on unknown ice than I'd turn props without a preflight. Someone who was running the risks that Horst was would just put the risks in with all the others she'd be balancing. Still, the landing and takeoff must have been bad.

"I don't suppose your pilot's hands have stopped shaking yet." I had to shout over the increased roar of the blades. Teller was balancing in ground effect and edging the last foot and a half to the ground.

"Oh Captain Standish, he is not my pilot." She said without turning around. She had that amused chuckle in her voice again.

I puzzled over it as the blades kicked up a blast of snow and turned the view ahead into a white glaze. It drifted away slowly as the blades stopped carrying our weight and stopped. The snow dust shone with flashes of blue and spots of red in the sun. The glare stabbed into my eyes so hard I feared I was going to slip away again.

They shoved me out and into the building at a run. They were doing the hurrying, I was sort of doing a shambling drag and trying to clear my head. I got a glimpse of a forest of antennae clustered on the roof, all steel spikes and cream colored fiberglass shells and gloss-black leads. A scattering of spruce pallets and packing crates fanned out from the doorway as though they had been tossed to each side the minute they were unpacked. Some of the three quarter ply from the crates had been used to block out the windows of the building where passing hunters had fired potshots through the double glaze. The plywood was all stencilled "Galetta Station" and slashed with black paint rectangles like the crates on the Otter had been.

Inside, some effort had been made to clear the hallway of ripped insulation, shattered glass, twisted fluorescent light fixtures and the rest of the flotsam left behind when the station had been shut down. It lay in long piles along the baseboards; a trail of useless garbage. All of it had once been flown in at enormous cost by U-S military cargo flights from the states. Nothing, and certainly not cost, had been allowed to hold up the rush to get the North Warning System built and working before the Soviets learned how to build ICBMs.

"A remarkable place Standish. Except for the damage done by the Eskimos, everything is still fresh. Why, do you know that all that the trucks needed were new batteries, a change of oil, and they started?"

I did know. It was the same at all the old stations.

When the government got around to salvaging the bases after buying them in the 1970's from the United States for a dollar it found itself with an unexpected fortune of salvageable heavy equipment. There were ten ton trucks with fewer than five thousand miles on them in new working condition. Refrigeration equipment and generators untouched by corrosion, their copper wires only slightly dulled by tarnish and still running sweetly in their oiled bearings. And endless stockpiles of like-new equipment; all persevered by the intense dry cold of the Arctic.

The glass crunched under our feet as we walked down the hallway to what must have been the control center. A plain band of white gold flashed on Horst's right ring finger as she talked and waved about at the walls. "It's as though everything here was kept in a museum only there are no exhibit labels." She was pleased by that remark and drilled me with her eyes to see whether I had noticed her wit. I only nodded again, but slower this time because my head still wasn't clear from the blow. I was also walking in a fog built up from extreme stress and no useful sleep. The brain was down to iron rail straight and linear thinking and was going to stay that way until I cleared the fatigue poisons out with some rest.

There was enough light coming from the unbroken and

unboarded windows to see that the walls had kept their sick green color above the shoulder high gloss yellow of the wainscoting molding. The place had that faint wax and disinfectant smell military barracks pick up. Here the smell was decades old. It had been trapped in the near perpetual freeze, apart from a few weeks in summer when the temperature briefly got above freezing. Now with the heat drifting from the control center door it was coming out of the very structure of the building.

I thought Horst was leading me to the old control room and I stumbled in surprise when I was hauled off to the left and down another corridor. Here it was colder. The air swept in through a break in the wall where a foundation had given away and opened a two foot slash in the ten ply and tarpaper. The litter was worse here as well. There was armored electrical cable conduit lying in loops and in the gloom the footing got tricky. Horst hadn't bothered with lighting this section.

"Here captain. We'll keep you here for a while." She motioned to Teller who leaned past his master and slid the bolt on the green metal door.

OLD CROW

$\mathcal{M}$y Swahili never had been good, and in the years since I had last seen him it had nearly disappeared, but I managed a few words.

"Two weeks," he shouted as he leapt to his feet and pounded me on the collar bones so hard that my heels felt like they were being driven into the gray linoleum.

"Uhali gani?" he said.

"Fine Phillip. I've been mourning you, crashing an airplane, trying not to get murdered, kidnapped, and God knows what else by that gang out there, but I'm fine." I was reeling as much from his pounding as from the shock of seeing him. "I thought you were dead. Where's your crew, Hadley and your loadmaster?"

The black face froze. "Killed when they captured us."

Phillip Tonguay, an African who wanted to fly so much in his early teens that he left what was left of Zimbabwe under the tyrant rule of Mugabe to emigrate to Canada with his parents on just the hope that he could get flying training.

With the help of an uncle in Montreal he got a job, and then several of them, working as many as four jobs a day. He worked tables in restaurants, ran dishwashers, and providing back kitchen help to finance his schooling. He went through secondary school, then university, and learned a new country. He used natural drive to beat through the doors and get into the Royal Canadian Air Force.

With all the drive to reach his goal of flight training he had never learned any of the social graces. While he could lay a table in a flash and was never at a loss for the right fork at a squadron dinner by virtue of his three and a half years in Montreal's restaurants, he never came close to mastering clothes. His idea of dressing would as likely include red socks and flashing blue trousers with a pink shirt as anything else. He had an odd clumsiness to his body too that made him look as gauche as he acted. His elbows stuck out when he walked and the drill instructors at basic never did get him to walk light-footed. Through the weeks of drill he continued to drive the soles of his boots into the parade ground with a flat footed snap. One day while still in basic training when we were still terrorized by our instructors he lost his winged cap badge.

He lost a lot of things and never missed them. Some people get sick to their stomach when they misplace something close to them. He hardly ever remembered owning anything.

The cap badge was something though. Every morning at six there was a fall-in and inspection before the march to the mess hall half a mile from the H-Huts. The instructors would look closely at our chins to see whether we had indeed used a razor and some of them would pull out a credit card and scrape it under a recruit's jaw. If it rasped, the poor bastard was in for cleaning toilets or extra drill during breaks. Brass had to be polished, bodies showered, and the toes of our black officer shoes, with a seam of stitching across the toes to distinguish them from ordinary airmen's shoes, had to gleam so much they became curved mirrors. It was serious stuff and we were all aware that we could be washed out of flying training before we ever got near a plane for a crummy performance in basic training.

Instead of Phillip recognizing that it really was important that he have a badge, and a properly shined one at that, and instead of getting a new one from stores, he simply fixed a pair of cheap white metal wings to his hat; the type of thing that pilots' organizations send out to prospective members as a subscription premium. One of the other trainees had picked them up in the junk mail that found us even at training camp. They were half the size of the real wings, blue and gold, instead of brass, and looked nothing like the broken necked albatross of the Air Force. So there he was that morning, chin shaved so every bristle nestled deep in his black pores, his shoes flashing in the rising sun, creases unbent and sharp, and this ridiculous tin badge stuck on the front of his officer's hat.

I was nowhere near him in the formation. At that point, I'd hardly said a word to him during those first weeks because I was busy trying to fit myself into this strange world of tight discipline and wondering when we would get to play with the airplanes.

The sergeant's peering eyes slid past me without comment. He lashed out at the guy next to me for having a tunic button at a cockeyed angle and snarled his way along the front rank to the right marker where Phillip stood straight to attention staring at the horizon.

The bellow scared me so much I tightened every muscle in my legs and nearly fell over. The sergeant had seen the badge and the abuse started.

"What in hell do you call that Mister?"

"Sir?"

"The badge you bugger. What in hell do you call that pile of shit on your head?"

"Sergeant I will thank you not to be abusive."

I choked. No one, probably not even the Station Commander, would ever have the nerve to talk back to our Sergeant. The guy was a walking nightmare of savagery and little controlled violence. I waited, we all waited, for the sound of guts splashing on the concrete.

"Abusive huh? You think I"m being abusive when I see some horrible piece of work like you have the nerve to come out on my parade ground with a hat looking like a pigeon crapped all over it. You are going to find out just how hard life can be."

I couldn't resist sliding my eyes to the side and gently easing my head so I could see, but without running too much of a risk of being caught looking. Everyone else was doing it too and we must have looked a crazy lot with our eyeballs rammed over as far as they could to the sides of our heads and the heads very cautiously turned toward what was without doubt going to be the biggest explosion we would see before the next war.

"Sergeant, I believe that you are referring to my hat badge."

"Of course you tall and useless tree stump. How dare you play dumb with me you insolent snot nosed puppy." His voice was raised hard and high. Its echoes bounced clearly back in the early morning air from the concrete barracks under construction at the other side of the parade ground. Other training units would be hearing that horrible voice coming over them as they too suffered through their inspections. "Do you know what I am going to do to you, you twisted pile of human wreckage? Do You!"

"No Sergeant," came Phillip's clear and controlled reply with its touch of British accent.

"I am going to make you scrub every inch of this parade ground," he paused to let the echo bound and rebound and die away, "with a goddamned toothbrush."

"Sergeant I feel I should state that you are exceeding your authority and I must remind you that Queen's Regulations forbid corporal punishment."

"YOU!" The echoes smashed about us, then left faded to leave a clean calm. Even the far off commands and tramp of boots from the other units stopped in silence. "YOU SIR! You remind me of a winter's day, short dark and dirty and very fucking miserable."

It has to be one of the oldest insults in the book from which drill sergeants learn their trade and I am sure that Julius Caesar's recruit instructors were using it two thousand years before. Still, coming the way it did, screamed over the whole base in the face of the only black in basic and to someone three inches over six feet tall, it collapsed us. It started slowly, like any great explosion will, with a slow deceptive building. The tensions in our bodies seemed to snap and spill their dammed energies over to the central nervous system. First came a teeth clenched grunt from someone behind me, then an explosion of expelled air from someone else and then the formation fell apart as we doubled over and reeled around in laughter.

We did four hours of extra drill that day. I became friends with him the same day and we went through our training together in a long series of suppressed jokes and wisecracks that stemmed from the day he had faced the devil and found him a milk snake.

Of course later it wasn't easy for him to be the only black in flying training. The competition was murderous. Pilot trainees are out for themselves because there are only so many spots open on the hot planes and that means lots of wash-outs. We never thought twice about kicking someone when they were down because once they were out out it eased the pressure just a bit on you. Phillip went the full year and a half through training with hardly a tightened neck muscle while they called him "blackie" or "jungle bunny" or any other racist slur that came along. But he made it through the training and a lot of them didn't. His skill as a pilot stopped the slurs. He had a major talent.

Now, after all this time here he was on an isolated hunk of rock in the Eastern Arctic.

"Well. What the hell you doing here and give me a cigarette." I hadn't had once since finding the burned outpost camp. The first deeply drawn breath sent my head spinning as the nicotine attached itself to all the empty brain receptors.

I'd been trying to quit for long time. There wasn't anything good about the habit and it was playing hell with my blood pressure and if I didn't do something about that soon, my pilot's licences would be in deep jeopardy.

We were in what probably had been the duty officer's bunk. The place where someone on duty would be allowed to sleep as long as he was fully clothed and ready to take the command if anything happened on the scopes. It would have been used in rotation by the officers. It held nothing other than two heavily upholstered red leather office arm chairs and a bed frame naked to the springs. Two shelves ran along the rear wall, separated by a window, and littered with scattered manuals, a crumpled map of the straits, six or seven coverless paperbacks losing their pages, and two brown mugs, one with a broken handle, the pieces lying on the floor under the window. A sheet of ply was screwed on from the outside. The screws poked their points through the window frame by half an inch.

"Jack I didn't know how they did it, although I do now. I lost all radio over the Old Crow Flats. Nothing but hash on all the radios and not just the comms. I tried HF too and that was just as bad; otherwise I would have tried to send on fifty two eighty." He crouched down, putting his back to the door and sat with his eyes closed. "Marteau shot Hadley when he came up on deck to see why we'd turned off course. The bastard pulled a gun on me when I was fiddling with the radios and then gave me a new course to fly. He didn't say a thing, just shot the kid in the forehead. Scared the shit out of me, I thought he was going to do me next and fly it himself."

Hijacked over the northern Yukon coast, that was a new one. "Who's Marteau. New guy?"

"Yeah, signed on with the company about a month ago and

came through the CFI checks like he'd invented Hercs. Seemed like a nice guy."

"What kind of co-pilot is he?" Lots of people can fly planes and a lot of them have trouble taking orders from a captain.

"Oh, he was fine, really almost too good. He'd have his hands on the flap selector before I hardly made up my mind to call for them. Same on the wheels. I mean it was like he was flying instead of me, not just looking ahead to what I might want, but really like he was the pilot and I was his cojo."

"How did you get here? You surely didn't fly the bird straight here did you."

"No. I guess they knew the word would get around pretty quick that the Herc was missing and we couldn't fly across the top of the Arctic without getting spotted. No, we cut south to the Alaska border and the Alaska Highway. There's an airstrip at Red Ore Creek. Know it?"

"I flew a few trips in there before the mine closed. Cessna 185 from Dawson running spares. You didn't land there did you? That strip's not big enough for a Hercules surely."

"Oh god, yes Jack of course it is if," he paused and reached his hands out in front of him so they were pulling back on the horns of a Lockheed control wheel, "you drag it in nice and slow."

I had slouched back in the armchair under the shelves so the back of my neck was resting on the rounded leather and feeling the heat of my body soften the leather so it molded to my shape. "Not nice huh." I was telling him I knew what that landing must have been like.

"Yeah, you're right. Blew a tire and burned the others on the gravel before pulling her back from the edge. I'm glad we were light. Could have been loaded with fuel but figured Anchorage would be better after we'd done the Prudhoe run."

"Why Red Ore Creek?"

He shrugged and spread his hands again. "Why not? It's deserted, in the middle of a fucking mountain range, no one goes near the place and if you wanted a place to work on a stolen plane for a while it can't be beat. It's also a great place to hide a small army." He jerked his thumb behind him at the door. "They had me out of the plane and a bunch of instrument and electronics technicians inside practically before I'd shut down properly. They had this huge mobile home thing that really was mobile on wheels and not just propped up on blocks. It was a shell to hide a fuel tanker. They had all these other motor home things, too all full of crates and stuff they just loaded straight into the C-130. Did a hell of a lot of work on that plane and a full servicing. Know what else they did to it too?"

He would have continued, but I was nodding. "JATO."

"How'd you know?"

"Really guessed I suppose. I saw the plane yesterday here except that it was all painted up differently of course. Recognized it too by the old burn marks. Course you had to use JATO to get out of Red Ore, didn't you?"

"Yah. Well, they loaded the thing right down with a hell of a pile of cargo."

"Any trouble?"

"No it was simple."

He wasn't a good liar. As far as I knew Phillip had never made a rocket assisted takeoff in the forces and rocket assisted takeoffs are never used in commercial flying, or much at all by anybody's military. It is just too dangerous.

I could imagine the kind of tension he must have been under at the end of the gravel with his props churning against the air and the brakes locked solid, wondering what the blast from the tubes would feel like and whether he could control the thrust. He would have known had he elected for transport flying in training instead of single engine fighter, but like a lot of us the thought of driving a bus through the sky was just too abhorrent a thought to bear.

We both paid for that attitude after leaving the forces. No

commercial outfit is interested in using a fighter jock to cart paying passengers around and the type of skills we'd learned sure didn't help in the air cargo field. Fuel management and steady instrument work are the order of the day in commercial flying, not high speed interception and weapons delivery.

Phillip was able to relearn quickly after he left the air force. He enrolled in one of those Texas pilot factories that make use of the constant clear skies to cram any amount of flight training into anyone with enough money. Phillip had the money. His family had been able to get out of Zimbabwe with most of their fortune. His father had been one of Mugabe's inner circle and had been able to steal about as much as anyone else until he fell out of favor.

At those schools you can go from basic flight training on a Cessna 152 to qualifying on the latest Airbus, if you have the money. Phillip filled his time in training to be an aerial truck driver with the same intensity he brought to bear on educating himself in Montreal. There was just enough irrational fighter pilot pride left to stop him from preparing for an airline job and turn him instead to heavy transports working the oil frontiers in the Philipines, Alaska and the Beaufort. At least on the frontiers there's variety. Airline work dries pilots' souls.

"You were in Resolute the night before last."

He nodded. "They had two armed guards in the cockpit with me the whole time. Made me fly from there into Hudson Bay below radar then head for Resolute as if I was coming in from the south."

"You can't get by the North Warning System stations that easy these days."

Phillip grinned again and shook his head. "Oh yes you can. These people have a guy in the back who works the radios for you and does all the talking with ATC. He sounds like an airline pilot, right accent, intonation, everything you'd want to hear from a bus driver, anything you want. He also works the ELINT."

"What? Radar and radio?"

"Yup. They have something really slick going for themselves. That plane just drops right off the screens when its working and they can screw up any frequency they want for incredible distances. They used it on me when they hijacked the plane and I know they used it on you."

I looked at Phillip on the floor, noting his almost new jeans and the cotton shirt under the wool cardigan and reflected that he seemed to have learned something about dressing. It was almost simply too incredible that we should meet after so long on an island in the Davis Strait. He'd used his opportunities better than I had after leaving the forces. I did it the hard way.

I did it the hard way by bumming around North America in the hope of finding some type of flying that could begin to match the thrill of Mach Two at 40 thousand feet and a weapons load that could wipe out a battleship. For a while, I did some flight instructing which consisted of smiling a lot at nervous people who were using their introductory offers clipped from flying magazines to have a look at what flying is all about. The smiling and the patter was to get them to come back because a flight instructor is paid according to the number of hours he instructs in the air and by no other means. It almost drove me to suicide to sit back and try as patiently as I could to instill in some half scared systems analyst, or over-eager teenager with the parents' money, the hunger for flight. Some were good and are still flying somewhere I'm sure. Others, if they didn't quit, must have driven their rented boats with wings into the ground harder than flesh can stand.

It was the lack of the edge that got to me after the air force. There's an edge to the world and if you go beyond it you fall off and never get back. That's OK and a sane person would stay well away from such a spot. But a fighter jock, or a test pilot, sometimes gets hooked on the need to keep peering over that edge.

There's nothing to equal taking a ten ton interceptor to the limits of its capabilities and to the limits of the pilot then pulling it back from the point of destruction.

That's why so many pilots are killed low-flying. They love to see how fast and how low they can push things before they pucker out or they pile it in.

Out to the edge and then back.

It's the name of the game and once hooked it can't be washed out of the system because it becomes a pilot's way of defining his place in the universe. It truly is a way of answering the question, "Who am I?" It has the advantage over any other way of describing existence in that it does provide an answer to the question, even if it does depend on scaring the shit out of yourself.

And it was just that insane view of life that had put me on the run across North Africa, chased by squads of bad guys.

NORTHERN LEGENDS

There used to be a bar at the airport in Montreal which had an entrance hallway tiled with stone slabs from all over the world. There was a castle stone from England, a slab of granite from the Canadian Shield, dolomite from some gigantic mine in the states and a chunk of something Nordair hauled out of the High Arctic. Each stone was labeled with the name of the airline that had flown it in. Fascinating stuff if you had the time to stop and look. Trouble is, I never did pay much attention because on the way into the bar I was always in too much of a hurry for a drink and on the way out I was usually trying to stop myself from ricocheting off the walls in front of the other guests to spend any time peering at a bunch of rocks glued to the wall.

I had been sitting in the bar one night, toward the end of February, the month when the bush flying world sort of takes a breather as it wraps up the winter contracts before signing the summer deals, wondering just where the hell my life as a pilot was going, when a pilot I knew casually drifted in, scanning for faces.

"Jack, you old sucker. How's it going?"

It took a moment to place him and at that I was lucky since it generally never does come to me early enough in the conversation with a passing acquaintance to figure out just who the hell I am talking to. This one though had some mental mnemonic behind it.

Just before Christmas I had been dusting oranges in Dade County. Miserable, dangerous work fifty feet off the ground, and often lower. All the time praying that a power line didn't cut across my route and end everything. Harry Townsend was one of the others on the contract and in the afternoons when we couldn't fly any more because of the turbulence and heat we, and most of the others, would make the rounds of the few small bars in Pubnical. As bars go, these were just that. Narrow strip fronts strung along the highway south. They are the sort of place that thrives on catching the passing tourist with a hamburger and hoping to pour in a few beers before packing him off again at sixty five miles an hour down the road. We and the occasional farmer made up the only steady clientele the bars would see that month.

Harry, over many drinks, had gradually filled me in on how things work in the southern United States, how the drugs are brought in low and through the steadily increasing radar defenses. He told me of the tricks of riding up out of the Gulf buried in a thunderstorm cell so no radar can get you, of air-dropping the cargo to boats inshore so the stuff can be landed and trucked out before the police can be directed from the air by the air marshals. It was an interesting conversation and it didn't take too much for me to guess that he was a fulltime part of it. The spray dusting was probably just cover and he was looking for new recruits.

Now here he was in Montreal. "Harry. You are a long way from the sun aren't you?"

"You're not kidding. I've never seen so much snow."

"Stick around, what we've got tonight is just fluff. If it weren't for the fog the flights would still be going."

He shook his head and grinned. To anyone used to the south the casual way northern winter pilots take the snow, ice, sleet and general crud is beyond them. They're too used to the perfect weather and too used to being able to hold up a takeoff for a few hours until things have cleared instead of having to power through and get where they are supposed to.

He raised one finger at the barman, didn't even look at him, and a triple scotch was delivered on the run. He must have either been there a long time, owned part of the bar, or tipped like crazy. "Where are you working these days?" he said, lighting a cigarette and raising the glass to his mouth so the smoke and scotch mixed on the way down.

"Here and there Harry, here and there. You?"

"Not too bad. Just on my way back from Morocco. Got a nice little contract to freight some things over. All I have to do is charter a Three and by this time next week I'll be set for a couple of years in West Palm Beach."

"Somehow I just cannot see you among the blue hair, white shoes and belt crowd."

We were half way through a bottle of Peter Dawson in my room before he offered to take me in on the deal. I was bored enough with myself and drunk enough to accept.

One of the thirty-three odd opposition groups and revolutionary movements in Morocco had somehow come up with enough cash to finance yet another takeover attempt against the King. Seems they didn't mind him being as high as a kite all the time, and I mean all of the time, but they did mind him turning mosques into swimming pools and pools into mosques as the fancy took him. Enter Harry Townsend, who seemed to know most of the world's mercenaries and arms dealers on a first name basis, that is if half of the stories he told me in my room that night were true.

Harry knew of a three plane operation in Fort Lauderdale going bust slowly and only too eager to charter their only DC-3 for a week. We made the hop to the Azores from Florida three days after Montreal. I was co-pilot.

Now at the time, I hadn't been in a Dakota in years. About all the preflight I could do was to check that the tanks were full and the crates were strapped down hard. Yet after just an hour out over the Atlantic and watching Harry handle the controls, just sitting there letting the smell and vibrations of the Dak seep through me, the old habits came back. Incomplete fragments of checklists wandered around my mind and after Harry handed over to me the feel came back too. I felt like a veteran Dak driver a few hours later and shot the landing myself at Tenerife.

Harry said he'd been told about a run of desert behind the Atlas Ranges where there was a smooth stretch of country that would take the plane. The rendezvous was near a place called Akka, about three hundred miles south of Rabat.

I think the guy on the ground who was supposedly responsible for making sure all the holes were filled in and the rocks kicked out of the way got his instructions reversed. Two thousand feet of ravine valley is no place to be landing a heavy Dakota. There was one good point about it. Harry was right when he said the army and the secret police wouldn't be there. No one in his right mind would ever consider an aircraft could attempt landing.

We didn't see the condition of the ground until after we crawled out of the wreckage of the cockpit. Actually there wasn't much to crawl out of because the whole nose section past the instrument panel had been torn away. When we stopped cartwheeling, there was nothing between my feet and the outside, just nothing of the forward flight deck at all. And not a scratch on either of us.

It took us a month to get out of Morocco through the back door of Spanish Sahara, Mauritania and finally Dakar Senegal. The Peoples Revolutionary Whatnot did pay us for the guns but not the plane. By the time I got back to Canada after we paid off the Fort Lauderdale people I had three hundred and fifty dollars total profit.

I did a lot of bush flying after that in northern Canada before ending up where Horst and Teller found me, flying for a company on the edge of nowhere, on the edge of bankruptcy, and me on the edge of nothingness.

MEET UP WITH PHILLIP

"ℳhen do we eat around here?" I asked Phillip. "I haven't eaten since yesterday morning."

Phillip sighed. "You white guys are all the same. Lock you up in a cage and instead of worrying or trying to escape you ask when the keeper brings the food."

I didn't bother correcting him. His captivity seemed to have awakened something of the hunter in him. His hands arced half closed and then open slowly in a strangling or grasping movement. I could feel the tension from him as he kept pressing his back and shoulders against the door and thrust with his bent legs at the linoleum. He was caged and didn't like it much. I didn't care yet about the cage because I was still trying to shake off the head injury and fighting the lack of sleep.

The smell of the seaweed he was smoking was hurting the inside of my head. I didn't care for Turkish tobacco, but it seemed like the only stuff available. "Why are you smoking these crappy things instead of a real cigarette."

"No choice. That's what they give me. Russian I think."

He tossed me the package and I looked at the Cyrillic characters. I didn't even know if I was holding the package the right way round, but it seemed Russian. I lit one and inhaled. I wasn't even sure that it was tobacco because the taste was so different. It could have been Bactrian Camel dung for all that I knew.

"You might try worrying about what they are going to make us do next," he said.

"Us?"

"Oh yes us. I need a co-pilot if they're going to make me keep flying that truck in false colors."

"Phillip I beginning to think we are in some kind of deep shit."

He rocked forward from the waist as the door pushed open. Horst was standing there. "Yes Captain you are in some kind of excrement as you put it."

Two of her bubble parka'd women were behind her with the muzzles lowered. "You are going to Greenland to pick up some equipment for me, then we will discuss your future." She turned away from the door, then paused and flipped a package of cigarettes on the linoleum so they skidded across the room and under the chair between my feet. "Since you don't like our brands, try these. I hope they are more to your liking."

I didn't say anything until the door was closed and locked then only got half the word out because Phillip was saying the other half.

"Bugged."

NORSKE OER

𝓘t was like sitting in a greenhouse. There was glass above me, to the right, and down along my right leg. I could see over the glare shield to the tip of the radome and out past Phillip on the left with no straining and twisting. The layout was made for a flight engineer, but we were running it ourselves. I couldn't see how Phillip had managed on his own.

It had been a very long time since I had sat behind the panel of a C-130 Hercules. After the years of crouching behind the panels of Cessnas where the intent of the designer appeared to have been to hide the sky from the pilot so he wouldn't be frightened by what was coming at him, and the years of fumbling in the cockpits of DC-3's, and aging Twin Otters, the Hercules panel was breathtaking. The flight instruments sat clear, in front of the eyes. Engines and fuel gauges sat in the middle for both pilots to watch easily, and the radios up high and center in the panel for easy tuning.

The Twin Otter had a nice panel as well. It was well laid out and logicial. But, it was cramped compared to the grand sweep of the flight-deck of the Hercules.

"How did you get by without a co-pilot?" I said.

"Third hand. No, really. This character here," he jerked his gloved right hand behind him to the man sitting on the rear bench. He hadn't said a word since we started. "he seems to know a lot about flight management and that's all I really need. If I have time to think it out first. Not a pilot though."

"Why is he sitting way back there? A flight engineer normally sat in the middle command chair slightly to the rear and between our seats. He could monitor the centre console engine intruments and handle the power levers from there.

"I don't want him anywhere near the controls unless I absolutely need the help. He can sit back there and watch the scenery for all I care."

We trimmed out at 21 thousand feet over the Greenlandic side of the strait. To the northeast I was catching glimpses through the stratus of the glare shooting off the ice-cap.

"Do you know this rock we're headed for?" Flying on the back side of the safety curve was not new to me. Still, I was getting leery about all of this flying by jumping into the cockpit business and slapping a bunch of switches and levers. When you start ignoring the preflight of the aircraft, checking the weather, flight planning and all the other pre-flight procedures you are a long way toward killing yourself.

"Mmmph," He was punching in the Sondrestrom beacon frequency. "Took a seismic crew off there a year, or a year and a half ago I guess. It's a North Warning System strip. Probably hasn't been used since then either."

There are lots of airstrips in the Canadian and Greenlandic Arctic that got slashed through the tundra in the big fifties scare then never used again.

I hitched my harness so it no longer dug into my right clavicle. "Glad I don't have to wear a parachute in this thing. It never seemd to make any sense to wear them in the Air Force in these planes. I haven't worn a parachute since, except for some dusting work."

"Jack, when does anyone ever get high enough in a cropduster to use a goddamned chute?" His laugh boomed through my headsets and made my eardrums ring.

"Ah well, these stories they tell about Kansas wheat growing so tall? Well, they're true. Why sometimes, right before harvest, you have to use oxygen to get over it." I was hoping the chatter would distract Alfonse. That was the name Phillip had settled on calling the flight engineer after failing to get any kind of response out of him.

"My white guy. Nerves of steel and telling jokes too. Tell another like that and you'll be wishing the company had insisted on chutes."

"Besides," he said. "There are two under the rear bench. I put them there while we were refueling." He was clearly trying to tell me something with his eyes but I wasn't getting it.

Phillip tuned the second radio to the international distress frequency. "Hey," he shouted over his shoulder to Alfonse, ignoring the intercom. "Check the APU line voltage, I'm getting surges." Phillip caught my eye and I switched the intercom circuit into the radio. Everything we said would go out on the distress frequency.

I was halfway through a semi conversational recap of what I had been through in past few days with Phillip adding in the necessary asides to fill in his side of things when Horst leaned past me and flipped the selector back to internal.

"It didn't go anywhere Standish," she said so softly that I barely heard her over the engines. She peered ahead at the coast of Greenland, now a rising black smudge fading into gray blue where the haze and cloud started. "The jamming works both ways. You cannot talk to anyone unless we allow it."

Two days of frustrations and anger boiled out. "For bloody hell's sake. You can't get away with this. When they get you, I'm going to be there to make sure you hang." Phillip laughed at my pomposity, Horst just looked at me.

"I'll be very much surprised, my two friends, if anyone is ever going to get me as you put it. No one is going to know anything about this."

"This what?" Phillip said with an innocent smile as if to say, "It's OK, we're all in this together, you can tell us."

"Let's just say that one of the deciding moments of world history has arrived." With that she turned back, clapped a hand on Alfonse's shoulder and slipped down the ladder to the cargo bay. We were silent for several moments watching the ice cap slide by until I said. "I don't care whether they do have this circuit tapped. I think they've finally done it."

Phillip looked startled. "Done what?"

"An atomic bomb," I said with assurance. It was becoming so clear and obvious to me. "Horst and her gang of foreign accented thugs have stolen, been given, or made a bomb and we're on our way to pick it up. Do you want to bet there'll be a submarine waiting for us when get there?"

"You missed it Jack. It isn't where we are going, it was at Jenness at the dock. An unmarked nuclear sub."

I remembered the odd shape the helicopter had passed over when returning me to the island.

King Frederick VIII couldn't have been too well liked by his subjects. Some of them named one of the most awful glaciers in Greenland after him. It's the size of Germany with absolutely none of the attractions. Phillip let down along the slope of the ice cap. For mile after mile of featureless white, a white cracked now and then by the dirty gray scars of crevasses, we eased down, until in the end we nailed Norske Oer.

The island was to have been the easternmost in the chain of radar stations east from Alaska, but something went wrong at the diplomatic level. In the panic to get the great radar defense lines done, the crews had been sent out ahead of all the formal permissions. When the approvals for Norske Oer fell through, the crews just packed up their equipment and flew away leaving everything behind. Eight thousand feet of unused gravel runway, hardpan taxi and parking areas, and one hangar big enough for the Globemasters that were to resupply the base, together with a collection of H-huts. All now showed the effects of thirty years of weekly blizzards sweeping down off the glacier. Each gust and blast of wind carried ice crystals that acted like silicon carbide sanding chips. The paint was gone, no planed edges were left on the wood. Glass looked clouded and the whole place resembled the way the world might look after mankind has killed itself off. Except for Phillip's seismic crew, I doubted that anyone had been there in years, Horst's crowd excepted that is.

It was warm for Northeastern Greenland and I was able to leave the plane wearing only a light down vest, the kind hunters wear in the cool fall weeks before winter in the south. Phillip wore just his flight suit. He rarely felt the cold and then only far past the point where everyone around him had long bundled up. He'd kept ordering Alfonse to turn down the cockpit heat all the way through the flight. Alfonse, normal like everyone else including me, had naturally kept sneaking it back up to avoid numbing his body. I silently supported Alfonse's guerrilla warfare with the heater.

We walked slowly toward the hangar behind Horst and her team. Phillip handed me a cigarette and I stopped to light it. Two hundred yards ahead the orange balloon parka crowd made a large splash of color against the grayed wood of the hangar and the eternal snow. There were patches of green showing through the snow cover. They were so few and beleaguered that I wondered why nature bothered plugging something into such marginal environmental niches.

"What are our chances of getting back out to the Herc and getting out of here?" I said.

Phillip raised his eyes to peer over the top of my head at the aircraft. But they focused just a few feet behind me.

I turned.

He said, "Well, what do you think Jack? Care to try those odds yourself?" Two orange parkas, just slightly larger than Phillip all of the way around waited for us to start walking again. They carried their automatic weapons at the hip on slings so the muzzles pointed ahead and down a few inches from our bellies to about our groins.

At the hangar, Horst had three men each on the hung doors trying to push them back on the rusted rails. The Judas door was open. We watched as they heaved against the rust.

"Jack," Phillip said, "we have to find a way out of this pretty soon. It can't be too much longer before Horst doesn't need us anymore and somehow I don't think she will simply let us go."

I nodded slowly. The screech of rusted wheels rose then eased down the scale as the door rolled back. "I've been thinking that since she picked me up. But short of running like hell and hiding in the rocks until they leave, then starving to death or freezing, I can't think of a thing."

"I can." he said. "I was thinking of the chutes. If we could get to somewhere inhabited, even a ship, we could just bail out."

"What about Alfonse?" The idea sounded nuts to me, especially the bit about jumping out over a ship. We'd last just seconds in the Arctic water.

"Have you ever rolled a Herc?" He was serious, but it was taking some effort for me to listen to him without snorting out loud and I didn't want to attract attention because this was the first time that we were sure of not being overheard. Everyone was busy with the doors or peering into the black of the gap exposed as they rolled apart from each other. The pause gave me time to think. "Rudder to skid it in and a kick over the top." I was musing more than talking to him.

"Right, and that kick will throw him hard against the side of the cockpit so he wouldn't be able to stop us going through the top hatch. If that doesn't work we'll bash him on the head with something." He paused. "Have to be done below pressure altitude of course but I don't know"

The Hercules has a round escape hatch in the roof of the flight deck. It was for use on the ground to give easy access to the top of the fuselage. I'd never heard of anyone opening it in flight.

I wondered what would happen to us as we came out into the full blast of air and with the propellers screaming at near supersonic speeds just a handful of feet away. And then directly behind us would be the vertical blade of the fin and rudder. Sliced pilot anyone?

"It'd be murder," I said it because that's what we would be doing to everyone in the plane and the idea didn't bother me. Phillip's private code of ethics saw the world as a collection of those who were for you and those who were against so there was no conscience worry there either. The guards moved up and we started toward the hangar mouth.

"Cape Dyer. When we go over," he said out of the corner of his mouth. Not for the first time, I felt some genuine depression about getting through the mess we were in. Cape Dyer lay just a handful of degrees off our course back to Jenness. Home of the North Warning System boys we'd been careful to avoid on the way over.

I was a dozen paces into the hangar and I could smell in the spring warmth the decades old Douglas Fir the hangar had been built from. I felt the grit under my feet against the poured concrete floor. Then through the gloom I started to make out shapes, familiar shapes.

Even after so many years of abandonment you could tell that this had been home to airplanes. There was a faint smell of grease, of aviation fuel, oil and quite a bit of kerosene. There was a heavy plastic smell to the hangar too. It came to me slowly that I shouldn't be smelling jet fuel in a hangar that had only known piston engines and that more than thirty years previous too. I shouldn't have been smelling plastic sheeting either.

As my eyes adjusted to the dark, I started to make out our cargo. It was in pieces, all neatly broken down and bundled in ten mil plastic sheeting. Through the cloudy white of the sheeting I was able to make it out bit by bit and slowly a picture built in my mind. Then, the bits matched in my memory and I recognized it.

There were enough holes in the curved roof of the hangar where katabatic winds had ripped off asphalt sheeting and fir planking to light the interior to a dim brightness. In carefully disassembled pieces sat a Mach 2.2 fighter-interceptor which in half a dozen models manufactured over twenty years represented the best all around attack aircraft in the world for its time. There were many fighters that could have knocked the old Starfighter out of the air, but none had proved itself so well over such a long time.

"Oh my god," muttered Phillip.

I was stunned. I couldn't understand what the thing was doing here only a few miles from the north pole, or what it was to be used for.

"It's the D Model," I said walking slowly toward the needle nose and past to the cockpit canopy. I couldn't see into the cockpit because of the silver quilted padding covering the armored glass. The gear was folded into its belly. The fuselage sat down on the lumber cradle just eight inches off the concrete. Not many of them had been built this way. Unlike almost all Starfighters this one had a dual cockpit for two pilots.

Phillip and I had trained on the G type built by Canadair. This one, so cold and quiet, might not climb as fast or as high but would in the end fly just like ours did.

"Drop tanks over there Jack and I think those look like Sparrows."

"Yeah, they're Sparrows. Looks like this is here to shoot something down."

"There is no way that those came from NASA. Air to air missiles in NASA? "Phillip shook his head.

"I wonder where they came from?" I said.

It took five hours for Horst's team to load the disassembled Starfighter into the Herc. It was another hour before Phillip was happy with its placement in relation to the center of gravity. He also did the calculations to see whether there was enough runway to get off safely. While he did that I moved the parachutes from the storage cabinet to the command chairs and clipped them into their fittings in the seat harnesses.

We were only able to get the pieces into the 130 because the engine and tail section had been moved out earlier. I wondered how the 104 got to the island in the first place.

The take-off was chancy and I breathed a lot easier when Phillip called for gear up as he held the beast in a shallow climb over the ice. He'd rotated in the last hundred feet of gravel.

"Should have asked some of that bunch to walk," I said.

"I should have gone with them and let you risk your neck alone." He turned back to Alfonse in the rear. "Go back and check the load."

Alfonse was entering engine and prop settings in his log and tapping out fuel consumption figures on his flight computer and didn't look up. "Do it yourself. I stay here."

"Hey kid," Phillip snapped in his imitation of the drill sergeant at St Jean, "I have a course to settle, my co-pilot is flying, and you are doing nothing that cannot wait. Now get down there and check that damned load." Alfonse stared at him for a heartbeat and almost defied him but Phillip was boring hard with his eyes. Alfonse looked away, took off his headset and left silently.

Phillip took his headset off as well and motioned me to do the same. We leaned across the throttle quadrants to talk against the four turboprops. "I'll let her drift a bit west of track so we'll be over Broughton then I'll roll her. You look after getting the roof hatch open while I keep it inverted."

"We'll be pretty high," I said. "It's going to be about minus sixty degrees and we don't even have boots." The winter gear was hanging in the aft locker. We couldn't have flown wearing parkas and snow boots and it would have looked as strange as hell if we'd tried. "And if we don't come down right outside the front door of somewhere warm we won't last long."

Phillip went blank around the eyes. It was the sort of look a person gets across a bar table half an hour before closing when all conversational subjects have been run to death and there are no drinks to order, and there's no reasonable excuse to get up and leave. It was a dead and blank unfocused stare into nothing.

I felt the same way. We had nothing else to try and what we had was so weak it was just this side of pointless.

I turned and looked at the hatch for what seemed like five minutes as the props throbbed away and a slight and slow thrill of vibration ran through the airframe and into my legs.

Although it had seemed like five minutes, five seconds was more like it before an answer came to me. "Do you know any way of cutting the heat, some way that can't be fixed by Alfonse?"

His teeth flashed in the cockpit gloom.

One half hour later I was starting to feel the bite of the cold on the outside edges of my little fingers. The single layer of black leather glove was doing nothing to keep the heat in and their tightness made it worse by closing down the blood circulation. If I were out on the land, I'd be starting to worry about losing all sensation and freezing them. As it was, I could barely feel the vibration of the engines through my hands. My fingers felt like they were encased in thick rubber.

"If you don't mind gentlemen, putting on the heat." Horst was on the flight deck.

I looked at Phillip and he turned back to Alfonse. "Well, you heard your boss, do something to earn your pay."

Alfonse fiddled with the heater controls under the stare of Horst for a couple of minutes. "It doesn't want to go any higher," he said to Horst. "I can't seem to make it work."

Phillip turned away from the instruments again and hooked

his right arm on the back of the seat so he was turned body to me and face to the rear of the flight deck. "Well goddamn it. If you are going to sit behind me playing prison guard instead of doing what I need a flight engineer for then you'd better just go back with the rest of the blasted passengers and let us fly." Phillip had just slapped Alfonse hard in the professional ego, telling him that he was nothing but a lump of cargo on the flight deck.

Alfonse began punching circuit breakers on the panel, then on the one to my right. We had rattled him. He was checking circuits that had nothing to do with the heater. Some of the circuits he was checking had more to do with the hydraulics of the engines than the heaters.

Phillip and I looked at each other. Despite the lack of even the slightest facial change, a message passed between us. I felt a surge of optimism that things were going to work out. Phillip had jiggered the panel. Until someone reconnected some wires he'd pulled off the terminals, there wasn't going to be any heat.

"You know Horst," I said, "there are going to be a lot more problems like this unless this aircraft starts getting some maintenance. It wouldn't be nice to have an engine fall off."

Phillip picked up my cue. "He's right. This isn't some made in heaven wonder. It's a collection of sophisticated systems, each one of which takes Murphy's law as its own."

"I don't think we will have to worry about that too much. It will fly long enough for what I want and you will do the flying. It doesn't look like he is going to get the thing to work. Better take her down where it's warmer." The last of what she said came faintly over the engines as she climbed down the ladder.

Phillip turned back to the controls. I pulled power and started down under Horst's orders. I marveled at how we had pushed events in our own direction for a change. "You know Phillip there's not a hell of a lot of difference between minus 60 and minus 25. Not going to change the temperature in here at all."

He nodded. "Just do what the man says my boy."

The difference would be life for us. By bringing us down Horst had increased our chances of surviving the parachute drop with enough energy left over to get to shelter. The Hercules swayed slightly, side to side, as it came down in a steep three thousand foot a minute descent. If anyone in the back had a blocked sinus they would soon be in deep painful agony as the pressure changes. The coast mountains rose in the windshield as we lost altitude.

Much later I clicked the intercom. "Broughton dead ahead captain. You're a little west of course."

"Well son of a bitch Jack, you're right. How'd we drift so much?"

I shrugged and played the part, not daring to say anything because I didn't trust my acting. I unclipped and stood behind the command seats, my hands on the opening bar of the hatch above my head as though I were stretching my muscles. I couldn't check how tight it was latched home without putting a lot more effort into my body. I hoped it was loose enough for us to snap the hatch off as we went over the top. The mountains started to fill the glass, Broughton slipped underneath the radome, and I braced for the roll.

Phillip called to Alfonse without turning his head or shifting his eyes from the altimeter. "Hey have you checked the APU? I told you before I was getting surges. That's what could be the matter. Go back and see if the heat exchanger is working."

This was it. The moment that Alfonse unstrapped and went down the ladder Phillip would shove out with his right foot and twist everything until we were inverted and stuck on the top of a roll.

Alfonse jerked the quick release of his seat harness. The snap of metal shot across the flight deck.

I think that in another two seconds the plan would have worked. But as Alfonse slipped out of his harness I heard Teller behind me.

"Come with me Mr. Standish. Ms Horst would like to see you now. Right now."

I looked back over my shoulder hoping that Phillip would go ahead anyway. There didn't seem to be any hint that Horst knew we were up to anything and the surprise might work in our favor. I risked it. "Phillip. What do you think?" He shook his head slightly and I dropped my hands from the latch.

"All right. Tell her I'll be there in a bit."

"Ms Horst said right now." No change of face or tone. A command to be obeyed. I unclipped my parachute and dropped myself into the seat.

The cargo bay was one great mound of metal and webbing. Bits of Starfighter peeked out from under tarpaulin and nylon cargo netting. I clambered along the side of the fuselage with difficulty. I had to walk almost sideways along the out curve of the fuselage to squeeze past the double row of sling seats we'd fixed for Horst and her private army.

"Captain Standish. I understand that you and Mr. Tonguay have experience with ...." she waved his hand with a loose wristed gesture over the netting.

I nodded. There didn't seem to be any point to denying it. She seemed to know a fair bit about both of us. "We flew them with the Canadian Air Force."

"This particular type." It was a statement and not a question.

"No, an earlier."

"But you can fly this can't you."

"You're the one that seems to know. Technically I suppose that yes we can fly it. But that was very many years ago. What's this about?"

"Captain. I suddenly find myself in need of a pilot to fly that aircraft. A most regrettable accident has struck down the man who was assigned." There was no pause between her words, they just clipped out in one long long string of syllables.

"Now to cut a lot of tedious arguing I'll just tell you this. If you don't fly that plane I will kill you. But not before I kill your friend in a way that you can see how it happens. I have not decided yet whether to throw him out of the helicopter or push him into one of the props of this plane."

The coldness and bluntness of the statement took my breath away. She was right, it did stop a lot of arguing. I didn't know what to say next. The throb of the props thrummed through the fuselage. For some funny reason I found myself studying the fine delicacy of the scratches worn in the plastic porthole behind his head. They caught the light and refracted it in tiny clusters of rainbow colors. The maker's name was printed very small at the base of the porthole and meant to be read from the outside. I found myself trying to make it out. It was the sudden cessation of the slightly out of sync props that brought me back. The fuselage settled down into a steady, smooth thrill of sound.

"I don't suppose it would do much good to say I think you are insane."

"I would not say so. As a matter of fact, I look on all this as a very sane enterprise, but then you still don't know what I am going to do."

"No, and quite frankly this is all making me very angry. Just what are you doing?"

She shook his head. "No, not now. When we have progressed."

"Why did you pick me to fly that beast. How do you know that Phillip isn't the better choice?" I wasn't trying to sound like I was passing off the dirty work out of cowardice. I was genuinely interested in the reasoning. My throat started to go raw from the effort of speaking above the noise. It takes a special effort to speak from the back of the throat to project above aircraft engine noise without screaming.

"He has been flying heavy transport since he left the air force whereas you have been doing a lot of small aircraft flying; crop-dusting, bush flying, and some rather questionable flying in other parts of the world. I would say from the way you were handling your Twin Otter until we shot you down, you still have the old reflexes. Yes?"

"I think, Ms Horst, you have probably more hot seat time than I do." It was a shot in the dark based on the hidden flight experience I'd detected on the flight down from Pond. She might have been an average pilot yet she had the eye of a trained fighter jock.

She chuckled, and again her eyes didn't go along with her mouth, "Perhaps Mr. Standish, but not in any plane you have flown."

I wanted to ask her which plane, Foxbat, Mig 21, or some other Soviet design but she waved her hand at me to end the discussion. She signalled Teller, who had been standing behind me, to lead me back to the flight deck.

"Have a nice tea party?" Phillip asked.

"Oh to be sure my dear sir. There was even some pepper cake only someone left the cake out of the pepper."

He rolled his eyes straight back into his head, it's a trick he does. Two gleaming white blanks in a black skull, clown or death, I didn't know how to interpret it.

"She wants us to fly the rocket. I told her you were the better, but I guess she just likes the idea of holding you a hostage."

He gazed to the right. There, the great valleys of Auyuittuq National Park started their run up from the sea and then southwest to the Pangnirtung Gorge on the far side of the mountain range. If it weren't for the leaping needle of the radar altimeter I would have thought we were only a couple of hundred feet off the ground. There wasn't anything to give scale to the immensity of the Penny Ice Cap and the fantastic gorges.

"I'd take offense," he continued, "except this is the first time I've ever heard a fighter pilot say someone else was a better man in the cockpit." He took off his headset. "And just why does she want you to fly the 104? What's she want with it?"

"I don't know. Said something had happened to the man who was supposed to fly it."

"That'd be Marteau."

"What happened to him?"

"He was the one flying the Hercules when you were shot down. They were real scared someone from Iron Island had seen what went on so Horst had him land by the camp. From what I gather there was a fair bit of shooting. Some of the hunters got to their guns first and one of them put a bullet into Marteau. Gotta say I'm real pleased it happened to the son of a bitch."

We swung on through growing moonlight, cutting across the fiords fretting the land.

JENNESS ISLAND LANDING

"**D**o you want to shoot this one?" Phillip said as he eased back the power for the approach to Jenness. I shook my head. "I'm sorry, I'm not feeling up to it. Besides, she's pretty loaded and that strip is short."

"Wow. Again humility from a fighter pilot." He nodded at Alfonse to run through the pre-flight landing checklist. I followed through on the plastic cards, item by item. Although the Hercules was still strange to me, and should have absorbed all of my attention, I couldn't keep my mind on the checklist at all.

"Jack. Snap out of it! Will you give me some flap!"

His bark shocked me back to reality and I pulled the flap to steepen the descent and allow the heavy transport to approach the strip slower. "Sorry Phillip. When do you want full?" I couldn't stop playing the conversation with Horst through my head. It didn't seem to make sense. What possible reason could she have for putting the success of whatever plan she had into a coerced hostage? That was not an effective strategy.

I also worried about her threats. It was clear to me that whether I got out of this alive or not was problematic. Aeva

Horst struck me as someone who would never want witnesses around. I had no doubt at all that they would be killed off and dumped in the middle of nothing. The Eastern Arctic sure is a lot of nothing.

There was something here, I thought, that wasn't adding up.. Something I was missing and it was bothering me.

"Maybe I'll just do it myself," he said through his concentration. There was a sheen on his brow. The approach was a bitch, uphill into the side of a mountain under a full load. I came awake and paid attention as we flew straight at the billion tons or so of rock.

We were going to be hot, shooting along the gravel relic from the fifties at a speed that wouldn't give us a lot of room if something went wrong. The thing had been built in an age when planes were slower and lighter. The only thing that pleased me about the run toward the side of the hill was the clear hard light of the moon that put every bump and runnel in the surface of the airstrip into relief. God knew what twenty years of cold so deep that even steel weakened and shattered had done to the under-surface. And how much of the subsurface had been washed away in the spring thaws? All it would take would be a blown tire and a skid into the rock along the sides and we'd be finished. If the tires held we were still going to have a hell of a job stopping before the last foot.

"Now!" he shouted. I dropped the flaps full and my shoulders pushed against the straps as we ran into a pillow of air. Phillip pulled back on the yoke to make the nose rear and the airspeed bleed away. I hauled all the power back then sat on the reverse thrust detent ready for the touchdown. I was doing Alfonse's job. He'd made no move to the jump seat and I wouldn't have let him anyway. Phillip held through the slight right turn curving down to the end of the strip as the airspeed sagged down to the bottom.

She hit the end of the runway in a dead stall and coming

down so fast I feared for the landing gear. The tail must have been inches from dragging its skid when he slammed her down. There was a crash and shudder that made the instruments shake in their mounts. I shoved the throttles through the gate and the engines and props screamed with the sudden shift to full power reverse thrust. The next instant Phillip was shoving the yoke full forward and we both stood hard on the brakes. At the same time I was dumping lift by bringing up the flaps. The tires crushed into the gravel. Dust and ice shot forward past the cockpit and curled in and up before us in a gray and brown fog that swirled away all sign of the airstrip. The deceleration made the shoulder straps bite hard and my head wanted to fall forward on my chest.

We bucked and pitched in a wild screaming of engine and prop noise, the hull slamming over the shattered tarmac. Rusted metal stands, the remnants of a runway lighting system flashed past in the glare of the landing lights as a flashing blur of brown and red. The Herc charged up the slight incline of the strip without any apparent signs of slowing despite the deceleration. I watched the jumble of boulders at the end of the runway, a deposit left there when the last of the glaciers went away. It grew and grew in the lights.

They sat there, thirty yards from the end of the strip, growing in detail with each half instant. The lights picked out gray and white lichen growing on them. Where the snow had blown away I could see last summer's grass. The lichen made some of them look like padded pillows. But soft they were not and I was afraid of them. A quarter of an inch of lichen wasn't going to save the landing gear from getting ripped off by those oil barrel size rocks.

I pulled flap again without waiting for Phillip's command. I hoped we were slow enough that the increased lift wouldn't send us ballooning back into the air or weaken the braking ability of the tires. Phillip kept the yoke full forward. I hoped that those huge sheets of metal hanging down into the air would add some badly needed drag.

I don't know if my action helped. At least we didn't go back into the air and stall. Somehow throughout that wild ride along the runway we lost enough energy and the Herc came to a bouncing stop. We were so close to the rocks at the end of the strip that we couldn't see them below the swell of the plane's nose.

"Phillip said. "Damned if I ever want to try that again."

My hands started to pour perspiration and I couldn't seem to wipe them dry on my thighs. "I hope those sons of bitches in the back shit their pants."

"Well, if they didn't, I came close." His grin was back, teeth flashing in the backscatter from the landing lights. "If they were paying me I'd give em all the money back and catch a boat to Bermuda." Phillip backed us away from the rocks with reverse thrust and turned the Herc in its own length with full power on the number one engine.

I turned around to see how Alfonse had made out. He was hunched over, dry heaving into his cupped hands. Served him right, I thought.

It didn't surprise when Horst bounced into the flight deck as if nothing unusual had happened. She looked as well rested and trim as the first time I'd met her in Resolute Bay. I thought it would take a lot to shake a woman like that, so obviously in control of her emotions.

Standing between us, she directed Phillip to the waiting trucks lined up at the side of the runway, halfway down. They must have had a stunning view of our controlled crash. Two flatbed trailers were there for the Starfighter parts. I couldn't see what Horst had in mind for the 104. It certainly wouldn't be able to fly from the island strip. We'd just proved that it was only barely long enough for the Herc.

"I won't be needing you two gentlemen tonight. I think you can appreciate that you will not be allowed to wander about, but we have some comfortable quarters for you, I assure you."

We nodded.

"What? No questions this time? You are learning."

HER LAIR

*W*e rode up the mountain in the back of a thirty-ton truck under the muzzle gaze of three automatic weapons. The guards pushed us into the old Dew Line station and down a different barracks corridor to the one that we had gone down before. It was open in places to the outside. Either the foundation had shifted over the years or wandering hunters had stripped away panels for their own use. The corridor was littered with shattered building materials and we walked on a bed of crumbled drywall that crunched like glass. The guards prodded us on to a T-junction where two adjoining rooms formed a kind of entrance to a barracks beyond. They must have been NCO quarters at one time and a lot more comfortable than the first room we had.

Horst was good to her word. It was a good room. The first thing I saw when we were pushed into the room was a table with a full bottle of Peter Dawson, and a carton of Players. I made for the booze.

Phillip walked over to a refrigerator that was giving out a low groaning caused by corroded bearings. "Feed the troops well and they'll fight their lives out for you."

I put down the unopened bottle and walked over to see what he meant. The fridge's middle shelf was piled with packaged meats, cheese, milk, coffee, and apples. The person who had been told to put the stuff in had done the minimum. It was all just dumped on the shelf as if someone had emptied out a bag. "Feed us well and give us drink too. I don't mind at the moment."

Phillip reached for the scotch. "Whall sonny, after that there brilliant piece of flying I don't give a skunk's kiss whether it is pee-cyco-lodge-ee-kill softening up. Ahmm having a drink."

"Yeh well I guess I'll have one too then. Maybe a whole bunch."

"You, you stupid bunny, you might have to fly. This is all mine."

I wasn't up to the repartee, "Like to see that character make me fly a 104 after drinking a bottle of this stuff, or anything else for that matter." I paused with the bottle in mid air over my glass. "Is there any way out of here?" There were two sharp snaps from the ice cubes in my drink and on cue, it seemed, a generator started up somewhere in the complex. We sat in the dingy green room quiet for a while.

"I don't think so. No point to knocking the guard on the head. Nowhere to run."

"Could try the Herc." I said.

"Nope, not all," he shook his head and swallowed scotch. "It needs refueling, somebody has to start it, and how long do you think they'd let us have to pre-warm the engines and top it off? That woman's private army would be down our backs pretty bloody quickly."

"There are snowmobiles. We could....No I guess not." I was thinking that there'd be little point to making a dash over the ice to Pangnirtung or Iqaluit. Apart from the vast distance we'd have to travel without food and proper equipment, there was no way we could carry enough fuel. A breakdown or more likely, getting lost, would end things for us. Then too there was the Bell 412 and I had no illusions about trying to avoid being spotted by a slow flying helicopter.

"If I thought there was any point to it," he said as he lighted a cigarette, "I might try to get a radio message through to someone."

"Like what?" I said, "Help we're being held captive on an Arctic island by a bunch of Russian spies with a private air force. Send in the Marines?"

"Does seem pointless I'll admit. Any ideas?"

I shook my head, spilling scotch around the corners of my mouth. "I just hope she isn't going to make me fly that beast. I have a feeling that even if I get it off the ground, and do whatever is in that mind of hers, she's not going to want us sitting around afterward selling the story to the networks."

"Huh," he snorted. "Reporters would really like this story I think for sure. It would be nice to know what is going on though."

I shook my head again, it was becoming a habit. "Beats me. What could she want that old beast for? There's nothing anywhere near here that could be a target."

"Who says she is going to use it for hitting something?"

"What else do you use things like that for?" I said. "It's definitely the most useless plane in the world for anything except destroying something." We kept knocking back the scotch as we talked. After the first drink when the muscles relaxed in my lower back and the old leather of the chair warmed more and molded to my muscles the world slipped away ten paces. We were getting pretty hammered when the guard unlocked the door and tossed in a blue plastic binder that skidded across the gray linoleum making a gritting noise on its way to Phillip's feet.

"Flight manual," he grunted.

"Spose," I said half to myself and waited for the door to close. "Must want us to brush up."

"Been a while since I saw one of those." He held the three ring binder in both hands and tossed it lightly up and down as though he was testing the weight against some remembered standard.

It had also been many years since I had seen a Lockheed manual for the Starfighter. Four full inches thick, more than half of it numbers and all of it written in a style that defied comprehension on the first or sometimes even the third reading. There'd been a time when we had both known the book as well as the test pilots and engineers who wrote it. Now, I couldn't even recall the basic layout of the cockpit.

I ran my finger tips over the star logo feeling for a raised pattern that wasn't there but almost seemed like it should be.

"It's funny how you forget," Phillip said.

"It's funny how you don't in a way. I can't remember all the details of this thing, but I sure can remember how it felt to fly one. Can't ever forget that."

"Guess not Jack but you got on better in those things than I ever did. There never was a day when I was able to take one off and put it back without feeling I was about half a second from instant death all the time I was in it."

I knew the feeling. The 104 had a terrible reputation with most people who know anything, or care anything about aircraft, most of it is undeserved yet like all reputations there is more than a grain of truth. The Starfighter has probably killed more pilots in training than any other aircraft in its class. It was not what anybody could have called a forgiving fighter.

Flown properly and with nerve it starts the adrenalin pumping and the world takes on a crystal brilliance brought on by what can only be an altered consciousness. There was hardly a better aircraft at the time for blasting straight up from the ground to altitude and striking hard, or screaming along fifty feet off the ground at Mach point whatever.

"I can't say I ever felt that way. I did finish every flight soaking wet though. Damn thing was fun to fly but it sure got the sweat glands working. You know, if you want to, I would be happy to let you have the honor of doing this damned thing."

"Damned thing my ass." He reached for the scotch on the floor mid-way between our armchairs. "No way man. It's your job. I'm just the truck driver."

"Jeez, isn't there any way you want to put yourself forward and advance yourself"

"My color is shining pure white with cowardice on this one Jack. There ain't no way I'm going to do anything here other than try to find a way out and go home."

We laughed and grabbed for the bottle at the same time. The manual dropped to the floor with a snap and in the silence that followed I heard the creak of the floor beams as they changed and adjusted to the plunging night temperatures.

We were in a bare damp green room with nothing to do but make stupid jokes and blast our senses away with Peter Dawson. I didn't want to fly the plane.

"You know Phillip," I stared at him for so long I think I almost forgot what I was going to say. "I am scared shitless."

"Me too Jack. This is going to get a lot worse and I hope we get out of it okay."

"There isn't any choice you know."

"Nope, guess not."

"If I don't do this, you get killed and there isn't the slightest doubt that maniac will do what she said. I wouldn't be surprised afterward either to find a bullet between my eyes too."

I didn't want to go along with Horst's plans yet there didn't seem to be any way out. The only way that would let us have a chance, not a good one for sure, would be to fly that 60 foot long monster, with its hellfire breath, off the ground. And while getting it off would be the trick, keeping it off without slamming myself into smashed goo would be the miracle. An overspeed, a moment's inattention, or a long forgotten rule or procedure would flip the beast onto its back faster than I could register what was happening. Stall and crash. The most common way of dying in the air since the Farmans, Wrights and Monets left the ground. Things hadn't changed in all the years since. In a Starfighter of course there is the added wonder of becoming part of an instantaneous fireball.

"Remember how scared we were the first flight in the thing?" Phillip said with a wicked grin.

"Not half as much as I am now." I was back to joking about the fear now instead of being open with it. "My reflexes were better, my brain was still sharp, we were just finishing years of flight training and we practically called the simulator home before they let us near the plane." I was sounding bitter but the hardness of my voice was taken away by the slurring that seemed to grow of its own out of my mouth. Every time I tried to form the words properly they got screwed up along the way and frustration was playing with my anger.

"Now some crap loaded asshole is putting a gun to my head and saying fly."

WAR CENTRAL

I awoke slowly. The guard was yelling at me to get to my feet. I'd fallen asleep in the armchair, passed out maybe. Phillip was shaking himself awake in the other chair. The empty bottle stood between us on the gray linoleum, its bottom a forest of cigarette butts all swollen and brown from the dregs of scotch.

"Okay, okay. I'm awake," I yelled, surging to my feet and immediately regretting it. The room spun slowly in a rising arc to the right. My head hurt. I could taste that slight bite of bile in the back of the throat that means you are at the point of vomiting unless you swallow hard and hold the stomach tight and still. "What the hell is all the noise about?"

They weren't taking any chances. A second guard was at the door with his AK-47 pulled close to the waist. The one that had shaken me awake was no fool. She stood two paces to the left to give her buddy a clear field of fire. They were a trained team and I had little doubt they were military trained. Civilians don't position themselves that way and have no need to learn how.

The air shushed slowly back into the seat cushion as I stood there trying to remember who I was and where I was. The noise sounded as rude as it ever did. Every military base in the world must have the same kind of leather chairs that wheeze air in and out with every movement of the sitter. I always feel like I should make some comment about it to anyone in the same room in case they thought I was having bowel trouble. The light was too bright for my eyes. My back was soaked in cooling sweat from the chair back. I shivered from the combination of hangover and the fright of being awakened from a coma like sleep by two guards armed with weapons that could cut all of my limbs off and still have ammunition left over.

"Oh brother," Phillip said with a slur that showed he was trying hard not to slur. "Can't you leave us alone?"

"Come." the one at the door said and stepped back into the hallway to cover me as I walked forward.

They walked us along the twelve foot wide corridor connecting the barracks to the other sections of the radar complex. The floor followed the level of the ground. We were going up and down two and three step rises every twenty feet or so. I stumbled several times and not always because I was drunk. The lights weren't working. The only illumination came from two foot square windows set across from each other at ten foot intervals. The dawn was on its way from the look of the gray light bouncing off the snow cover. In the light from the still hidden sun, reflected from the northeast past the horizon over the frozen Davis Strait, and off the cap of snow on the island, I could dimly see the walls and floor. The daily thaw in the past couple of weeks had started the ice on the walls melting and refreezing. In places, the wood frames and gypsum wallboard were rippled with miniature frozen waterfalls. The place reeked of engine oil.

They guided us through the obstacle course, down the corridor, around a couple of bends, and into another long hall until we came to a steel covered door. It was closed as well as guarded by another of Horst's men. It opened stiffly to the guard's push and we entered the former command post of the station, now brought back to life.

I'd heard many stories about the abandoned DEW Line stations.

Those were the days when suburbanites debated at cocktail parties about the merits of various underground shelter designs. Some built them, everyone thought about them. Schoolchildren were given practice drills in what to do when the big one dropped. The advice, duck beneath your desk and keep your eyes shut was useless but then so was much of the air defense planning that was being done. The DEW Line stations faded out of use gradually with the development of stronger radars which reduced the need for a station every fifty miles.

Today they have all been replaced by automated robot radar stations operated remotely from thousands of miles away, backed by fleets of polar orbit satellites.

In Iqaluit, then known as Frobisher Bay, where the main base for that part of the Arctic had been located, there is a prevalent community legend that the Corps of Engineers drove several million dollars worth of road graders, trucks, jeeps, parts and surplus supplies into a ravine and bulldozed thousands of tons of gravel over the lot. They also buried thousands of drums of aviation fuel and diesel. People have been searching for that little cold war gold mine ever since.

At Padloping Island, north of Broughton, Inuit hunters found a complete fifties vintage hi-fi sound system and a library of thousands of records all in perfect condition. At Resolution Island there was a complete kitchen and a library consisting of just about every mystery and thriller novel published in the fifties and sixties.

There was a lot left to Jenness as well. I could see racks of electronic equipment against the left wall, electric cables swung across the ceiling, some to end in a tangle of disconnected wires and others running deeply into a mass of gear. In front of us were the consoles where crews once manned the radars round the clock. Now there were empty gaping holes where the screens had been, debris piled on the writing fronts and all dark except for an arc around the raised dais in the middle of the room. Here the consoles were alive although I could see that none of the original equipment was working. Instead, modern portable radar and computer terminals were propped in place. The center of the room was bathed in blue-green light from the screens. Someone sat at the central command desk in the middle of the circle. I knew who it was despite the lack of light.

"War Central Jack," Phillip said as we moved in. He swung his arms to take in the room and got a rifle barrel across the left forearm for the trouble.

Horst sat in the swivel chair where generations of commanding and duty officers must have sat waiting for the word from one of the operators in the outer ring that blips were rising to the north.

The flicker of red diode lights rippled across the front panel of one of the portable units. There was no sound other than the scrape of my feet as I moved into the room and the far away roar of a generator. As I got closer to the inner circle I saw two thick glassed radar screens, at least three feet in diameter. I'd seen them before in air traffic control centers. They were at an angle to me and I couldn't make out what they were tracking. I thought I saw a grid of curving lines that faded and brightened as the scanning lines swept across the display. The diode lights flashed strings of numbers that the two operators weren't bothering to look at. Their gaze was to the screens. Two men sat on the far side of the circle from us and behind Horst's back. They were manning radio receivers. Their earphones leaked none of the traffic that they must have been tracking.

I stopped because I got a tap on my right shoulder with a rifle barrel. It tapped again and I moved forward. I've always thought it better to obey the threat of a gun rather than try to become a movie-land hero by grabbing for the barrel. You get very dead very quickly that way.

Horst didn't seem to notice the incident. "I am truly sorry Mr. Standish and of course Mr, er ah..., to have disturbed your rest but you see events are moving more quickly than I had anticipated."

"What's this," Phillip said through a tensed jaw as he fought the pain of his arm, "the walking computer making an error."

"No, not an error. Other very fickle people have changed their minds." She said it in such a way that it was clear she believed those fickle minds were of a much lower intelligence compared to her and we weren't much better than them either.

"My plans must move more quickly, that's all. I am grateful that there is enough time for the captain here." She said this while looking straight into my eyes but talking as though she was addressing a gathering of doctors around a patient and discussing the diagnosis without acknowledging the poor bugger in the bed. "Enough time for him to regain the use of his higher faculties and do some very essential work for us."

In other words, time to sober up and follow orders or get shot.

I was intrigued by her constant self referencing. "Is there anyone else other than you involved in all this?" She was not the type of person who I would have thought that dark Russian plotters would encourage. She was too correct and determined, too self driven and self assured to win the favor of any ambitious politician bent on dominance. Independence breeds rebellion.

"Why should there be anyone other than me captain? Do you think I represent the vanguard of the Russian hordes in the final attack on capitalism? Or do you think I'm a renegade trying to bring back Communism? Perhaps I might be working for international finaciers. Do you think that?" She mocked me and at the same time made it clear to me that perhaps she was in complete charge of events.

"It seems pretty obvious that you have some pretty big backers," Phillip said.

"Yeah, you sure do," I added. "The planes, this equipment, the flights back and forth over the whole damned north. I'd say you had some backing all right."

"You forgot the submarine." Phillip said.

Horst nodded and smiled. "There is a school of history gentlemen that holds individuals have no lasting effect on events, that events are independent of generals, politicians, rabble rousers or even the likes of you two. It matters not at all whether you live or die, this philosophy holds."

I wanted so much to sit down and rest my head in my hands in hopes of easing the pain. Horst continued and in the torrent of words I saw the gleaming of an idealist.

"I do not hold to that school. Without Lenin, there would have been no Soviet State as we knew it. It's doubtful that there would even have been a sustained revolution. Now while that would please me more than the present state of affairs it is still clear that the function of Lenin's presence was to be in the right place at the right time."

I swayed and heard Phillip mutter to me, "My God, she's a fruitcake."

Horst continued without a pause. I hoped I wasn't going to double over with the nausea in my gut brought on by my hangover. "The United States has had many insignificant presidents who were ruled by events instead of shaping them. Yet would America have reached the moon without John Kennedy? I think not. Lincoln, as overrated as he is, nevertheless commanded a nation's leap forward. Hitler dragged his nation out of the slums and out of a depression; another example of a strong individual shaping fate and not the other way around."

She's no fruitcake, I thought. She was obviously a woman obsessed with an idea. "Dangerous but not mad." I said aloud to Phillip.

Horst smiled slightly at my remark and looked at the two giant radar screens for a moment. "Come forward and have a seat."

"You," she said to someone in the shadows, "Bring coffee and aspirin."

The thought of coffee brought a strong surge of emotion in me. All I wanted at that moment was to swallow gallons of the stuff.

"You gentlemen will have to regain your sobriety in a hurry if you want to stay alive."

"You mean if your plan to conquer the world is to work." Phillip said.

"Conquer the world? What gives you any idea that's my goal. In a way, Mr. Tonguay, I hope to prevent the world from being conquered.

I pushed my body back into the metal folding chair in front of the console where'd we'd been sat. My head was hurting and Horst's philosophizing was making me angry. It was as though all the alcohol I'd drunk instantly burned out of the blood stream and my head cleared as the rage built.

"I've been kidnaped , beat up, dragged around the godamned north at the point of a gun, violated ADIZ and who knows how many air regs. I've been threatened so many times now it is beginning to seem normal to me. You tried to kill me by shooting down my plane. Now you turn around and tell me that I am now essential to your grand scheme? Yet give us a bottle of scotch then tell us to hurry and get sober because your schedule is out of whack? And on top of that your whole scheme relies on an obsolete aircraft flown by someone who hasn't even seen one for almost a quarter of a century."

I swallowed hard to clear the spittle that had sprayed from my mouth. The anger shook my whole body.

"You know what? You don't seem like some great brain to me, not the way you try to make out to be. Look at the mistakes you've made. You had to wipe out a whole Inuit village because your plan went wrong, didn't you. Oh sure you carted them off to Port Helliwel and that's a mighty big flaw because any passing bush plane could drop in there any moment and then where will you be. You are playing this by ear, and you don't know what the hell you are doing."

I sat down again feeling ill once more. I expected her to have me dragged out right there and shot, Instead, she nodded and smiled. "Valid points Mr. Standish. You have spirit. You shouldn't think, however, that you will be allowed to get away with another outburst. Do not taunt me Captain. I need you to fly the Starfighter but that won't stop me from ordering some of my more unstable people from inflicting some temporary, non debilitating, pain on you. The best way in your case would be the attachment of a couple of electrodes." She looked briefly at the female guard to her left and they exchanged glances.

I'm no braver or more fearful than most others and only a fool would have pushed things after that. "All right, all right. I'll settle for some idea of what this is all about." I flicked my left hand to indicate the room.

She didn't answer right away because she was taking a tray from someone outside the circle of green, blue light. The coffee and aspirins had arrived and my hangover woke up in anticipation. Horst stepped forward with the tray and put in on top of our console. "Death. Death Mr. Standish is what it is all about. The death of important men."

"Who?" Phillip said, but Horst didn't respond or even look at him.

"Very dangerous and powerful men who you will murder for me Jack Standish."

She didn't pull punches. No words like, assassinate, do in, bump off, liquidate, or just kill. I forced the top off the pill bottle and after my head stopped pounding from the effort, fished for several seconds with thumb and finger to pull the cotton batting out. Phillip poured two cups of coffee without looking at either one of us.

A silence grew.

I began to hear the mutter of chatter between some airliner requesting clearance to climb to 32 thousand feet to avoid the westerly head wind over the Atlantic, the same wind that I was now aware of rippling around the old radar station. I wondered how the poor bastards who had been stationed at Jenness put up with the endless sound of wind, a wind that hadn't stopped blowing for thousands of treeless miles on its way to thousands more miles of ocean. The wind and the separation from home must have turned quite a few mad.

"You want me to shoot down an airliner."

It was the only answer I could see. The radar set-up, the radios and the use of a high speed interceptor armed with Sparrows all added up. Jenness sits to the north of the main transatlantic flight routes from the west and mid-west states. We were within easy range of some plodding 747. The crew would be so bored by the sight of a featureless horizon they'd rarely look out the cockpit and never consider the need to watch for another plane. "You want me to blast down an airliner. A plane with somebody important on it right? Who? The President of the United States, the Secretary General of the United Nations or is it someone from the other side?"

"Go on Mr. Standish. This is interesting."

Phillip grabbed me by the right arm and I almost dropped the coffee mug. "Jack. The President of Russia is in the States for trade talks. He's supposed to leave Los Angeles this week."

"That's it isn't it Horst? Phillip has it right doesn't he? You are going to have me shoot down the Russian leader's plane. You want it done by an American plane and leave enough evidence lying around this place to pin it squarely on the United States so no amount of cover-up will work. That's why you have left such a big trail isn't it."

There wasn't the slightest flicker of emotion from Horst's face. "You hardly need any briefing at all do you? There's no point to me telling you anymore," And she got out of the swivel chair then snapped a command at the guards who had us on our feet and practically running from the room.

My head started spinning again from the rush out of the room and what I had guessed was Horst's plan.

"Jack it's not too late. Did you see the way she panicked?" We were once more back in the NCO's room. It smelled of stale sweat and stale smoke.

"What do you mean panicked? I only rocked her back a little on her self assured heels by figuring it all out before she could tell me."

"Fraid not friend. Had nothing to do with you." Phillip took a package of cooked ham from the fridge and stripped away the plastic. He shook the meat in his hand in my direction for emphasis. "There was a trace on the radar screen, the one closest to her. While you were spouting off, that radar tech warned her. Jack, that trace sure looked like a high speed flight down from Thule straight for here."

"Military?"

"What else comes from Thule? Besides nothing civil could move that quickly."

"Might be a ferry flight south?"

He crammed a third of the ham into his mouth and chewed a bit then spoke once the meat had been chewed down enough to go to one side. "Sure, but it was coming through the center of the screen so it's either coming to have a look, or some jet jockey just happened to pick here as a waypoint."

I sat forward, charged with energy. "If he's low enough he might figure something is wrong or maybe somebody is getting suspicious about this place. There must be a search on for my plane."

He smirked. "You've forgotten that rack equipment in the Herc."

I had too. If Phillip was right about the effectiveness of the gear then the search would be going on hundreds of miles off track, sent there by the electronic distortion. The poor bastards, I thought, they're probably searching the Meta Incognita Peninsula trying to track the fragments of ELT signals that the equipment was shunting over there. It also occurred to me that any aircraft headed for the Iron Island camp would get vectored away by false transmissions pretending to come from the nearest ADIZ station. It wouldn't be too hard. Pilots in the north rarely put up too much of a fuss when they're warned away from an area by the military. It's either a military exercise that we wouldn't want to mix in with, or it is something they want want kept quiet. You don't mess with military secrets.

We also put up with it because the military provides too many services for us; the occasional use of an air force strip when flying a charter, radar vectoring in poor weather, passing on messages with their high powered radio equipment when ours cannot punch through the atmospheric hash, and the occasional free meal or drink in the mess.

But the secret doings of the different militaries in the Arctic were quietly told tales among the old Arctic hands.

There was Edmonton and a very dark secret ...

PHANTOMS OVER THE ICE

*H*e wouldn't have told me those secrets if he hadn't been into the second half of the bottle by the time our tall tales switched to the doings of the American and Canadian forces in the north. We were both staying in the Outlander Hotel in Edmonton waiting for morning commercial airline flights. Franklin Merkle sat in his hotel room and told me things that the security people would have gone nuts about if they had known he had talked.

"Know what Jack? There's a son of a bitch of a bunch of crap going on in the islands." We'd been hangar flying for hours and the switch in conversation befuddled me.

"What do you mean?"

"Ever see how they hunted subs in the islands in the eighties? Course not. You do know about the subs don't you?"

"Yes I know about the submarines," I told him. The stretch of water between Ellesmere Island and Greenland had been a super highway for nuclear submarines belonging to the Soviet Union and the United States. They got to each other's shores quicker and with less chance of detection from the spy satellites by going under the polar ice. But where they went through the straits they could be tracked for a while by the base at Alert which meant, among many other things, a network of undersea listening devices.

"I was flying from Qanak. Know it?"

"Yeah, close by Thule, Greenland."

He continued. "On my way to Alert in a twin with dogs for some of those pole runners."

I nodded again. Pole runners is the slang term given the annual spring crop of would be and serious adventurers trying to get to the pole by foot, by sled or however they hope to get into the record books. Supplying them is good business for northern charter companies, if their credit is good that is.

"The flight track on that route goes over the strait at its narrowest," Franklin said. "Doesn't look like much on the map, just a thin strip of blue so far north that most atlases don't even bother showing it. But it's wide there, must be a dozen miles and deep. Don't know how deep but sure must be the way the shores go down at each side. There was this guy who told me in Thule that both sides seem to prefer leaving the strait open. If the Americans or the Canadians tried too hard to close the door, the Soviets would retaliate by sprinkling the floor of the Atlantic with their own listening gear and then no one would get any spying done."

"So what happened?" I said in an attempt to get him to the point.

"I guess someone in Washington must have decided to show whose waters they really were." Franklin paused.

"Of course, they're really Canadian and Danish but the Americans play around in that part of the Arctic so much they for all practical purposes own it. Anyhow, I was climbing out past a string of little islands. Nice slow climb you know, from Qanak. Just sort of left the trim up a bit and let her fly up, the way the airlines do it. Well just there," he pointed to a spot on the polyester carpet by my left foot and I stupidly followed the finger.

"Just there, was a Sea King, about three thousand feet down, right on the ice crud. You seen that stuff?"

"Yeah," I said. "I fly the north remember. All that loose stuff that keeps breaking away from the landfast. Water's not water and the ice isn't."

"Right. This guy has a sonobuoy right in it. I could see the wire as clear as anything. He wasn't moving an inch. You could see the mess his rotor blast was making of the crud. Then I see an Argus. Must have been the last year you Canadians flew them before switching to the Aurora."

"I'm Scottish."

"Sfunny, you don't have an accent."

"Been here since I was a kid. Kids lose accents or get beat up at school." He nodded and used the moment to break from the story to pour another scotch. I did the same, filling my glass halfway with tepid hotel room water from the bathroom. He used the melted ice water in the bottom of the bucket.

"Anyway, I was pretty surprised by this. Never saw that before. I was so busy watching the two, the Sea King on the deck and this big mother of a four engine piston job doing these mile wide circles not fifty feet off the water. Took me a good five minutes of watching before I saw the F-4's. Whole fucking flight of the buggers just sitting way up there at maybe 15 thousand. They weren't even bothering to hide their exhaust smoke or contrails.

"How'd you know they were Phantoms? Couldn'a been 15 thousand for you to recognize them."

"Well sort of. I mean I didn't really know that's what they were then, but a few minutes later I got a hell of a better look. Besides I knew that the only thing flying then out of Thule in those days, like fighter you know, was the F-4. That and the smoke. Nothing poured out exhaust smoke like a Phantom."

"How close?"

"Hang on a bit I'll get to it." I was going to have to let him tell it in his own way.

"This Argus all of a sudden sort of straightens out of its turn, goes on a bit, then did the damnedest left turn. The guy driving this was a pro in a big way. Christ he dropped that wingtip right down. I swear Jack it was about that high off the water," He stood up and raised his right hand, still clutching his glass to the level of his ear. "He had that bugger in a 60 degree bank. Jeez I've never seen anything like it. If his heart skipped a beat it would have been cartwheels all across the strait."

"So what was going on? Did they find a sub?"

"Yeah, but hang on. I figured I was getting too close to something. I thought maybe an exercise but I didn't want to get any closer cause they sure don't like it when you screw up an exercise or anything else they're up to. Pulled power and turned away a bit so it wouldn't look like I was trying to mess with them.

"Figured, leave those guys alone and they'll leave me alone.

"Boy you should have seen those Phantoms. They came out of the sky so fast I swear to God they had these little streak lines behind them, you know like they put in comic books to show speed. Those mothers were moving.

"They came down one and after another in this long line and every one pulled out so hard those pilots must have blacked out. You could see these pure white vortices of supercompressed air coming off the wingtips. Looked like the wings were coated with white smoke." He stopped to light another cigarette and I did the same.

"So what about the sub?"

"All I saw was this black thing, maybe a hundred feet long sort of half break through the ice, I guess the conning tower. It never got all the way up. Those F-4's let go with everything. Cannon, rockets, whatever. There was smoke and water and fire going everywhere. Those poor buggers in the sub never got out. By the time the spray cleared enough for me to see, the Phantoms were climbing through ten thousand and all there was on the water was a bunch of junk floating around."

"They knocked out a Soviet submarine?" I was astonished. It was the first time I'd heard first hand that the cold war had turned hot. "How come I've never heard of this before? It would have made headlines around the world if it had happened."

Franklin was angry. "Say guy. That's what I saw and it's no bullshit. Christ I shouldn't be telling you all this either and you don't want to believe it. I know this. There must be a lot more things like this that go on that we never hear of. And I'll tell you why. By the time I got to Alert I was ready to tell the world but I never had a chance. They had security people all over me and the Twin Otter the second I turned off the props. They had me in some stinking little room scaring the shit out of me if I ever told anyone what I saw. Fuck I don't know why I told you cause those guys play real hard."

I never saw Franklin Merkle again, but I thought of his story often whenever a flight took me anywhere near the Kennedy Channel.

It's that kind of super secret activity that fed rumors among pilots in the Arctic and ensures that military orders about where to fly or not are followed. No, I thought, there was no chance that any search plane or any other aircraft would get near Iron Island or Jenness. But that trace on the radar Phillip saw made me think a bit.

PLANS

"*P*hillip, how about making a run for the radios and shouting for help. Maybe that would get the plane to have a closer look."

"Jack. How are we going to get past the guards on the door? Then how do you get along what must be a couple of hundred yards of corridor, through a steel door, fight off Horst and her army, and then, and then, figure out what knobs to twiddle on the radio? That's after you've figured out which ones are the radios in that electronic supermarket. And then what are you going to do? Guess at a frequency?"

"Okay. Still if we got to a radio we might reach someone. I doubt that their jamming gear is blanking out the island. They wouldn't be able to track the North Atlantic flights if it was. How about the Herc's radios or even their helicopter?"

His eyes glazed again as he concentrated and a slight smile came. "Okay. All right. How do we get out of here?"

"I don't think these guys will fall for one of us pretending to be sick and then allowing us to smash their heads in. How about....," I didn't finish. I saw a look of disgusted shock on his face.

"Have you ever thought," he spun about to smash his fist into the drywall. It made a shallow moon crater in the gypsum, "that whoever was zapping across the screen is probably long gone by now?"

The hangover had made me miss it. A high flying jet would have been over Jenness and gone about the time we got back into the room. "Not much point I guess."

"Nope. Another plan?"

I didn't answer. I was thinking that even if we had got to the planes the radios weren't powerful enough anyway to reach Thule or any other location that had the equipment to hear us. They were powerful enough at altitude, say eight thousand feet, but from the ground, even if that ground was several hundred feet up an island mountain, there was no chance.

I stared at the moon crater. Crumbled gypsum had trickled out and sat against the baseboard molding in a small heap of white granules. An idea was also trickling past that curious mixture of hopelessness and hangover clouding my mind. It sat somewhere between my eyes and the wall and refused to come into focus. I searched for it, chasing that elusive thought which must have been there, or might not; I wasn't sure. I might have got it if the door hadn't burst in so hard the door knob punched another hole into the wallboard.

We were on our way again.

Horst wasn't in the swivel chair. The radio operators sat in their places. The radar screens were now double banked with two people each to ensure that nothing slipped through this time. One of the screens was the long range stuff. The other was limited to the immediate area around the island. It provided high definition tracking of anything coming across the ice, or any aircraft which might try to elude the long range scan by flying low through the ground clutter, or by using radar avoidance gear.

A bank of four, ten inch, tablets were ranged across the top of the console where we had sat less than twenty minutes before.

The coffee was still there and I ached to get some of it. I wasn't prepared for the hiss in my ear. I jumped when Horst spoke behind me.

"You would have been interested I am sure to have seen what was going on here. You will appreciate, though, my need to have distractions eliminated in a crisis."

I don't know what she thought I was, some form of noble adversary, a worthy opponent, matched wits in the scheme of life or what. She came across as the type willing to say, "Well played sir," as she someone beat into the ground with a club.. A private school mentality steeped in games, clearly set enunciation, and choice of words. Horst's character seemed to lean more to the British upper class than the proletariat of Gorki. Although, perhaps it was a private school for psychopaths.

The so-called classless society is remarkable for its indulgence in those tiny signs cultures use to mark members apart from, better than, lower than and just different from others. She didn't seem the type that the Russian leaders would trust a mission of this type to. If it had been me in one of those gray carpeted offices behind the red walls of the Kremlin scanning the lists of officers for someone with the strength needed to set up a guerrilla organization in a foreign country solely for killing my country's most senior leader, I would have chosen someone who owed more to the homeland than Horst with her uncontrollable psychoses and decadent ways. I would have chosen someone with a record of unfailing loyalty to his immediate leaders rather than a woman who spoke impeccable english and bantered a liberal philosophy of history. Such people as Horst are far too independent.

I couldn't see her acting on her own. The complexity of the operation she had mounted was staggering. It must have been in the planning stages for many months.

The expense must have been terrific. She couldn't have been able to steal and hijack everything she needed. I was ready to bet she must have paid out a lot of money to some group in the United States to steal, then smuggle that NASA research Starfighter out of the country.

God knew there are enough para-military wacko types in that part of the world who would have been happy and capable of meeting her needs.

And no matter how much money she might have, I thought, there's just nowhere she could have got hold of that submarine. From the size of it as it had sat at the dock it appeared to be a late generation nuclear powered missile carrier.

"Should you be wondering Captain; an aircraft from Thule was tracked heading for the island, so you see I was not able to have you around while I dealt with it."

I was irritated with her always calling me Captain and snapped at her. "What'd you do general, shoot it down with a Klara class missile? Spread the poor asshole all over the strait?" I knew as I said it that she wouldn't have done that. The heat from the missile would have flared over the receptors of whichever satellite was around, and quite possibly by Thule if they were running a full telemetry on the jet.

"Hardly. I did the most sensible thing... nothing." She handed me a coffee in an off white porcelain mug. It was the type that only lunch bars in long vanished department stores used. And of course, in military messes, at least every one I'd ever been in. They withstand the inept washing skills that untrained military kitchen help inflict on the crockery. Like every such mug this one had been through the dishwasher cycle so many times that no glaze remained on the rim. Added to the coffee taste was that sensation of grit on the lower lip so everything tasted as though it had been strained through a sand filter. I also swear that when they were designed the human index finger was much smaller. You either have to force a finger through the hole and give up hope it will ever come back out, or cradle the whole mug backwards in the hand. The base kitchen was obviously still stocked with the things.

"I suspected the plane, an F-16 by the way, was just using the island as a waypoint. Destruction would have brought complications."

Phillip broke his silence for the first time since entering the room. "Doesn't your hired help ever get tired of you taking all the glory?" I sensed he was as tired of the charade as I was but showing it far more. His lips drew back across the teeth in a grimace, which in Phillip passes for a sneer. "I mean, to hear you talk one would think you were the only one here."

Horst didn't bother to notice Phillip's presence. I could see by the slight narrowing at the corners of her eyes though that she had heard and wasn't going to react. I didn't know whether that was because of some prejudice against his color, or because Phillip was nothing more than the hostage in this affair. He didn't count in her equations as long as he was alive to be used to make me do what she wanted.

The radar technicians perched on the front edge of their chairs over the screens. Radio traffic muttered in the background mixing with the faint roar of wind.

Things just weren't adding up. I said, "I can't see how you can really believe that I will shoot down an airliner with what, a hundred, two hundred, people on board? Just because you're threatening to shoot Phillip? You know you can't force me to weigh one man more than that." It hurt to say, but it was right. I knew that I wouldn't be able to do it just to allow Phillip to live.

It's one thing to kill a man under war-time conditions when given the chance he would do the same thing to you, but that's not the same as shooting down a plane load of people who couldn't know what was going to hit them. We were trained killers Phillip and me and I suspected Horst too. We were trained by the air force to kill the other pilot as quickly and as easily as possible.

That means taking every opportunity to slip into the blind spot, creep up to missile or cannon range, and shoot in the back. We were trained to swoop down on truck convoys, factories, troops, anything on the ground that couldn't shoot back with anything heavy enough to do us harm. We were trained to cut them to ribbons at no cost to ourselves, all in the name of warfare.

It was that, kill or be killed, philosophy which dominated our training and those who couldn't or wouldn't grasp it found themselves flying heavy transports or, god-forbid, helicopters.

"I have no doubts Mr. Standish, that you will do exactly what I want you to do. You see while Mr. Tonquay here will be in front of a gun on the ground, you will be too. Teller is going with you."

Teller took a step down from the dais and the swivel chair. I've known men with cold eyes, but this was the first time I saw dead eyes. There was not the tiniest crinkle to the corners, not the slightest flinch in the face, or the barest widening of the irises. The flesh of his face was without life. Teller had frightened me in Resolute the first time I saw him and now he terrified me. With him in the back seat I had trouble. Here was a man who not only felt nothing when he killed, he felt nothing of his own death. I knew he'd be sitting in the radar operator's seat behind me in the 104 ready to blast the back of my head apart if I even looked like trying to screw things up. He wouldn't even bother pulling the ejection handle when the jet went out of control with me dead in the front chair.

There is a price to all morality and in this case my life was it. Intellectually I could argue that my life did not stack up against the lives of those in that airliner any more than I considered Phillip's life did. Yet I felt the emotion flaming inside me. I did not want the back of my head pushed through my eyesockets and splattered across the armored glass of the windshield. I did not want to stop living and the price of that was what Horst wanted.

"Teller is an unusual man, Mr. Standish. You will find it

impossible to stand in his way or mine. You will not be able to become even the smallest obstacle to my path."

"We haven't been doing too badly so far." I said.

Phillip shook his head as I spoke. "If I have to listen to this lunatic at least I want to know what the hell this is all about."

"Yes, I suppose there is no reason why you shouldn't participate."

MONTREAL SNOWSTORM

I reached for the coffee mug again and wished the aspirin would start to work on the woolly headache living behind my eyes. The coffee was just at that point where it would be cold if not drunk in one go and all the better as a thirst quencher for being lukewarm.

"No there is no reason, but I don't think we have the time." Horst turned to her left and the steel doors. My mouth fell open with the suddenness of her change in mood. The woman was playing us like she was on some psychological deep sea trawl.

Then I thought I saw the reason for her switch about. One of the guards was backing a two-wheel dolly into the room. It was piled to the curved handles with green painted ammunition boxes. Someone had obliterated black writing with silver spray paint. Teller nodded to Horst from the radar screens.

"I am afraid we will have to continue our talk some other time. My plans are back on track." Horst said.

You were right Mr. Standish to say I was improvising a few minutes ago. You see, even the best planned exercises are prone to outside influences. The mark of a good planner, you might say, is to know when and how to abandon the plan and ride with those influences."

Three men I hadn't seen before entered wearing down-filled green parkas with telescopic hoods, the type of parka most worn by oil workers and construction workers in the Arctic. They followed the cart in. Their white plastic soled boots stamped hard against the linoleum. The men nodded at Horst and continued past to the consoles, ripping the Velcro sealing off the zippers with nasty shearing sounds and dropping the parkas on empty chairs. I smelled the cold on them as they passed.

"In this case Captain, a plane I was waiting for was held up for twelve hours longer than I would have expected by a snowstorm in Montreal." She jerked her chin slightly and our two guards prodded us in the backs with their rifle butts. I was too busy trying to get a better look at the ammunition boxes and walked out of the room with the coffee mug still in my hand. The feel of that thick porcelain cradled in my fist worked its way to the shoulder muscles and they tightened as I estimated distances to my guard and tried to guess how hard I would have to hit him. I wondered too what we'd do if I did get him on the floor. We were some distance from the main entrance and even then there was nowhere to go that would hide us from the guns. I might have tried it, but the guard at the door saw the mug and took it from me.

Phillip led the way by half a step. He picked his way over the occasional fragment of wallboard that had crumbled to the tile over the years. The gypsum lay in chunks the size of road gravel among the soggy and half frozen remains of paper surfacing. Armored electric cable looped across the hallway. I kept my eyes on the floor to avoid tripping. The cable gave me an idea.

I kept my eyes searching the gloom for the right length of conduit. In the glow coming through a split in the corridor, at the head of a two step drop, a basketball sized hoop of cable conduit rose out of the shadows at the edge. A free end curled a couple of feet up the wall. I guessed there was enough slack.

Sharply. "Phillip!" And my hand reached past the base of the loop away from the free end. I turned and lashed overhead with eight feet of three quarter inch flexible steel armoured cable. The corrugated skin acted like a dull chainsaw as it whipped across the face of the tall guard farthest from me and cut up across the mouth of the other as I backhanded through the blow. The cable made a sound like a stick hitting a wet pillow.

The guards screamed and dropped their guns to clutch at their faces. The blood looked like black paint in the gloom.

Phillip lunged up from the base of the steps and kicked the AK-47's to the other side of the hallway from the guards then went after them. He tossed one to me and I gave the unfamiliar mechanism a check to see how to use it. Phillip stood still for a moment staring at the guards then moved forward and smashed them across the backs of their heads with the butt. They looked dead. He bent to the closest and started to drag him out of the hallway.

"No. Leave them there. Can't waste time." I ran down the corridor to the door leading to the barracks wing where our room was. At the far end of the wing was what I was hoping for; a door to the outside, the fire escape. I hit the door at full run with shoulder and hip and it snapped open and crashed against the hinges and the outside wall. The wind shot into my face. "Come on," I screamed and ran out.

"Hold on Jack. We need gear." And he ran back the length of the barracks leaving me standing in the minus whatever gale in a down vest and clutching the cooling metal of the automatic rifle without gloves. The cold curled down my open shirt neck and edged across the tops of my ears. I panted from the exertion and strained against the sound of the wind for any sign that our escape had been noted.

I had no idea where we were going to go, no plans, no goals, other than to get out and away. And I had no brains if I expected to stay on the loose for more than 15 minutes without winter clothing. If Phillip hadn't thought to go back for the clothing, we'd have been giving ourselves up in ten minutes just for the chance to sit in front of a heater.

Phillip returned with the parkas and gloves. "Where to?" I said.

"I don't know. You should have thought of that before. Airstrip I spose." Phillip zipped his parka to his chin and we drew the hoods forward against the wind.

We stumbled down the rocky spine the station was built on and tried to get our bearings. It was difficult to see the hollows and rises of the slope and we kept falling against rocks and into snow patches. "We'll try to get one of the radios going." I gasped as we ran.

We got off the spine and started through the cluster of four machine buildings at the head of the road. I was running past the largest when Phillip grabbed my arm and spun me to a stop in front of the metal tambour door. It was a garage.

The garage sat inside the last curve of the road from the airstrip. The wind had piled snow in fifty foot drifts to the top of its roof, but the door was crosswise to the wind and the ground was bare to the rock and gravel. Phillip grabbed the looped chain on the ground and hauled on it. The door didn't move. I grabbed the chain too and added my pull to his. The door broke free of the ridge of ice holding it tight and shot up in a harsh clatter of metal.

SUNDOGS AND ICE

*S*ix snowmobiles sat nose out with tracks off the ground to stop them freezing under the weight of the machines; all had ignition keys. We tossed four of the keys into a corner filled with a jumble of empty oil cans, scraps of shipping pallets, and discarded truck parts. I knew that throwing away the keys wouldn't slow down the hunt too much. There's nothing elaborate about the keys. They're mostly just key shaped metal lugs lacking the intricate saw-tooth edging and veined lock slides of real keys. On some machines a penknife blade will start the engines. But the extra minute or two that Horst's men would spend checking to see whether someone else had the keys or whether they were stored somewhere in the garage might give us an edge.

We started two machines and ground them over the gravel floor in a shower of spitting sparks from the runners and onto the road.

The sun was up. A faint golden ring flung wide around it through the pale blue told me there was bad weather on the way. Almost past the limit of visibility in the ring was a slight thickening of glow at the three and nine o'clock positions. Sundogs.

I pointed at them to show Phillip and opened the throttle. I heard Phillip's snarl in response and we went down the road fighting the steering arms as the runners bit unevenly into the shallow snowdrifts in our path. At times, I had to pull the brake lever right to the handlegrip to slow enough to avoid the worst. I didn't want to be flipped into the path of Phillip's machine.

There were stretches of road that the wind had cleared down to the rock and we skidded across them in screams of ripping metal and six foot long sparks. They spat out from under the wear bars in showers of dull yellow clusters. Long straight lines of fire that forked and forked again at their ends until they were gigantic versions of hand sparklers. We plowed through lakes of fire.

We left the road as it cuts across the end of the airstrip, just past the clump of rocks where the Herc almost came to an end. We crashed through the little outriders of those rocks in a wild charge of bouncing machines and slapping drive belts. The springs bottomed on my machine with every jolt and the chassis must have been permanently distorted from then on. There seemed to be half a mile of rocks in front of us. Some of them I was able to steer around, but I hit a lot straight on and the machine would ride up and crash back down so violently that I would be thrown half over the windshield. Once my left ski tip caught straight on a boulder and the steering arms whipped out of my hands and the handlegrip drove into my side. The snowmobile started to go over. I was almost thrown straight under. Somehow, I pulled it back and pushed on with the steering dragging to the left.

Phillip moved ahead of me and to my left. His machine was taking a terrible pounding. Mine must have looked as bad. The driving track was split. A long strip of it had caught up around one of the bogies. Blue smoke streamed back from it as the wildly rotating little wheel burned the material. A huge dent distorted the nose of his snowmobile and the windshield was cocked forward where Phillip had crashed into it and pushed it ahead. His skis were rattling and waving so badly I knew the shock absorbers had gone.

Then as I fought to keep from tilting right over again as I rounded a boulder the size of a small car his machine smashed straight on into a steep pile of loose rocks. His entire machine reared back and lifted clear of the ground. The tracks screamed. The sound ricocheted against the rocks, as the engine raced at full throttle with no load.

Phillip clung to the handlegrips as the nose rolled back. His legs and body slipped from the seat cushion and they formed a tent shape hurtling through the air with his snowmobile leaning back toward him and him at a forty five degree angle.

Aircraft stall the same way, the same ungainly arch up and then the agonizing wait until the fall begins and the mushy sag of acceleration to the ground. He and the machine hit the other side of the mound. The rear of his tracks bit into a hollow and the machine shot forward to land flat and hard. There was a spurt of rock and snow as the screaming track dug in and two hundred and fifty pounds of machinery ripped away from under him. The deadman's throttle closed, but that track had been going at a hell of a rate and the snowmobile raced straight at another rockpile and drove itself into junk.

There was no sign of movement from Phillip. When I got to him he was cradling a rock in both arms and lying face down in a frozen patch of lichen. His left glove was gone and lay near the wreckage. His fingers were still curled from the grip on the bar. Apart from checking to make sure there was no blood coming from his mouth there was little first aid knowledge I could remember to help. His legs looked normal, so I assumed no major damage and hauled him unconscious onto the rear seat cushion of my snowmobile. He started gasping and spitting while I was trying to prop him into position and feel for any bits of splintered bones or the wet of blood. I rolled him over and that turned the gasps to a groan.

"Phillip, are you all right?" That is the other side of the unconscious person's inane comment, "Where am I?"

He clutched his jaw, "Oh God. Son of a bitch." There was a dark welt against his skin where his chin had scraped a rock. His eyes were open and bright.

"Can you move? They'll be after us. Can you hang on?"

He nodded and I got on the machine. He leaned against my back as I moved off. I heard his groans every time I hit a rock too hard. I kept looking back up the slope, but I saw no sign of the cavalry charge I expected.

I drove the rest of the way through the rockfield at a walking pace, me standing up on the running boards with my right hand on the throttle and my left behind me on his shoulder to steady him. We made better time once I got onto the airstrip and the rush of bitter air brought him back to something feeling more human like.

The Hercules was where we'd left it, halfway down the strip. The 412 was tucked close behind the starboard wing as though sheltering from the wind. There was no sign of the Starfighter or trucks.

The vague plan, now all of ten minutes old, had been to get a radio going and call for help. Now I started to think about getting the Herc off the ground. There wasn't enough fuel in the tanks to go far unless Horst had them filled in the meantime. Still there'd be enough, I thought, to get away from the island and put down on the sea ice close to land and then take things from there. I could, I thought, coast crawl to stay over thick ice and make it as far as I could to a settlement before putting the plane down with empty tanks. It would save a lot of walking and would get us far enough away.

I drove straight for the plane while I counted the DayGlo

fabric strips dangling in the wind from the control surface locks, the pitot tube, and antennas so I would know whether I had got them all off before takeoff. I didn't want to try taking off with an aileron locked.

Phillip screamed my name against the noise of the engine and the rattle over the gravel. I turned. He was staring back up the mountain slope. It took me a moment to make them out although I knew what I was looking for. The glare of the sun on the snow patches make the bare rock an impenetrable black. I caught movement and saw them. Three of the thirty ton trucks making the first turn from the base now hidden beyond the top of the mountain. It had taken them a longer time to start the diesel engines in the cold and organize the hunt than I expected.

I almost ran into the radome of the Herc by watching the trucks. "Come on. Let's get to the radios."

A hopeless idea.

There was a time when aircraft, in the days of grass fields and nice minded people, when all pilots formed some sort of brother-hood of the air, didn't have door locks. That was a time before the general mounting level of savagery, drug smuggling, hijacking and just straight thievery. Now there are locks on everything that flies and while they still aren't as good as the cheapest of car locks they're impervious to the snowmobile penknife trick. We didn't have the key to the Hercules.

The two of us stood there listening to the growl of the trucks coming down the mountain and staring at that stupid lock.

"What about the radio in the Bell?" I asked. There was no answer so I ran over the frozen gravel and mud to it and almost ran into one of the number three engine prop blades on the way. "The damn thing's locked too." The words were still coming out when I saw the last chance and an unexpected one at that. I hadn't seen it before because we had come down the strip straight to the Hercules and from that angle we couldn't see behind the port wing shoulder. "Lookit that," I yelled to Phillip.

Nose on just ten feet behind the cocked tail of the big transport sat a friendly looking little Twin Otter, black snubby nose and fat paw balloon tires.

The pilot door was locked and the passenger-cargo door too but that didn't worry me. The one thing no one ever seems to lock on a Twin is the small baggage door at the tail. That's where you keep your engine covers and odd bits of tools and things like that which the ground crew are forever needing. Phillip boosted me up and I scrambled through a litter of Arctic survival gear, a crushed cardboard box and an engine cover. On some Otters there's a partition sealing off the luggage space. I've yet to see one. They're all removed so the flight crew can get at the stuff without having to leave the aircraft. I wriggled through the bulkhead cut-out.

"Pull off the covers and get the flags off." I shouted and ran up front.

This was the plane that had brought the strange load of ammunition boxes. I judged from the layout of the auxiliary fuel system that it had made the flight from Montreal in one trip and could have gone on much further. Two 45 gallon drums were lashed in the cabin near the tail and connected to the main system with fuel lines. It's a modification seen on Otters doing long distance work where airstrips and fuel are either not available, or the work demands long hours in the air; flights such as magnetometer surveys and long hauls over the Arctic ice-cap. I didn't stop to tap them. I didn't care whether they had any fuel. All I wanted was to get into the air and away from those trucks and the island. On the way forward I lifted the passenger door latch for Phillip.

I wasted half a minute rummaging through the map pockets for the spare ignition key that I knew would have to be in the cockpit somewhere. Aircraft like the Otter that depend on charter work for a living are home to several pilots a week switching from one job to another. Since keeping track of the keys is always an impossibility the common practice is to leave them either in the ignition or a map pocket. Sure enough, I found it in the ignition after wasting that thirty seconds going through the pockets. I hit the starting sequence before I was even in the left hand seat. The port engine ignited and spooled up. Phillip was still dragging the cover from the starboard engine on board when I started the blades on that one turning. The blades spun and spun faster with the rising whine of the turbines. They changed pitch from feather ground to fine, and then the PT-6's started to howl cleanly. I didn't bother with any checks other than to glance at the annunciator panel to make sure no fire lights were on. I felt the plane rock as Phillip threw himself through the rear door.

I couldn't see the trucks. The road was behind us and to the right. They had to have been close I thought, although perhaps slowed by the washouts at the head of the strip where the runoff from the mountain slope cut across.

I don't know how I was able to twist that plane out from behind the Hercules. I didn't have the time to waste going into full reverse and backing clear. Phillip jumped into the right seat as I twisted the throttles. I suppose the starboard wingtip must have all but wiped the ass of the Hercules as we pulled clear.

"Give me flap," and I shoved the levers forward. Phillip tapped the back of my hand so I let go and held the wheel with both. The plane bucked and slammed through the clusters of snowdrifts between us and the strip. We were so lightly loaded I was able to pull us off, just shaving the stall speed. The plane mushed diagonally across the airstrip. I felt, rather than saw, the end of the ragged drifts and the flat of the gravel and slammed the wheel forward to push the Otter back closer to the ground. I held it down to build better speed so we could climb out of ground effect and get away.

"I'll hold it here," I shouted over the engines. I got her up about fifteen feet then ran downslope to the sea ice. The airspeed built up horribly fast and went into the red arc on the airspeed indicator. I was pushing toward the Never Exceed speed. I know the limits are there for good reasons but figured that I had a better reason for ignoring it this time.

In simple terms the limits say, "If you go any faster the wings will fall off and you will never walk home." The limits are not something to exceed capriciously. What a lot of pilots don't know, however, is that the engineers and test pilots build in a fudge factor. "Here, we'll knock off ten percent for the old cowboy who tries to wreck this beauty."

So, the test pilot will drive the plane out past the limits of the flight envelope, the conditions beyond which the engineers figure it can't fly safely, and he'll come back to the guys with the calculators and say, "Son of a bitch of an elevator was fluttering so bad at 269 knots I almost bought it."

The calculators will work for a few seconds and the Never Exceed speed will be set at 240 knots. At that point, empirical guess work goes into action and makes nonsense of the silicon chips and sets the Vne at 234 knots on the theory that a little bit off the top might provide an extra bit of safety. And the idea of picking a weird number like 234 is rooted in the popular psychology that says to a pilot, "Hey, don't fool around out here. Our computers and wind tunnels and the lives of three test pilots confirm that at EXACTLY 234 knots the wings WILL fall off."

So I knew about that kind of design thinking and something else too as I let the speed keep building and throwing us toward the jumble of shore ice. Northern pilots know and manufacturers sometimes acknowledge in the flight manuals that the numbers arrived at over the test ranges of the desert western United States don't always apply in the cold, dense air of the Arctic. The wings can carry more. The props are also a little more efficient. As a result, you can carry more cargo, even if you are in technical violation of the regulations according to the figures arrived at by the manufacturer and the FAA.

Of course, steel and aluminum gets a little brittle in deep cold. According to the book, a pilot could theoretically fly away with an elephant tucked in the cargo bay in warm weather. But in the Arctic cold he had better not try any sharp turns without being good at making forced landings with the wingtips touching each other.

Phillip pointed to an island rising like an office tower about three miles to the northwest. "If you get behind that we can get lost in the fiords."

I nodded without taking my eyes from the shore ice and gently, delicately, started to pull back on the yoke using just my fingertips, hoping the spars were good at holding. Slowly, but slowly, the speed dribbled off as the nose came up and finally I had the needle back below the red.

"What do you want to do, head for Pangnirtung or Iqaluit?" I said.

"Neither," he said. "Think we should find a good spot and sit and wait a while. They'll have those aircraft in the air any moment and with the radar in the Hercules they'll pick us off real quick unless we're down on the ground." He buckled his harness. Mine was still unfastened and it made me uncomfortable not having it tight around me as I pushed the plane down close to the ice and headed for the island.

"Phillip. Keep calling out the height from the radar altimeter." I was having trouble judging height off the ice. Open leads looked half a mile wide one moment and about ten feet across the next. I was afraid to take my eyes off the ice and the island to check the altimeter. I didn't want to find out in one hell of a hurry that the fifty feet I was trying to hold was nothing.

"What the hell Jack. The thing doesn't read well enough this low. Feel for the cushion."

"For god's sakes. At 210 knots you want me to feel ground effect cushion?" The controls were stiff at this speed although the needle was still slowly falling back. "I'll take it up a bit."

"Ok got it. The thing's registering. Hold there."

"I hope you're right Tonquay. This thing doesn't have floats."

"Forget the floats on the ice, idiot. Try for wheels and those rocks." He pointed straight ahead at a billion tons of island coming at us so quickly it seemed to swell to fill the windshield.

A LINE ON THE CHART

*T*he square edge of the cliff face came straight on. My palms went wet. "Son of a bitch. Thing's closer than I thought," I yelled as I twisted the controls to the left. The lack of depth perception in this world of black and ice and no visual cues had almost got me again.

We went around that stump of rock like a souped up Harvard cutting the pylons at the Nevada air races. If there had been any early spring birds getting ready for summer nesting on the ledges they would have needed all summer to regrow the feathers the Otter had blasted off them as it grazed the cliff face.

"Kind of makes you wish for railroad tracks eh?" Phillip said after we had finally cleared the island.

I laughed. "Iron compass, depth gauge, sure, you bet." I thought of how easy pilots in the south had it with real cues to indicate altitude for them, things like houses and trees and railroad tracks to navigate by. Every once in a while I'd run into one of those southern trained pilots up for a summer of Arctic flying. They either flew around with their eyes glued to their altimeters or roller coastered all over the sky when they tried to fly altitude visually. It scared them silly until they got used to it.

What had seemed to us to be an unbroken wall of rock and mountains as we scooted across the bay to the island now opened into a maze of twisted channels, black islands, blunt headed peninsulas and dark cliffs.

The maze stretched back off into haze and fog and seemed to break into a series of fiords all pointing at us.

Ice leads threaded through the drifted pack ice painting black slashes through the ice glare. Shards of ice thrusting vertically out of the pack ice where it had rafted flashed sun into my eyes. Soon my vision filled with purple afterimages.

Phillip found a pair of sunglasses in the right door pocket and passed them over.

"Oh, boy that helps." The deep creases in my forehead smoothed out with the relief. Now I could see clearly through the glare.

There were little islands that looked like whales, medium ones like freighters, and others resembling churches, castles, small villages at sea and monsters enough for a couple of nightmares.

The islands stood straight out from the ocean all dappled and streaked with packed snow ice crammed into crevices by the winter wind. The larger ones were snowcapped with cream colored domes that I knew hid jagged island tops.

"See anywhere?" Phillip said.

I shook my head. Nowhere was there room enough to even park a car.

Phillip kept craning his head from side to side and peering ahead into the haze. "Ice looks too broken by the current and tide to risk a landing."

"Maybe those floats would have been the thing after all."

"Head back there!" Phillip pointed across to my side of the cockpit. His arm almost hit me in the face. "Back there quick." He chopped his hand down in a small arc to show me the way.

I don't know why we don't just point. Every pilot seems to

indicate direction as though using a meat cleaver to slice out the precise heading.

I turned and lined up on a fiord running into the channel at an angle to the others. "What is it?"

He had the navigation chart out. His finger traced through the blue shading. "Airstrip."

"No way chum. I know this area remember. There's nothing here."

"I tell you this, it shows a strip. Look!"

Sure enough, on the map there was an airstrip, or rather a line on the chart. "Let me see that." I said.

In quick glances while I flew on I picked out the markings. "Ruins, it says."

"Little box too for a building." he added.

The Twin Otter bounced through a wind bubble that had been shot off from an islet under us. I wondered about the strip. We had nowhere to go and a big need to get down but anything on the charts would be investigated by Horst.

"Well I don't know. It shows a mark for ruins and the word "station." That's gotta be a weather station. Doesn't it? They always have airstrips even if they are abandoned."

I pulled back the power and dropped ten degrees of flap. We floated along slightly nose down for visibility and about as slow as a car moving through late Friday afternoon commuter highway traffic.

The sun streamed through the glass onto my face so I let the Twin slip gently into cliff shadow and followed Phillip's fiord inland. The cliffs got higher as we went and the wind stronger as it shot down the valley from the plateau. The controls constantly bucked in my hands. There was no beach anywhere. The cliffs dropped straight into the sea and kept right on going for all I could guess. Blackness and black with slashes of white danced ahead of us as we flew on through shadow.

Phillip had the map in his hand now. His eyes constantly

flicked between it and the fiord, trying to match the contour with what we could see. "I know what we'll find," he said. "An old whaling station. They didn't have airstrips eighty years ago you know." I nodded without looking at him. The same thought had occurred to me. Station could mean weather or whaling very easily. The Eastern Arctic is dotted with abandoned whaling stations.

The coasts of Baffin Island and Labrador at times seem crusted with loose stone foundations and rusting iron cauldrons left over from the heavy days of whaling at the turn of the 19th century. New England whalers would drop off small crews to handle a few dozen carcasses and pick them up in the fall for the run home. Sometimes the crews didn't get picked up because their mother ship had perished, and the small bands of men would freeze to death in a winter they didn't know how to handle. A few, a very few, lived through those winters with the Inuit and returned to Hartford or Boston or where-ever months later. Others never did, opting to live in the new land and their bloodlines live on in the modern Inuit.

"I'm afraid you're right, Phillip. This place isn't going to be much use for us, even if we do find it, and I don't think we will in this light."

"Oh Yeah?" he whooped, half raising against the seat harness to peer forward. "That's what we want. Right there Jack, right there." He stabbed his fingers forward and down several times.

MONSTERS IN THE PACK ICE

I sometimes get this urge to pitch smart-ass co-pilots out of the aircraft when my expert opinions are questioned, and it doesn't matter if they are right.

It was indeed an airstrip, or to be accurate, more just a thousand feet of cliff debris that had fallen to make a narrow shelf along the water. The construction crews had picked off the large boulders and filled in the low spots so it was just barely flat enough to take a plane with fat tires and strong struts.

I figured there was just enough room to get the Otter down without wiping away the wing tip along the cliff.

"There are the ruins." Phillip said.

"Where?"

"Those black lines at the end of the strip. There. See it?"

"Think so. Don't look like a weather station though." It puzzled me. Three straight lines of black rock foundation near the water covered to their tops by drifts and a scattering of pine timbers. There were bits of red brown iron mysteries poking out of the snow along the beach and around the foundation walls. I was sure it was a whaling station.

"I don't see anything here Phillip. There's nothing here but junk." Then I saw it. "No. Hang on. Under the cliff. A hut" I pushed on power as we sailed past just twenty feet off the beach and then climbed around to the right to line up for another pass.

"I see it," Phillip said. "White hut in the overhang."

The overhang was a tremendous undercutting of the cliff about fifty feet high and deep. It ran about half the length of a city block before narrowing down to a slit and disappearing into the rock face. If the hut hadn't been there we wouldn't have been able to see it against the black. The hut was once white before years of snow and ice crystals had stripped away the paint yet against that rock it gleamed like a pearl in a black velvet lined box. Out on the beach sat two of the beehive like structures on stilts, louvered and capped with slanted roofs, that weather people use to house their barometers and thermometers. Just from the empty look to the place I could tell no one had been around for a long time.

"Can you get it down?" He said it more like a statement than a question as he pulled the landing checklist from the map pocket.

I didn't bother with another fly over. We were set up nicely for the strip at the end of the climbing turn. I pulled the power back and slowed things down for the easiest touchdown I could get. The Twin Otter is superb for this kind of work and can take a pounding that few other aircraft can.

"Hang on." We slammed through a foot deep drift at the edge of the strip, exactly where I had not intended the wheels to hit. There was perfectly good bare gravel in front of and behind the drift where the Twin would have liked better to land, but no, I somehow had to choose a spot that sent us lunging forward into the shoulder straps.

As we hit I prayed there was no rock buried in the snow otherwise we'd be like those poor marooned whalers. The snow smashed up through the props and a thunder of snow crust ripped away at the belly. The plane danced hard with vibration, and then we were landed.

The slow touchdown speed and the wind coming down from the valley, as well as the braking effect of the snowdrift, had the Otter stopped in little more than a few times her own length.

I said. "Try that in a Herc and see what happens."

He let the air out of his lungs with a puff. "I'd rather see you try it in a 104. But don't ask me around as co-pilot."

I smiled and used almost three-quarter power to bounce over the drifts to the overhang.

I had an idea.

"If they come this way they're not going to have much luck."

He looked at me, and then at the darkness ahead. "Gotcha Jack. Figure tail will clear?"

I didn't know. "Better hop out and guide me in."

With Phillip waving me on I taxied the Twin Otter nose into the overhang slowly and nervously. The turbines thundered and shrilled against the rock so much I began to worry about the vibrations triggering a million ton landslide on top of my head. As soon as Phillip raised his hands I had the turbines spooling down and set about shutting down all systems. The silence after the chaotic roaring went as deep as the blackness of the rock.

"If they come this way," Phillip said when he opened his door again to pull out his parka, "they'll never know we were here."

"You're assuming the hut is livable."

"Think so. We should wipe out the tire tracks too."

"Yeah. let's do that now. Those guys could be here anytime. Probably won't see the plane right away but those tracks will really stand out."

A wooden bar held the hut door closed. When I lifted the bar out of its clamps, I found the door unlocked. Inside was an oil furnace and an empty fuel tank.

But there was a Quebec style heater in one corner. It was not much more than an old oil drum on its side with a door for loading in wood on one end and a stove pipe going through the roof from the other end.

"We'll have to drain some fuel from the Otter if we want to run the furnace." I said. "But it would probably be easier to use some of the wood lying around here and get the stove working instead."

"They must have put it together themselves to save fuel. There's sure enough wood lying around on the beach." Phillip kicked at the trash lying on the floor.

I could see a Time Magazine from November 1961 with some vaguely familiar world leader on the cover. A Field and Stream with a cover article titled, "Field Dressing Your Kill in Seven Minutes," and just the front cover left from the November 1961 National Geographic, "Italy Marks its 100th Year" and a painted map of Italy,.

Phillip said, "This place is a time capsule. There hasn't been anybody here for like fifty or sixty years or more."

There was also an empty Carnation Milk can, the paper wrinkled away from the tin by the damp, but still freshly colored. A half rolled gray wool sock lay under the stove. A twisted coil of barograph paper looped through all the grit and sand left behind when the men stationed here had tramped in and out on the last day. They hadn't bothered to leave things tidy and I couldn't see that they should have.

The mattresses were gone from the green painted metal beds. I had seen and slept on beds just like this in half a dozen barracks. I suppose soldiers worldwide are still sleeping on the same model, and will sleep on them still when we are sending peace keeping troops to the eastern deserts of Mars.

"Nice place huh?" I said as I kicked away at the rubbish.

Phillip flicked through the Time. "At least the windows are fine and we've got shelter."

"What about the smoke?" I wasn't going to start a fire if all it would do would be to send up a location beacon for Aeva.

"Let's get it going now and get it burning hot. That way what little smoke gets up the cliff will be so thin that no one will see it."

The gloom in the fiord turned to night with the disappearance of the sun behind the mountains and soon we had a home. The Quebec heater pumped out heat like a nuclear reactor as it chewed through the 80-year-old pine scraps we fed it. The almost freeze dried pine caught as though it had been soaked in gasoline. It burned so hot there was no smoke at all coming from the stovepipe.

As the ice melted in the hut the place took on the damp, musty smell of a summer cottage opened on the first warm Saturday of April after the winter shutdown.

We sat in the glow from the cracks around the stove's door. The barograph paper was tacked across the windows to trap the ancient magazines against the glass so no light could leak out into the night. In this black wilderness even a small flashlight would be seen for miles.

The wind had ended with sundown.

In the dark of the deep fiord, it now became very easy to start believing in the Inuit legends of the demons and foul monsters that live in the pack ice. They are said to lurk in the dark for people foolish enough to go out alone without the shaman's charms and amulets.

I could believe in the beast that heaves itself out of the ice-cracks behind you so you never see it. It will always be behind your back no matter how quickly you turn. It'll snatch you down into the black water the instant you let it jump.

"I figure that if they haven't found us by tomorrow night we'll have a chance of getting out to Iqaluit."

I nodded sleepily in the heat. The lack of sleep over the past few days, together with the beating my body had been taking from crashing aircraft, extreme levels of adrenalin, inadequate food, and screaming tension pressed down over my eyebrows. I sat on the floor with my back to the bed, bathed in the heat and the quiet. There wasn't a sound apart from the low crackle of the flames, my breathing, and the slight shuffle now and again of Phillip's feet.

The outside was as silent as though there was no outside, had never been and would never be. We were locked in our tiny universe of the hut and had no ken of any other.

Sleep crept through my head.

I roused myself just enough to yawn out the words. "I don't think they'll guess we're anywhere nearby. They must have assumed we got clean away. That means they'll be clearing off Jenness as fast as hell before we get the law down on them."

"Mmm maybe," Phillip said. "If the wind doesn't come back up and blow the engine covers off we might even survive a flyby."

Phillip was the one who had suggested using some of the twelve and fourteen foot long pine timbers from the whaling station to prop against the tail assembly of the Otter. We stretched the dark canvas covers over the horizontal stabilizer to break the outline of the plane and hide some of its white paint. We piled snow against the timbers in the hope that from a distance everything would look just like another pile of wreckage from the station, and nothing like the tail of a Twin Otter.

"If the engines start..." he yawned and I nodded again. There didn't seem to be any point to worrying about what a night and a day of cold-soak would do to the plane. Either the batteries had enough in them to spin up the turbines and ignite, or they didn't. There was nothing I could do about it. With the fuzzy thought of how I would go about trying to push start a Twin Otter drifting through my mind I fell into sleep.

ANOTHER DAWN DEPARTURE

*T*hey did start — eventually. It took some doing and in the end it became a race between building up shaft speed to ignition and the batteries running down into inert lead. The glue-like oil baths held back the shafts so the propellers at first only turned with a sickening slowness. I got number one going first and ran it up well for several minutes before switching to number two. It started almost easily with the full amperage from the hot engine.

I left them running and climbed down to help Phillip drag away the timbers from the tail. By the time we'd kicked the snow away and repacked the engine covers we dripped sweat, and I feared for hypothermia if we had to remain outside before we had dried off.

The heated cockpit felt like a warm bed.

We'd waited for the sun to pass well over the fiord so the shadows would hide the takeoff. All through the day we'd listened for the sound of engines and heard nothing but the cracking of the shore ice and the dancing of the snow crystals blown down the valley by the glacier wind.

"You ready?" I asked Phillip. He had finished reading me the checklist and was now trying the radios.

"Guess so. Any trouble with this one?"

He was not used to short field takeoffs. A Hercules doesn't operate out of thousand foot airstrips that are nothing more than roughly cleared rock. He was apprehensive.

"Hey guy, that Jenness takeoff was worse than this."

"But that happened so quickly I didn't have time to think about it. And it's just occurred to me that I haven't even checked to see whether your licence is good for this thing."

He laughed once then slapped the glare shield. "Let's go cowboy. Get us home."

"Right chief." I pushed on the power against brake and scanned the instruments quickly and rolled us on. I shouted above the thunder of the props. "I'm going to stay in this valley until we reach the glacier and stay low from there." A dangerous way to fly through unknown mountainous terrain yet safer than popping above the horizon to be seen twenty miles away.

The run was short and far smoother than the landing. The Otter leaped up into ground effect and clawed up in a shallow turn away from the cliff. Empty, and getting short of fuel, the Twin flew like a fighter.

The glacier came at us in a rush of white and glare when we climbed out of the fiord's shadow. Phillip tried the radios again and got nothing but a rush of static that varied in volume up and down through all bands and frequencies. I wasn't too worried about it. We were too far from anybody to reach with VHF and transmission is notoriously unreliable on the lower frequencies in that part of the world.

Phillip jotted numbers on the the map. "Iqaluit's about 95 miles that way." he gestured due west or he should have been gesturing west and meant it as west but the magnetic compass means nothing in those latitudes. The Otter was equipped with a sun compass, but still, I was more than a little concerned about navigation.

"Look Phillip. I've never eyeballed my way over this part of Baffin without navaids. We're miles away from what I'm used to."

"You telling me you're lost? We only just got going."

I shook my head. "Not lost yet. Not yet, but I will be pretty quick. The sun's no damned good the way it hangs around the horizon. Got no radio fix and the map is too general for what I need."

"What do you want to do?"

"Not what I want to do. It's the only way, otherwise we're going to be in a hell of a spot. No gas to keep running around looking for Iqaluit."

"You're not telling me you want to go back to Jenness?" His eyes widened with alarm.

"No, not that, but almost. I figure if I get the sun just ahead of the left wingtip we might be going southwest. Then if I'm right, we should pick up Frobisher Bay, and I can follow the coast to the town."

"If the light holds you mean. That's not the midnight sun. It's going to set pretty damn soon."

I'd started the turn to port. As the sun swept across the cockpit, the light reddened as we turned. It was like being bathed lightly in blood. A bloody halo wrapped Phillip's head.

I put the sun just ahead of the wingtip. The sun was already so low that it would disappear behind the higher hill tops. I kept the de Havilland as close to those hills as I dared. We were running a serious risk of clipping one, but I didn't want to be spotted by any radar equipped plane like that damned Hercules. The darkening red glow wrapped Phillip's head in a bloody halo.

"You watch for the water and I'll concentrate on the ground. If we don't pick it up in ten minutes I'll climb until we can see it."

The Twin flew on across the Beekman Peninsula and into the

Great Hall Peninsula with its maze of valleys and glacial deposits. A land of chaos, lost and alone.

I worried about the fuel. The tanks were low. I wondered whether there might be some still left in the drums behind us in the cabin. We hadn't checked them. I didn't know whether there was any fuel or how much there might be. Until I got over the bay I wasn't going to send Phillip back to start transferring anything that might be left. I needed his eyes.

The flying was hard in that flat red light.

Hills leapt out of the ground in front of me with no shadows to warn me. Valleys dropped away beneath us without warning and left nothing before us but the purple and black trail that led to night left by the setting sun. It could hide a mountain and the soonest I'd see it would be when the nose plowed into the granite. My back ached with the tension. I kept wiping my palms one at a time on my knees. The silence between us stretched with the minutes.

"We should have been there by now." I said. The sun kept disappearing behind hills and casting everything before us into nothing. "I'm going to climb before it's too late."

"Hold it!

There it is. You're too far south."

I couldn't see what he was looking at, so I turned 20 degrees.

"Ok. You're heading right at it. Coast is about a mile ahead. You made it Jack. You made it."

"Hang on friend. Made nothing yet. Can't even see the damned water and besides we still have to fly the coast to Iqaluit. Know how hard that's going to be at this altitude?"

Then it was under me. The waters of Frobisher Bay spread out under the wings. A cluster of house sized islands skittered past under the rush of the plane. I banked steeply to the west and let the plane creep closer to the shore so I had some depth perception.

Far ahead up the bay a snap of white shot out. I thought it was a star flicking through the cloud cover but two seconds later it flared again.

"Trouble Phillip."

I felt him turn to me in the darkness of the cockpit. The instrument lights were turned low. He was a black shape sitting with me in the cockpit. "Engines?"

"No. Nothing that simple. There's a plane ahead. Watch." The strobes flashed far ahead, sometimes dimly and other times brightly.

"Pretty far away Jack. Probably one of your colleagues."

I forgot the darkness and shook my head. He couldn't see that.

Phillip said, "That's more likely one of First Air's planes or maybe even the Montreal sched."

"No way." I said. "It's low down. And it's way too far east to be a sched. They come in direct from the south to the airport. I think it is the Hercules."

"What the hell are we going to do now?"

"Try the radio. Should be able to get the tower now we're over the water."

Five minutes went and all Phillip could get back from his calling was the repeated rushing of static.

"Jack I don't like this. There's nothing wrong with the radios. We're being jammed. Fuck they must be jamming the whole region. I think you're right. That's them up ahead, and they're pretty sure we're around."

"That thing's got search radar hasn't it?"

"Yeah. Whole set up they installed in back. They had to rig all sorts of antennas to make it work.

"Then we've got to get the hell off this water." I flicked the right wing down and shot toward the shore, dropping as I did. I wanted to lose the Otter in the ground clutter. If we stayed over the water, the radar would have a nice clean horizon to pick us off from.

"How are we going to get past them?"

"Get back there," I said gesturing to the cabin, "and transfer every drop of fuel that might be in those drums. I"m going to try sneaking in the back way."

"How are you going to do that man?"

"I'm heading back into the hills. If I'm right, I should pick up a series of long valleys that point right to Frobisher. If I can get into a nice wide one we can ride up it almost all the way to the airport."

"God I hope you're right. But for my sake will you be careful. I really don't want to get slammed into a hillside at my age."

"Fuel, boy. We need fuel."

I hunted through the dark, trying to pick out the ice covered lakes and the drifts on the hillsides until the land changed and the sweep of the rocks stretched to the northwest. I was in the valley system and below the horizon.

Phillip had done something to the fuel system. The needle on the main tank took a tiny jump, and then another, and in a few minutes I had enough fuel to keep us in the air for another hour and a half.

LOST

*I*t was a crazy landscape, all boulder, rock and gravel. Ice and lichen showed through the bared hilltops. In summer and hard sunlight, with grass and speckled wildflower colors, it's beautiful. At winter's worst, when the sun really doesn't want to be seen for very long over the mountains of Meta Incognita, the country holds beauty only for the Inuit and a very few southerners who have spent their adult lives learning a new sense of beauty.

This night the beauty was far away. The only light I now had was a glow of twilight through light clouds and a faint cast of moonlight. It all looked like midwinter to me, cruel, alien and savage. There was nothing for my eyes to lock onto and hold; no reference points to fix the Otter in space.

"What a fuck of a place to crash." Phillip said. "I hope you're right about this."

"Me too. You ever see anything so lonely?" It was a world of loneliness translated into a monochrome abstract.

"You want me to fly for a while?"

I thought about it. Phillip was a talented flyer and had more time than me on transports. He was also in a strange world. "No.

I'll keep her. I think I know this region. You watch the board. I don't want to take my eyes off these hills."

"Right. You fly and I'll keep the rubber bands wound up." The old joke that never dies.

At twenty or 100 or 500 feet the Otter roller coastered up the first valley and through the small hillocks of rock. I never quite knew how high I was from moment to moment. I couldn't keep to a constant altitude without reference points. The radio altimeter was useless this close to broken ground. Everything looked like it was right in front of me or a couple of miles away, at the same time.

It made me sweat trying to keep from slamming into the landscape. Every now and again as I realized that I really was a little too low I expected the gear to catch and rip us into a fire ball. The plane flew on in a series of wild climbs and dives as I tried to follow the contour. I was torn between trying to stay alive by keeping altitude and the fear of being spotted by the Hercules if I got too high. I flew down ravines and gullies in the flat darkness with no idea of where they were leading, or whether they had anywhere to go other than to the base of a hill I couldn't climb over.

Phillip stayed quiet for a long time.

"Everything OK?" I asked.

"Sure Jack. Fine."

"Tough as hell to see where we're going."

"Tell me about it. It's no fun sitting here not doing anything." The tone of his voice betrayed the tension.

"Pilots should never be passengers," I said. "Can't stand sitting in the back of an airliner while some clown I don't know is punching through overcast on a minimums landing."

"Me too. I always figure I can do a better and safer job of flying an Airbus than the guy up front and I've never even seen the inside of the cockpit of one."

I sympathized. Pilots make the worst of passengers. They all want control. I've seen the pilot types in the terminals. They're the ones who scout over the heads of the passengers boarding. They peer over the seat backs checking out the location of the emergency exits. They check the emergency cards in their seat backs while the non flyers pretend endless airline experience and ignore the whole thing. And pilots never have to be told to buckle the seat belt.

But it's on the takeoff roll that the pilot betrays himself.

Legs stretch slightly when the engines spool up and the fuselage bobs on the brakes. The right hand flexes half open and the left takes a cupping, sideways, almost benedictory shape. It's the shape of the control column. The legs are out to imaginary rudder pedals. The right hand is for the throttles.

They sit still as the jet runs down the runway then the left hand starts a gentle come hither flicker. The hand is feeling through the column for the rotation, trying to second guess the guy up front.

Rotation and lift. The passenger pilot eases back in the chair and waits to feel the wheels retracting, and waits again with a stiff lower abdomen for the flap retraction.

That one gets me every time. It damn well feels like a stall is coming. There's a quick mush forward and a slight sinking, which is really just a lowering of acceleration, and then the climb continues normally. But it's that tiny moment when the cerebellum is convinced a stall is coming that causes the trouble. Priority codes shunt through my spine shutting down the non essential body functions to route energy to the motor nerves. I can feel the muscle nerves firing up and the fibers tightening to just below threshold, a microsecond from instant movement. Then as the acceleration resumes the alarm system shuts down and my body relaxes.

Phillip spoke again. "You know, I never feel like this when I'm flying, no matter how nasty things are getting."

"I'm only glad it's me here and not you then I'd be really scared."

"No, I'm serious." he said, "I mean even when I'm in a turn on final, and it's a bit too tight -- the airspeed a bit too low. And you know that little shudder it gives, the pre-stall buffet? Even then it's okay. I just don't get tense or anything. You put me in the back seat of an airliner in turbulence though and I'm pissing sweat out of me."

I pulled the column back a bit and sailed over the top of a hill with a couple of feet to spare and sent the Otter sliding down into the next valley. "I think it's because when you're at the controls you have every bit of information you need when you need it." I said. "It is almost as if any potential problem is kind of telegraphed ahead of you. You know what's coming. In the back of those pop cans you're always reacting after something happens with no chance to anticipate."

"Yeah, a pop can. But what pop can is lined with stuff that'll burn like hell and poison you with the smoke? You know all I can think of at times when I'm getting bounced around in those pop cans of yours is jet fuel cooking the wreckage while I'm lying trapped in the seat and the aluminum starts to melt.

I tried to look at him and almost immediately lost ground contact and had to get us back into the valley groove. It's like taking your eyes off the expressway traffic for a second to look at the passenger and suddenly finding your car drifting across a lane. "Are you afraid of flying?"

He was silent for a bit. "I suppose in a way I am. I mean not when I'm flying of course, just when I don't know the guy up front. Yeah, I guess every time I get on an airliner I think about it crashing."

"Me too chum. Me too. How about now?"

"Oh shit yeah Jack. You're the worst of the bunch. If we weren't so low I'd parachute out of here."

We were both afraid because we knew how dangerous it was and both sure in each other because we trusted. Yet we had both spent a lot of time on the edges of flight envelopes, out beyond the lines where designers and manufacturers' compromises can add and compound to a terrible, what the investigators like to call, "departure from controlled flight." We feared because we knew what could go wrong down here just a few feet above sixteen thousand year old shattered remnants of glacier debris. We were in the near black of night with no navigation aid to point the direction.

Lost.

Phillip tried the radios again but once again there was nothing. "Might as well be flying this thing with your eyes shut Jack. Won't make any difference for all I can see."

I was worrying about the light too. A couple of times, only the faint gleam off a chunk of snow near a hill crest had alerted me to sudden death. The valleys were all right. There was generally a good bed of snow or ice on a lake left to reflect the little light we were getting. The hills though were bare as a result of the spring sun and the constant wind. They almost merged perfectly with the cloudy night. "I'm taking it up a bit."

"What about the Herc?" Phillip said.

"I don't really care anymore. We've got to get up before we lose it all." As I spoke, I pulled the nose up until gradually I once again had a stretched out horizon. A hundred feet off the valley bottoms felt like a thousand after the ride we'd been through. "Should be good here. Some of the hills go a bit higher, but I think we can see them better at this height and the tops might screw up their radar."

"Would be nice if it did. Frankly I don't care whether it gets us. I don't want to go back down into that." He jabbed his thumb down at the floor. Already we were feeling better with the increased height. My hands started to dry.

"You ever hear about the DC-3 that went down around here?" The shape of the land reminded me of the crash.

"Ran out of gas or something didn't he?" Phillip said and pointed out a hill dead ahead.

I sucked in my breath and banked left around it and straightened out. "Yeah. Strangest damned thing. Almost makes you believe there really is the ghost of a Dorset Culture shaman guarding this coast."

"How so?" I saw his face for the first time in a flare of moonlight through the clouds.

"This Dak see, is carrying a bunch of delegates back from some Inuit Tapirisat meeting in Pangnirtung. They're heading for Frobisher at something like 12 or 14 thousand over solid snow cloud. Imagine this. Over this kind of country, on top of snow and high level crud hiding the stars."

"About as black as you can get. Solid instruments all the way. So?"

"So this. Everybody in the back is asleep, pilot probably thinking of Frobisher approach and wondering what the ground conditions are like. Then one of the Pratts burps. Just a bump in the engine see."

"Guy's heart must have gone into his mouth. Can't stand that feeling myself when an engine goes silly for a split second. I think it'd be better to have the damn thing quit cold instead of making you suffer waiting for more trouble."

"Oh this guy didn't have long to wait I'll tell you," I continued, "Half a minute goes by and the engine sputters and stops. Before the bugger has a chance to do anything, away goes the other. So there he is. Twelve thousand feet up over country that hasn't been flat since the ice age, above a white-out, at night, and no damned fuel." It must have been a heart stopping feeling. The feeling that there was no way out of this one. That you were going to pile into the ground at the blunt end of several tons of metal and a dozen or so people in the back would soon be crumpled jelly against your spine.

"Son of a bitch earned his pay that night." Phillip said.

"You don't know it. The guy comes down into the crap with both props feathered, lowers the gear and sets up for approach speed and sets her down through the muck."

"Those poor passengers must have been having fits. The pilot would have had it bad enough, but those sons of bitchs in the back. Must have been about out of their minds. How'd he get it down?"

"Only God or that shaman ghost knows. Pilot still doesn't know what happened. He puts it down into the white-out, feels a ground flare and rounds out. You know where he ended up?" I didn't wait for an answer. "In the only son of a bitching valley anywhere around that could take the Dakota. He put it down hard in a valley only just long enough."

"Injuries?"

"Nope." I shook my head. "Not even a scratch. Plane lost its gear and bent the props, but everyone was okay. They got picked up the next day by the search.

Some guy bought the salvage and figured he was going to fly it out. Spent a lot of money too but once he got the fuselage jacked up and the gear straightened he discovered the back was broken. Pretty well stripped now I hear. They hauled the engines and instruments and radios back to Iqaluit by snowmobile. But you know the funny thing is that there just was nowhere else the plane could have been put down without a lot of dead."

"Ran out of gas eh. Pilot must have been cited in the report. Remember what they kept hitting us with in flight school."

I remembered. It is hard to forget after someone has drummed it into your head almost every day through flight training.

"Gentlemen. A pilot who runs out of fuel, for whatever reason, is guilty of a court-martial offense. There are no exceptions. It is always possible to avoid getting into a situation where you will run out of gas."

That made me think. "How are we doing for fuel?"

Phillip peered at the fuel gauges. I had the lighting turned to a minimum so I could have a better view of the ground. "About half an hour's worth I think. Fuel rate is way up though."

I nodded. That was to be expected running so close to the ground and constantly on the throttles and charging about the sky like a fighter. "Should be way more than enough."

"Should be if we get there."

I chuckled and my heart wasn't in the joke. If I didn't soon start to recognize something I was going to have to admit we were lost.

The control column was writhing and slipping in my hands like a live eel. The sweat was coming back. My eyes burned at the inner corners from too much concentrating on the way ahead and from not enough blinking to clear the debris from the eyeballs. I prayed that the rest of the plane was holding together better. If we lost a compressor blade at this height in my condition, I might not catch the yaw quickly enough to keep us off the ground.

"Is that it?" Phillip pointed slightly to the left. I peered into the black and blinked madly looking for what, I didn't know. Then I caught it. A sudden bloom of yellow and orange haloed a hillside perhaps a couple of miles off.

"Gotta be. Nothing else out here to make light."

"Could be a volcano." he said lightly. I was too tense and wanted to snap back at him to shut up while I worked.

"Not the airport beacon. I think we're on the money. It's gotta be the power plant."

"Where's the airport?"

"Other side of the town and we're not going anywhere near it." I had the Otter slowed right down now and the flaps partly out. We couldn't be heard a quarter mile away if there was any kind of wind scrubbing the snow.

"So where are we going Jack? Do I get to know or is this all your show."

"Sorry friend. This is getting a bit much for me." I felt his hand clap my right shoulder and somewhere along with the touch came some energy.

"You're all right Jack. You got us this far. The rest should be okay."

I clenched my teeth and straightened against the seat. "There's a lake they use for the town water supply. It's just this side of the power plant. It's plenty big enough and no one will know we're there until daylight."

"You sure it's big enough?"

"Of course I'm sure you asshole. You think I'd deliberately pick one too small?"

My outburst made him laugh and I realized he'd been prodding me into full alert.

"I'll give you flap when you need it. Just call."

I nodded and concentrated on the last hill before the lake. "This one's going to be a bit hairy. I want to come over that hill as low as possible and down the other side. It's the highest one anywhere around and I don't want them spotting us.

Hang on!" I shouted, and rolled up and to the left into the hillside, pulling back and back on the controls, staying off the throttles. The Twin seemed to almost sink upwards as it crawled slower and slower up the hill in a thirty degree climb. The speed sagged away. I felt my stomach tightening.

I saw Phillip's left arm out of the corner of my eye going up for the power levers. He was doing the obvious to stop the coming stall. "Stay off!"

His arm stopped halfway up and stayed there. His fingers were loose but within inches of the levers, ready to slap forward and save us from the rocks. He waited, which is something I wouldn't have done if I had been the one sitting in the right seat.

I knew that hill. I'd tramped the area half a dozen times looking for some Peregrines that were supposed to be nesting in a cliff face.

But in all those treks I never even saw a falcon let alone found the nest. Instead, I acquired just the knowledge I needed for this last flight and I prayed I remembered the shape of the hill well enough.

The props weren't biting well at all. The stall warning came on first with a tiny burble then a constant shriek. I ignored it, trusting instead to the denser air and a fudge factor. Still I could feel the buffet and there was no doubt I had her down to within half a knot of a clean breaking stall nose into the hill.

The buffet and bucking built. The crest of the hill crawled down the windshield to us as a black semicircle surrounded by the bright glow from the diesel generator discharges. It was too late to call for more flap. That would send us straight into a stall. Even if I had more speed, the pitchdown might have driven the gear into the hillside and we would have been pressed ground meat instantly. I hung on and prayed. Phillip's hand remained at the throttles.

All I could think of as my hands and feet worked on the controls was how unprotected the pilots of a Twin Otter are in a crash. There is nothing ahead of the instrument panel capable of stopping much of anything. The tiniest of compact cars stand up to highway speed crashes better than the average aircraft to slower impacts. If we went into the hill at 70 knots we'd be dismembered.

Then the hilltop was gone under the nose in a flash of windswept bare rocks. As the break started I pushed sharply forward on the column until it went to the stops. We charged over the crest and fell down the hillside. I felt the speed build and with it the bucking then the buffeting died away. Phillip dropped his arm and I exhaled. The Otter was not going to rip its belly out after all. Blood began running through my body again. I felt my leg muscles ease up.

I hunted for the lake and couldn't see it. It just was not there. We were coming down a three hundred foot high hill in a steep dive at what was supposed to be an ice covered lake and I couldn't see anything.

"What the hell..."

The base of the hill charged toward us as a black slash and above it was nothing. Not featureless, just nothing. I was staring at a gigantic blind spot, a huge hole in my vision, a hole without color or form. The dark gray splotch was the lake ice and I couldn't tell where it started or where it went. There were no shadows in the night and no horizon. My eyes had nothing to focus on and my mind had nothing in the cerebral cortex to interpret. I could have been a hundred feet from the lake or a hundred inches.

"Hit the lights! Hit the goddamn landing lights."

Phillip's hand flashed to the switches and the world turned to flaming white. The twin beams slashed at the lake and I could see. And in that instance of seeing I had to act faster than I had every acted in a plane.

We were about to smash through the ice into the lake.

I pulled that control column back so hard and so quickly it's a wonder nothing broke. "Kill the engines. Quickly."

His hand was still at the quadrant; it hadn't moved. I yelled again. His hand slammed the throttles back as he yanked off the power.

The Otter shock stalled.

de Havilland would have had my head for treating their beautifully designed plane so badly, but I would have gladly given them my head myself in deep thanks for them building a plane strong enough to take the treatment.

If anybody had been around to watch they would have seen a twin engined high wing bush plane scream over the top of the hill, so close to the rocks that the wheels would have looked like they were rolling on the ground. Then they would have seen the Otter shoot straight down in a wild charge to the ice, two sudden beams of actinic light, a snap pitch of the nose upwards, and then the wings would have disappeared in a dense fog of condensation as the airflow separated from the airfoils.

I heard the master switch as Phillip killed all the power to reduce the risk of fire in the crash and we hit the ice with just the slightest nose up attitude.

The wheel assemblies sheared away with a tremendous crash. The plane plowed ahead, propped up by the nose gear which hadn't ripped entirely loose so the fuselage continued nose high through the crash. A violent death tremor hammered under my feet as the nose gear cut through the snowpack and sent it smashing at the belly. Chunks of fractured ice and bits of main gear thundered through the aft section. The wing struts pulled loose with a terrible scream.

We stopped with one last neck snapping jerk. Silence and blackness, the first edges of cold seeping in through the shattered hull.

"What's the takeoff going to be like?"

I stared at Phillip then started to laugh a bit too hard and loud.

He waited until I finished and added, "You are getting very experienced at crashing Twin Otters. Should look really good on your resume."

I laughed again, but without the shrillness this time and groped with a shaking hand in the map pocket for cigarettes, but there weren't any. "I'm not going to pretend I planned it this way. I had something a little more gentle in mind. Couldn't see the ice."

"I don't know how you did see it. I never did."

We sat for a few moments in silence until the cold made me move. "We've got to get away from here. I don't think we made enough noise to matter, but we're going to get pretty cold soon unless we move it."

"Yeah let's get out of here. I have this uncontainable urge to have a leak."

THE POWER STATION

*I*t looked like a seaplane.

The plane sat as though floating on an ocean swell. The fuselage sat on the crest of a snow dome a hundred feet long. The landing gear was gone, ripped off in the landing and buried in the snow.

"Somebody should write a letter to de Havilland about this."

"Not me," I said. "They'd probably hire hit men to make sure I never talked about what I did to one of their beauties. If de Havilland was still in business that is."

"Do you know where we are?" He shrugged into his parka, flipped up the hood, and gazed at the light glow.

"Yes. It's a bit of a walk to the plant. There's always someone there so we can get a ride down the hill to the town."

I set off through the thrown up debris of snow blocks and ice from our landing and made it to the hardpan. It squeaked even at this time of year. It made me think that spring wasn't so close after all. The daily melt should have been pouring enough moisture into the snowlayers to loosen them up. Instead, they squeaked with dryness.

Low cloud scuttered by. The wind started to rise. I thought I'd been lucky there had been no wind for the landing. This wind was getting stronger very quickly. It soon had the loose snow shooting along the hardpan and we walked through a foot deep cloud of flying snow.

"Weather's breaking to the west." Phillip said, trudging beside me through the drifts.

"Uh huh, always does. From the west, I mean. Wind is getting a hell of a lot stronger. We could be in for a storm."

"Much further?"

"Round this headland and about three hundred yards I guess."

"Hope so. I can't take this cold as well as you."

"Comes from where you were born Phillip, comes from there."

"Bullshit."

"It's always windy here. Windiest spot in the Arctic you know." And the way it was picking up there was little doubt. The crystals bit into my cheeks.

"You putting me on Jack?" His words were thin in the night.

"Nope, truth for sure. Wind's almost constant here. It funnels through the Nettling Lake chain and then down the bay. They were going to fix Iqaluit up with a windmill power system, but it didn't work out."We trudged and squeaked fifty paces before he spoke. "You going to tell me why anybody would want to stick up windmills here. It's not exactly Holland."

"No idiot. Those super sophisticated things, all bent metal and stuff like some graduate abstract architect's thesis. The thing was supposed to produce power in anything over twelve miles an hour or something but the bearings kept burning out. The way the wind is around here it would have been going almost all of the time."

"Be going like hell tonight." He was bent to the left to hide his face from the wind and all I could see of him was a parka back and hood. I felt my breath being sucked out as the air rushed past me from behind.

"Makes more sense than using petroleum," I shouted and it sounded louder than I had intended in a sudden lull. "The place is heated from oil and the power comes from oil fired generators and the bloody oil comes from Venezuela by way of Montreal. You know how much fucking oil there is in the north right now they could use?"

"I sure hope we can get that bunch of crazies rounded up before they catch up with us," Phillip said.

I didn't say anything. Horst and crowd would be pulling out all the stops to get at us. That plane in the bay had to be them and that meant the hunt was still in full cry. I worried about what we might find in Iqaluit. But right then, I felt more concerned about staying alive after surviving two crashes and the wildest flight of my career, than about that crowd of killers.

The snow crystals weren't drifting into piles anymore, they were flying straight out along the lake. Runnels of snow swept across our boots and ran to the rock shore. I pulled the corner of my hood closer to my face and let the wolverine fur cover my eyes. The headland came closer in a fog of hazy white gray. The glow from the plant stacks was gone, wiped out by the snow and the deeper darkness that came with the snowclouds. I stepped up the pace and passed Phillip.

"Jack, it's starting to snow." His black face disappeared against the rocks.

"Whiteout coming. Better get moving before we get caught." The thought of getting trapped so far from shelter in a whiteout and wandering around the lake aimlessly until we dropped from exposure scared me. I shambled into a toe trot, the best that can be done in winter wear over a frozen lake. The wind shifted again and blew directly from our right. The shore was on our left. I edged closer to it. By following the rocks I knew we would eventually reach the power plant. It sat at the head of the lake where it narrowed and ran into a stream leading down to the bay. If I lost sight of the shore, we'd be lost. But I couldn't get right on the shore because of the heavy drifting and ice hillocks.

"It's getting colder too," he said.

I pulled my leather mitts over my gloves and made sure the forearm gauntlets were pulled well over the cuffs. The boots were keeping our feet warm and the exertion of the trot was helping too but nothing other than hard woven nylon windpants would keep our legs warm. The wind sliced through the denim into my thighs and turned them numb.

"Give me your hand," I shouted at the fading bulk behind me, "Don't let go. We'll try to get closer to the shore. Keep the wind to your side."

We staggered through the newly formed drifts and the pace dropped to a heavy footed slog. I heard him gasping in the wind. The cold burned my throat. I couldn't seem to get enough air. It stung as I sucked it in through my mouth. It was impossible to breath through my nose.

Conditions were getting worse by the minute. Visibility dropped to just feet. At times, the shore disappeared in a swirl of snow and when that happened we were left in a featureless bowl of dirty gray. The storm was building. We fought through the drifts.

"Jack!

Listen!"

I stopped. Above the wind there was a sound, a sound that fell and disappeared and rose again and rose higher.

Engines. Turboprops.

The sound built and came clear. A heavy engine transport was flying somewhere close and low. The engines strained against the wind, extended landing gear, and flap.

"Some poor bastards earning their pay tonight," he said.

"Bastards is right. That's gotta be the Hercules."

"Well, I don't envy them trying a landing in this shit."

He was right. These weren't anywhere near adequate conditions to put down a Hercules. Iqaluit has a bomber length runway and an instrument landing system, but they don't help much when the runway lights are hidden by an Arctic winter storm. The pilots would be fighting a plane that was getting bounced around in a full storm and praying they could pick up the lights. I supposed Horst was flying, and wished her to hell.

Our slogging march went on for what seemed like hours yet it couldn't have been more than forty minutes. Then out of the blackish gray before me something swelled into shape so quickly that I walked into it and bumped my head against it; the power station.

It took many frustrating and cold minutes to creep along the panel steel wall, over oil barrels and wrecked snowmobiles, bits of power generating equipment, scraps of cargo pallets and debris, before we found the door. I only found it because of a single light glowing faintly above it. The tiny bulb in its wire cage hardly had the strength to cast a yellow light more than a few feet out into the storm. At first it was just a fuzzy bloom of light in the black.

It was enough to guide us to safety and warmth.

The shift boss gave us muddy instant coffee and powdered milk to lighten it while we tried to soak heat from the steam radiators in his office.

He was dark from tan picked up in a recent Caribbean vacation. He'd be working as much overtime as he could get to recoup what he'd blown out during his break from the ice, wind, and isolation of the Eastern Arctic

"Pilot aren't you?" he said as he handed me the plastic foam cup. It was marked by the teeth and fingernails of who knew how many other coffee drinkers. The inside had turned a dull beige from the coffee.

"Yeah. How'd you know?"

"Seen you around a few times in the Legion. George Frank."

We shook hands. "Jack Standish. This is Phillip Tonguay."

Frank seemed to shy a bit from contact with Phillip's skin. Phillip noticed and didn't react.

"We had to put our Otter down on your lake because of the storm. Couldn't get into the airport." I was too tired and cold to get into the real story. That could wait for the RCMP. Phillip huddled over his coffee to draw the steam into his open mouth.

I took a tentative sip of the phoney coffee. "Look. Could I borrow a phone?"

Frank waved at his desk. It was a catch-all desk, a steel and Formica surface for piling paper and storing tools on. I could see that not much paperwork ever got down on time in the power plant. A summer windjacket was buried in a crumpled Montreal Gazette and weighed down by an empty Ballantines bottle and a discarded oil burner. The coffee jar and one of its ancestors stuck up through the shuffled pile of paper, clothing and bits and pieces as though forming a central point for the cluttered composition. The phone had a clear space all to itself on the front corner showing that it was in constant use. A Penthouse Magazine lay at a steep angle between the phone and the mess as if to act as a dam. I wondered what the contents of the drawers were like.

He shook his head as he pulled a package of Gauloise from his hip pocket, my least favorite cigarette. "The storm must have knocked out the lines. Went dead about quarter of an hour ago. You can't goes anywheres anyhow."

I took the cigarette although I just didn't feel like it at all. Smoking was getting to be a pointless drudge.

The bolted steel panels of the roof vibrated and banged in the wind. The noise almost overcoming the throb of the diesel generators deeper inside the plant.

Phillip stretched his legs in the office armchair he'd dragged to the radiator. "Well I for one don't care. I'm too tired to give a damn." He arched his back so his long body was suspended on his heels on the floor and his shoulders on the seat back. He splayed his fingers wide as his back arched, tensing every muscle and tightening every tendon. He filled the room like some great black butterfly spreading wing.

George Frank stared with an expression of slight distaste for a moment before turning to me. "There's no way down in this stuff. You'll have to wait until it clears and then you'll have to wait until the road is cleared

I knew what he was talking about. Whiteouts can last a full day and more. I'd sat through one in Resolute that had kept me and three mechanics trapped for a day and a half with nothing to eat but rations from the survival kit in a Dakota. We were unable to cross the hundred yards separating us from the Transient Downtown. The worst part of it had been the lack of anything to read except outdated NOTAMS. They warned of things I didn't need to know about. Just dozens of pages of Notices to Airmen about things like new power lines, changes in radio frequencies, migratory bird routes and endlessly on into deepest trivia.

Conversations between the four of us had been exhausted with the last of the dirty jokes and the realization that not one of us had any interest in any of the others.

"You wouldn't have a couple of beds would you?" I asked wistfully.

"No. There are some foam slabs. Might be a little dirty. I use them when I go out Caribou hunting."

"I don't care. I think I could sleep on the floor." I doubted he ever got near a Caribou and the trips out were a chance to lead the good old boy life with fellow drunks away from the families.

Phillip spread his foam slab out on the floor, filling the space. That left me the desk top. I drew a breath and swept up the litter in large armloads and dumped everything in the desk kneehole. Frank left us alone promising to wake us if the phones started to work.

I settled my body deeper into the foam mattress by letting my back muscles loosen. The wolverine trim around the hood of my parka tickled my nose as I tried to adjust the heavy coat to cover me as a blanket.

Phillip said, "You'd think that with all the storms this place gets they'd make sure the wind couldn't blow down the telephone lines. I mean this place must get bigger storms than this."

I thought of the Hercules making its approach through the storm, of Horst, and of those racks of electronic equipment in the cargo bay and of sophisticated jamming equipment. I thought about it for a bit and was still running things through my mind when I fell asleep.

The first full five hour sleep since it all started left me brighter and more alert than I had been for a very long time. I had awoken to the noise of Frank fumbling through the junk pile under the desk for the coffee jar.

"Phones going yet?" I could see perhaps a hundred feet out through the window over the stacks of empty oil drums before the snow cut off the world. The light was bright and that meant the cloud cover was thinning. If the road down the three hundred foot hill to the village was not too badly drifted we'd be able to walk into Iqaluit and find the RCMP depot.

"No, and the radio isn't working either. Lots of static so it's probably the storm. No loss I guess. Just willy wobbling anyway."

It took me a second to realize he was not talking about a communications radio but was commenting on the local radio station. There's only one radio station in most Arctic communities and that's run by the Canadian Broadcasting Corporation. Since the majority of the people in the Eastern Arctic are Inuit, the bulk of the programming is in Inuktitut. Frank obviously had little sympathy or liking for Inuit or he wouldn't be calling their language willy wobbling.

He poured boiling water into the same cups and dropped the powdered milk in too quickly and it floated in a congealed ball on top instead of dissolving. I tried to pick out the same cup I had used during the night. I had a vague hope that the bacteria I had left on it might have cultured and grown over that left by former drinkers. At least I was immune to my own germs. It probably does not work any better than wiping the neck of a bottle passed around yet it did at least have the psychological benefit of making the coffee more palatable.

I scrounged another Gauloise and listened to Frank prattling on about the overtime he was piling up because the storm had stopped the day shift from coming on duty.

"None of them made it in so that makes two full shifts plus fifteen percent and now double time, meal displacements and pretty soon penalty payments." I doubted the Power Commission was getting its full day's work from him even at the vastly increased rates.

"How many men keep this place going?"

"Well, there's only three of us now. Supposed to have more but turnover is pretty high and we run the night shift pretty light on crew. Just keeping the generators going. Don't bother with the maintenance schedule at night."

I wondered whether the day shift was more efficient under a different shift boss.

It was past noon when a truck-mounted snowblower followed by a grader showed up and the shift arrived. Frank ran us down to the RCMP in his Suburban. I told him we had to report the forced landing on the lake. He was off to the Legion and his overdue beer ration before we had reached the front door of the depot.

"There's no one here," Phillip said it quietly as if afraid to show disrespect. Churches and police stations have that effect on people. We stamped the snow from our boots and brushed it from our parkas before it could melt and dampen the down. We stood still and listened hard for any sound to come through the partition wall behind the counter. Finally, Phillip saw a bell push and soon I heard a door slam somewhere in the back and then the sound of rubber soled boots coming along a hallway.

"I guess I'll start at the beginning and you fill in things," I said to Phillip in a whisper, "We'll probably have a hell of a time convincing them we're serious. These guys are going to take some talking to."

The inner door opened as I was talking.

"No captain. You will not have any trouble at all convincing me. None at all."

Two of her men jumped through the door and levelled their AK-47s at us. We stared at Horst.

She laughed.

VIDEO SELFIE

*T*eller held an automatic pistol on us from the front seat of the GMC Wagon. The driver was one of the men I had flown down from Resolute. Another, who I had not seen before sat crunched into the back right corner of the truck with her rifle pointing at the back of our heads. I sat behind the driver. Phillip, also with a bench seat to himself, sat behind me on the left. Teller had his back to the passenger door. We were both in a crossfire zone.

The ring road circles across the landside of Iqaluit then sweeps down through the town to divide the high-rise complex of apartments and government offices from the Inuit community and the airport. The graders had the snowpack down almost to the blacktop. It's the only paved road for a thousand miles in any direction, the legacy of a government contract for the resurfacing of the runway. The road was smooth, there were no bumps or potholes, so no chance to grab at the driver and hold him as hostage. Besides, I thought, Teller would probably shoot me regardless of what happened to his man.

"How did you people get here so quickly," Phillip knew the

answer already. He was only talking for the sake of saying something.

"We're not stupid." Teller hoarsely and painfully pronounced the words. English was still new enough to him that he was translating as he went from his native language. "The commander said you would come here so we came here too."

"Aren't you worried that someone is going to find out you've taken the mounties hostage?"

He didn't answer me. I hoped that meant they were worried about it, which might also mean someone could rescue us before Horst had us shot. My fear that we would be shot was growing. We had screwed up her plans and she did not look like someone who could forgive that.

It seemed ridiculous to me to be driven through the village in an RCMP truck. About a dozen eight or ten year old kids kicked a soccer ball in the Nakasuk school-yard. Snowmobiles and trucks passed us in both directions. Mothers towed their children on wooden sleds. Snow crews cleared the side roads. Ordinary life was just feet away from me and all the more frustrating for that. I thought wildly of some way I could draw the attention of someone, anyone, and let them know something was wrong but there didn't seem any way. No one in the truck wore a uniform and yet that would not raise attention because the Mounties often dressed like civilians when moving their vehicles around off duty.

I thought about popping the door open and jumping. I gave that idea up because the truck was rolling through town at better than fifty miles an hour, past kids, dogs, snowmobiles and pedestrians.

The door was on the other side of the truck from me. That meant Teller would have to take his eyes off me long enough so I could lunge across the seat, figure out how the latch worked, then hurl myself at the road side. Apart from the good chance of smashing into the ice chunks along the roadside and splitting my head open, or picking the exact moment to launch myself head-first into a power pole, I'd still be leaving Phillip behind.

I did not want to do that.

My other thought was that even if we were both able to get out at the same time there was nowhere to run to.

In a place where the houses were fifty feet apart to guard against spreading house fires there's not enough cover to disappear into before being spotted.

"We're going to the airport." Phillip said.

The driver turned left at the old FARA Club corner ruining a theory I had been developing that Horst would have made the abandoned DEW Line station on the hill west of the village her new temporary headquarters. There was no basis for the theory other than it seemed the sort of place that Horst would use to get rid of us.

We came to the gas station.

Five snowmobiles parked nose on to the pumps like cattle at a trough. Their komatiks spread about the yard at the end of thirty-foot rope hitches. Wooden boxes three-foot square and covered in blue plastic tarp were lashed at the ends of the sleds.

The Inuit hunters were filling ten-gallon drums with gasoline, preparing for a seal hunt now that the weather was clearing.

As we bounced past them, I was overcome with a sharp longing. I wanted to be with them to sit at the floe edge in the bright and warm spring sun. I wanted to hear just the sound of my own breathing, the creak of the sea ice as the tide shifted it, and the far off swooshing sound of wind going past a raven's wings. The only thought that I wanted to have bother me was whether I would get a shot at a seal.

It seemed the most important thing in life at that moment to do nothing but the simplest of tasks and forget the horror of what we faced. The hunters going about their preparations made me think of those familiar warm things we take so much for granted that they became the markers of a boring and safe existence. Those trips on a Saturday afternoon in the car to do the weekly supermarket shopping. Cutting grass on an oppressively humid July night, wishing for a beer.

I longed for the chatter of people so consumed with the tiny details of life and holding them so seriously that they became the most important parts of their lives. I wanted a life without someone chasing after me with a gun, for a reason I had no knowing of.

Then we were past and there was nothing ahead but the gaudy orange mess of a plastic building that the government had built as a poor excuse of an airport terminal.

The truck ran around the back of the terminal. "It's your Hercules Phillip." I was stating the obvious. "Who flew it Teller? Was it your boss?"

He didn't understand so I repeated the question slower.

"That is not for you. The commander tells you what to do."

Both Twin Otters used by First Air were gone. I wondered whether they were on the search for mine, the first one that I had crashed, near Iron Island. I tried to see down the taxiway to the DND hangar, but the line of truck mounted snowblowers was in the way.

The Hercules was being refuelled. Horst leaned against the lowered rear ramp watching the 18 year old Inuk at the controls of the pumper.

"Mister Standish. You once again have caused me a great deal of trouble. If I had not found you, my assignment would have been completely disrupted. You are lucky to still be alive. Do you understand me?"

I stood still and erect before her. Her rage didn't show in her face or her voice yet it lapped out from her in rolling waves on some other level. I felt hate, and near death.

"You!" she pointed at Phillip, "Get up front and prepare to fly us back to the island." Phillip jumped onto the ramp and I started to follow but Horst stopped me.

"Your task, Standish, remains the same. You are to fly that interceptor. If you attempt any more escapes, or in any way obstruct my plan — I will shoot your friend."

"You know Horst, or whatever your real name is. You must be right out of your fucking mind." It was my turn to let the rage wash out. I no longer cared if she shot me. It was now obvious that we were going to die.

One way or another we would die. "You won't last a day. Those Mounted Police officers you have tied up in the depot are going to get loose or someone is going to find them. They're probably on the way here already. There's a DND base here too and they can have aircraft up from the south in three hours. In fact, they've probably got enough stuff here now searching for me that they can have you shut down for good before the day's over."

She smiled. "No that is not true."

We climbed the ramp and walked a few paces into the empty cargo hold. She was silent for a moment as she bent and looked through the porthole to see why the sound of fuel pumping had ended. One of the men was signing the fuel slip. I doubted the bill would get paid.

"No one here can phone or get a radio message out. The Mounties are heavily drugged and even if they are found they cannot possibly tell what happened to them for at least another twenty-four hours. Who would suspect just another cargo plane refuelling?"

"What do you mean no one can get a message out? This place is on satellite phone service you know. Anybody can direct dial from here to the rest of the world."

"They cannot without a satellite dish. The storm allowed some of my technicians to wreck some of its vitals last night. As for the radio. Well, we have installed one of our little jamming devices in the town. Nothing, but nothing, that uses radio frequencies can send or receive. Now, as for your Air Force, such as it is, the Aurora is looking for you between Pond Inlet and Clyde River. That too is thanks to one of our little devices. It imitates a very weak and irregularly operating emergency locator beacon. Just enough to keep them searching in the area, but not enough to let them lock-on to the right spot."

"There's going to be a First Air flight in here in about an hour and that will fly out a message." The whine of the auxiliary power unit began to grow. Phillip was powering up. The noise of the APU made Horst raise her voice.

"Possibly it could, if anyone here realized there is anything amiss. As far as they are concerned the phones are not working because of the storm. That I will admit was a fortuitous event. Similarly, the lack of radio service will be put down to atmospheric conditions, at least for enough time to allow me to get on with my job."

"And just what is your job? You cannot be serious about shooting down your own president's plane?"

Or could she? A thought struck me.

Teller and the other six came through the side door. Horst nodded at me and turned away to the crew telephone on the front bulkhead. As she talked to Phillip the number one prop started to turn. The low whine of the compressor spinning up rose in pitch. The rear ramp gave a jerk then slowly lifted from the ground. I sat in the last sling seat and watched the snow-blowers creeping along the taxiway casting solid streams of snow far into the air. The ramp rose past the horizontal until all I could see was the road leading across the threshold of the runway, the road that runs on the top of what the United States Air Force had built as a second runway. They had never used it because the wind was never in that direction.

The road leads to the ground satellite receiving station. The white disk was horizontal to the ground and pointed toward the northern stars.

It took me a few seconds, then it came to me what they had

done. The disk should have been almost vertical and aimed at the southern horizon to catch the Anik stationed over the equator. They had wrecked the dish mount. Until it was realigned, the disk would be sending messages to the nearest stars.

The ramp went to 15 degrees as I stared out, the snowblowers and the road were now cut off. I thought about the hunters I'd seen going to the floe edge and what Horst had in store for us.

A bullet in the brain was guaranteed.

There wouldn't be any simple life on the floe-edge for me. I started to see that more and more clearly.

I waited until the ramp was almost too high, but not quite. There was just enough gap for me to roll through after sprinting up the inside slope.

I fell far and hit the taxiway hard.

It hurt badly but the adrenalin kicked in and I moved fast.

I ran like hell under the left wing and almost into the howling blades of number one before I remembered and ducked.

It was fifty yards to the terminal, which is about a four-second run for a track sprinter with shoes weighing ounces. I carried twenty pounds of boot rubber and full winter clothing across the ice patches at a pace not much slower than an Olympic trainee.

I got to the glass entrance door and pulled it open as the first shot smashed into the bottom door hinge. It sent a stinging vibration through the aluminum frame into my left hand on the handle. I dived in full length to land on the green carpeting.

The people waiting for their flight froze as I slid in and rolled away from the windows. They hadn't heard the shot. They froze and watched me scuttle along the long wall to the back door trying to stay away from the windows.

No more shots. I leaped over baggage and around a couple of three-year old toddlers and petrified knots of families. I risked a glance to look behind. None of Horst's team followed.

The C-130 moved slowly in a tight circle, all engines going, then shot off under full power down the taxiway. Phillip had bought me time.

A purple Arctic Cat Panther, years out of date, sat in front of the door. It started instantly and I had the track spinning before the recoil spring wound up the cord. I shot down to the road then lost time making the sharp right turn from the terminal to the gas station. The front skis lost their bite on the hardpack and until I felt the track braking I thought I was going to plunge into the ravine at killing speed.

Five weaving snowmobiles and straggling komatiks covered the road. It was too late to stop. I went sliding sideways into one sled, bounced off it into a snowmobile, sending the driver onto the road, and causing the driver next to him to swerve violently into the snowbank and overturn. There was a sharp shock as my machine snagged a towline, then it broke loose and the road was clear. I sped through and gave a sled dog a close brush with death by riding out of the road and cutting across the front yard of the corner house where it was tied up.

The track banged furiously from the rough handling. I kept the throttle lever right down and concentrated on staying with the machine. The suspension bottomed out hard, banging continuously. I was making a habit, it seemed, of busting up planes and snowmobiles.

The building I was after sits at the intersection of the paved ring road and the side road I was on. I'd noticed the changes to the building when we drove past in the truck and paid little notice. Now it was going to be my way out, I hoped.

I guessed it would be a full ten minutes before Horst could overpower Phillip and get the plane back to the truck and start the search for me. I thought it might be enough time to run to cover. Of course, it wasn't going to be hard for him to track me. Half the village would be able to point out the route of the crazy snowmobile driver who seemed bent on killing himself and anyone in his way. They'd be only too willing to help the men in the RCMP truck.

I almost piled the snowmobile into the side of the Taqravut building by leaving the brake to the last instant.

I was inside and using up second after second of that precious ten minutes trying to convince John that I was serious and he'd better act. John Nesbitt worked for the local office of the broadcasting society. He'd started out teaching people how to make videos of their own Inuit lives and concerns. Then he stopped leading them and instead worked for the Inuit as an adviser, paper handler, and electronics troubleshooter while they ran their own television transmission service.

"Look Standish, this is all too wild. I can't believe you." I had him backed into a corner of the office and combined studio; a time base corrector unit on one side of him and a lighting rack on the other. All through my wild garbled story he'd been backing away until he was trapped.

"John I don't have any time before they get me. Listen please and help."

His eyes stared and his nostrils flared. He was trying to act calmly in the face of a man who he thought had gone nuts. I would have felt the same.

"All right John. Listen. I've told you about the phones and the cops and the satellite dish, and about everything else. I've got to get out of here before they get me and I've got to get word out. How about this? Set up a recorder and I'll have my say on video. You hang onto it and after I've gone you check out my story. Go up to the cop station and have a look for yourself. That should convince you and then you can do it. Okay?"

He had no choice. It was either stay in the corner, helpless before a madman, or humor him and let him clear out. He made up his mind in a couple of seconds, a couple of seconds that went by like long minutes to my speeded up metabolism. "Okay Jack. I'll do it that way."

The telling to Nesbitt had helped clarify events in my mind and I was able to pack a considerable amount of detail into my account on video without scrambling it out of sequence. I must have looked like hell on that recording, a half bearded and black-eyed wildman wearing a parka, crouched behind a desk and front lit with one light dead on. I talked for seven or eight minutes without pause before I had it all out.

"John that's it. I can't stay here any longer. I've got to find somewhere to hide and I don't want them catching me here with that video file around. Hang on to it. Will you check it out?"

He switched out the light and snapped open the video recorder to remove the memory card. He had an urgent look about him. "Don't worry about things here Jack. Watching you do this convinced me. I'll get it out."

I opened the door, had a quick look around, and ran around the back of the building without another look at him. The town seemed quiet. There was no unusual activity, no sound of vehicles coming or snowmobiles searching for me. I ran through the houses to dodge the main road and made for the hill to the complex. I had one long stretch of open ground through the Nakasuk school-yard before the hill. It was here I expected the trouble because I'd be in the open for two hundred yards then at least another hundred yards in full view of the town as I made my way up the hillside. I hoped I would look like anyone else at a distance as I went.

I was wrong.

The four-wheel drive truck plowed through the snowbank along the road beside the schoolyard and charged for me. I was far too far away from cover. Teller drove. There were two men with him. I didn't see any guns. They'd be kept out of sight.

I ran anyway. Desperately and blindly for the steep path up the hill. The truck got to within three feet of me and I thought Teller was going to run me down, and perhaps he would have except he had to swerve out of the way of a boulder.

The long steep slope of the path was slick from the sliding of the children. I'd have to try scrambling up through the scree formed by the dynamiting of the hill top to form the foundation of the complex to gain any lead on Teller and his men. I was losing heart. There was no way, I knew, that I could make it through the chaotic tumble of rock and concrete waste. The snow would be packed into crevices like mortar in some places so I'd have no purchase for my feet. Other gaps in the rocks would be covered by a light and soft dusting of snow and I would never realize that until my leg plunged through and broke. I charged on regardless.

I pushed through a fresh drift that hadn't been packed by the wind, just twenty feet from the base of the path. I felt my right boot catch under a loop of wire, another DEW line relic, part of the thousands of feet of heavy electrical conduit and cable strewn about the base of the hill. The stuff had lain there for years because no one bothered with the immense work of clearing it away and now it had me.

I smashed forward onto my face so quickly that I hadn't been able to get my hands up fast enough to protect myself. A lichen softened pillow of rock caught my forehead. An instant of flashing yellow fire then a soft fall toward dark and warmth.

ICE BADGERS

*J*enness was the same, the same upthrust hump of a sea mountain ringed by bands and slashes of white, blue, gray and black ice. The air was free of ice fog. The scene had that acid-etched clarity so characteristic of the Arctic. Colors vibrated with intensity. It's a clarity and sharpness that a camera can never duplicate because the photographic process cannot reproduce the resolution available to the human eye.

Phillip let the Hercules down slowly through the approach. The island sat nicely framed in the cockpit windows, drifting and bobbing slightly as the plane settled through the light wind. My forehead felt squeezed. A nasty swelling feeling of pain arced from the midpoint of my eyebrows to the downtown of my brow.

The pain had been worse when I had come to on my back in the cargo bay with my fingers going numb in the cold. Somewhere in my wild attempt to flee I had lost my gloves. A metal track channel used for sliding pallets into the cargo bay cut under my right shoulder and the first thing I did, before even figuring out where I was, was to roll over away from the agony. The vibration and noise told me first where I was and that allowed the brain to interpret what the eyes were picking up.

The jumble of shapes and light snapped into clarity. I recognized the curve of the hull, the rise of the stringers intersecting the frames as they made their way from the tail to the nose. A round glare of light turned blue as my irises narrowed; a porthole. A line of tangled green bouncing became the canvas sling seats. I sat up and breathed on my fingers in an attempt to put some heat into them. I saw Horst. Her head was lowered to her chest as if she was sleeping. Then her eyes opened.

"I promised you that you and your friend," she nodded in the direction of the cockpit, "would live once you had carried out my orders. Your actions and those of your black colleague tempt me to renege on that promise."

I tried to say something and found my mouth dry and my tongue heavy. I wanted to lash out at her and call her liar. I was relieved to find that Phillip was still alive. I'd feared that my escape, and his efforts to taxi the plane away from the terminal, had resulted in a bullet in the head.

She continued. "I have gone to immense trouble and some danger to the operation to regain you. Time is leaving us behind. But I will make another promise.

If you jeopardize this mission once again I will torture Mr. Tonguay and you will watch.

I will not kill him, but he will wish I had.

If you cause this mission to fail then I will have Teller kill you in the slowest most painful way he can devise."

I was unable to think. I seemed to soak up everything around me as I waited for my senses to collect again. The violence of the woman was something that could be felt and strangely my body heated up as the words chilled my spirit. I nodded.

"Get up to the cockpit." Her head lifted as she said it and she drew a deep breath. A slight tremble in her left arm made me think that she was under extreme stress and things were not going as planned.

Phillip was alone on the flight deck. He turned to me as I eased into the right seat. "Did you get a chance to tell anyone?"

I searched for the shoulder straps. I didn't speak until I was buckled in and the boom mike in place. "Thanks for giving me that time. What'd they do to you."

"Nothing. There was too much pandemonium. Teller came crashing up here and fired out of the side window at you so I just reached out and flipped the throttles. I claimed Teller had pushed me into them when he pushed past me." He laughed. "You should have heard Horst when she realized Teller was trying to kill you. Boy I'm telling you, that woman really needs you bad to fly the 104."

"Yeah but you tell me for what?"

The island floated towards us. I let Phillip handle everything while I sat back and let the pain ease from my head. He ran through his checklist from memory without saying a word, leaving Alfonse to race about opening switches and setting controls without the protocol of a spoken checklist. Phillip enjoyed the game. Despite my lethargy and pain I kept an eye on the instrument panel to make sure Phillip's harassment didn't result in trouble for us in the flight. Once again I was as nervous as a passenger.

At Jenness, he lined the Herc up nicely on final for the strip with everything hanging out and dirty so the C-130 came down steeply and slowly. "This truck is going to need a month's over-haul if it ever gets back south," he said. "You should see the flow rate records I found. That Horst sure isn't used to flying heavy transport. It's a wonder she got into Iqaluit with half the systems set up wrong or not even turned on."

"Just another jet jockey."

"You think so too? Kinda makes you wonder why she isn't flying the jet instead of you."

"Yeah I keep wondering that too. I thought maybe it was because she really can't handle a 104, but that doesn't make sense because with the planning that went into this thing she would have had time to at least get checked out with the manuals. I mean, if you can fly a MIG, and I'm sure she can, then she can damn well fly a Starfighter. The thing is decades old and no trick pony for anybody with modern fighter experience and the operating manual."

The Hercules came down to flare height but the nose was not even over the end of the airstrip. Phillip was trying to touch down as close to the end as possible so a missed approach wouldn't mean kissing the top of the island in a go-around.

He pulled back on the yoke with both hands. "You know what I think." he said, his head turned slightly to the left to watch for the ground rise.

"Yes, yes I do." I tensed, waiting for the sink to the gravel. "One way trip."

He nodded and the Hercules hit the ground on both mains with a crash of scattering gravel and a blast of propwash.

No chances were taken with us this time. We were back in the round control room, kept barely above freezing by the heat of the electronic equipment and two portable heaters beamed at the back of the two radar operators. The dregs in our coffee cups, still on the console where Horst had outlined her plan to us, were still liquid.

The two guards we'd taken out in the corridor stood behind us pointing their weapons at our backs. One carried a two-inch wide strip of dressing down her right temple and cheek. She was the one I had caught with the conduit. The other had bandage over most of his jaw. They didn't speak and we weren't going to give them an opportunity to make up for letting us escape. We sat there in silence for a quarter of an hour before a large pot of vegetable soup was put on the console. We hadn't eaten since the night in the weather hut and then it had been just the survival rations from the Otter.

I was spoon fighting in the tureen with Phillip for the last of the soup when Horst stepped up on the dais and sat in the swivel chair. She spun around once to look over the radar screens, then to us. She steepled her fingers before her nose, looked at both of us and smiled. "You are both very dangerous men. You, Mr. Standish, are probably the most dangerous I have ever met. It is truly remarkable how you have let nothing stop you. There was a time when we would have been friends."

She was right. There was something about her that I couldn't dislike. She had a precision to her character. She lived by some internal ethical code that colored her personality. Her rigidity of speech, and the sense of controlled tension that came from her, spoke of a woman who wouldn't be anybody's servant.

"I don't have friends who go about kidnapping villages. Two so far isn't it? Or have you been laying waste in our absence?" I did not want to give an inch to her apparent mild and conciliatory manner. "No one I know murders, steals planes, and arranges political assassinations."

She paused for a moment before replying. She rarely ever seemed to blink and it unnerved me.

"Tell me. Would you kill me if it meant your escape from here?"

Although Horst was talking to me, Phillip nodded.

"Then there is little difference. I will kill for a different kind of freedom. I and the people I represent see a horror facing the world brought into life by opportunistic politicians paying lip service to ideology but selling out their people and the rest of the world for the sake of power. We want freedom from the coming nuclear holocaust. Killing is the only way to win that freedom and that is the way it will be. I argue that my actions are as legitimate as yours."

"My head hurts Horst so please let's pass on the philosophy.

Okay?"

Phillip leaned his arms on the ledge of the console and played with his spoon. He made snake tracks of soup across the plywood for a few seconds then spoke. "What the hell is this all for?" He raised the hand holding the spoon. His thumb was in the bowl of the spoon, the handle hidden in his clenched palm. The hand rose to eye height and the elbow went out slightly. It looked exactly right for a dagger throw. I glanced away from him so I wouldn't tip off Horst and got ready to move.

There was a harsh click of metal and the spoon dropped from his hand to clatter dully on the linoleum. The muzzle of an AK-47 pressed into the back of Phillip's head so forcefully that he was forced to lean forward onto the ledge. The second guard moved past me and swept the soup tureen and the other spoon onto the floor.

"Well it seems Mr. Tonguay is just as dangerous as you Mr. Standish," she continued without change of inflection.

"Philosophy is everything Mr. Standish. Philosophy dictates our lives and our deaths. Everyone, and I must say that most don't realize this, has a philosophy. The farmer works his fields in a year of drought and pest convinced his is the best of worlds. The office worker with mind numbed from the futility of the work, knows that there will never be a life of riches or escape from the mortgage and the children who won't come to heel under discipline. He lives to another philosophy that surrenders the spirit to an existence of unremitting uselessness. That philosophy dictates that there can be no change and no escape despite the dreams. The tragedy is that escape is available to that office drone the instant the personal philosophy changes to allow for it. Unfortunately, people are like leopards and cannot change. Outside events will change a person far more easily and surely than a person can change themselves."

"Look. If I have to listen to your rather naive views can I at least have a cigarette." I deliberately needled her. My irritation was pushed along too by my genuine need for nicotine. Any more of this odyssey back and forth across the Eastern Arctic at the point of a gun, I thought, and I would have to quit smoking out of the sheer impossibility of maintaining my habit. To my surprise, because the thought had never occurred to me before, I felt myself concluding that it really was a good idea to quit.

She motioned to someone in the gloom behind the radar screens and a flattened package with two Camels was lobbed over to me. It came so quickly I didn't recognize what it was and let it slap down past me to slide on the floor. Horst looked hard at the package and said sharply. "How many more of those are there?"

A short stammer from the gloom and a defensive voice. "Just a few packages ma'am. Really I'm sorry. They were packed by accident I think."

"Anyone else with American cigarettes or magazines, gum? Anything?" Her voice shot around the room leaving a silence that told of hidden supplies.

"You!" she shot at the defensive voice. "Go through every box and bag here. Search every square inch and gather up all of that material and destroy it. Every cigarette butt, every scrap of paper not allowed must be cleared up instantly." There was a rustle of Gore-Tex fabric as the man made his way around the room and left. The radar operators looked at each other.

"There is no time left. All must be ready when we leave."

Phillip chuckled deeply. "Nothing seems to go just right for you does it? Even your people can't help screwing things up."

She didn't reply directly to him. "You have one hour Mr. Standish to get ready to fly then I want you down on the ice and in that plane."

"On the ice?" It hadn't occurred to me she would use the ice as a runway for the Starfighter. I hadn't given the matter any thought at all yet it was obvious now that the only way to get the Starfighter into the air was to use the sea ice. The gravel airstrip was thousands of feet too short. "How the hell do you expect me to get a 104 off on ice? Planes like that need smooth concrete. Starfighters aren't bush planes you know."

She smiled. "Believe me it has been looked into. My people are finishing the preparations. You will find the ice sufficient. It is remarkable how smooth the ice is once the snow cover is removed."

"But ice for God's Sake. How much braking control do you expect me to have? One gust of wind and we'll be a fireball. It's spring too. All that weight concentrated on three wheels so blasted small -- why that beast weighs twelve tons at takeoff."

"The idea is not new. The use of ice airstrips for military aircraft has a long history in your country. It was you Canadians who developed the idea of floating bomber bases on icebergs in the second world war. Even now you bush pilots land routinely on ice."

I shook my head. Flying prop jets off an ice strip is old hat sure but I didn't think anyone would have seriously considered using ice for a supersonic fighter, especially a plane as murderous as the Starfighter. "There's a big difference Horst, between using ice that has been prepared with a wire grid braking surface and reinforced against fracture lines, and what you are talking about."

"The old Soviet Union," she said mildly and still with a smile, "flew Tupolovs off forward ice bases in the Barents Sea."

"Those Badger tests weren't done from the kind of ice you want to use. Those strips were prepared weeks ahead of time. They used, or should I say you people used, pumps to flood the surface with seawater and let it freeze. Those strips were built twelve, fifteen feet thick. This stuff might be five feet, I don't know."

"Precisely Captain. You yourself flew the necessary pumps here from Resolute. There is eight feet of new ice waiting for you. That is far more than necessary. I can't provide the metal grid but the surface is rough enough I am sure."

"What about the landing?" There was vehemence in Phillip's question.

"Oh gentlemen," she bared her teeth fully, the same way a wolf does just before it attacks, " there will be no landing."

It took my breath away. She was actually admitting that I had no chance of surviving. It didn't seem to make sense for her to admit it and run the risk of me refusing all threats to go. I got so angry I almost stood to throw myself across the console at her.

Before I could move she added, "It is unlikely that you would be able to land safely on the ice so the two of you will have to eject over the island and we will pick you up in the helicopter."

I did not like that idea either. Ejection, even in an emergency and in a warm climate, is not without a considerable risk. The thought of doing it in subzero weather, over a mountain island, was beyond considering. I turned around to look for Teller to see what reaction he might have to the idea of ejecting in these conditions.

"No Mr. Standish. There has been a change of plan. Mr. Tonguay will be going with you instead of Mr. Teller."

I was shocked, then puzzled. How could he make me do the intercept, I wondered, if his ace card hostage was out of his control and sitting in the Starfighter with me? I could be at Thule before the echoes of my afterburner stopped vibrating the wood frame walls of this control room. Phillip turned and rolled his eyes at me. I stared back at him and Horst continued.

"While you two were away from us it occurred to me that I would have a lot less trouble here on the ground from either of you if you were both in the air together. Naturally, you are now thinking that I would lose my hold over you. Well, not at all."

The radar operators had turned to listen better. "It's obvious that the only way to get you to do what I need Standish, is to have you at the point of instant death. Accordingly, an explosive device has been embedded in the plane."

She paused to let that sink in. "It is wired to the transponder

circuitry. You will be tracked from here and all your radio transmissions monitored. Should you deviate, I will detonate the
bomb. Remember Captain, the faintest suspicion that you are
attempting to take the plane away from the target, or that you are
trying to communicate with anyone else, will result in your
death. And that of Mr. Tonguay of course."

I pulled in a deep breath, let it out and lit another cigarette.
"Okay, I really don't have much more heart left. Just what is it
we're supposed to do?"

"As I told you. I want you to kill a man for me. The details will
be given before the takeoff. In the meantime I suggest you look
over the manual again." She threw the Lockheed binder down on
the ledge, knocking away the cigarette butt stood on end because
there was no ashtray, and left the room. I stared at the binder.

Phillip lowered his voice so the guards couldn't hear. "Well
Jack. What the hell are we supposed to do now?"

I didn't know. I felt like a white laboratory rat being run
through the maze time after time after time and knowing always
that there could never be a way out. We weren't going to live if
we didn't shoot down the Russian plane and we sure as hell
wouldn't live afterwards either, I was certain of that. Either Horst
would detonate the bomb or we would be forced to eject over
open water and freeze to death in less than three minutes. I
flipped the manual open at random and hit the ELINT section.

"Remember any of this stuff?"

He shook his head. "Seems to me you should be looking up
takeoff parameters, not this junk."

"Spose. Still, it's what the plane was designed for after all. We
must have had this memorized once."

"I'm more interested in you remembering how to fly it, not
messing around with the electronic intelligence gathering crap."

"One-way trip chum. Just keep holding onto that."

He paused for several seconds. "What's the difference Jack?
Buy it on the roll out or when she pushes the button."

"I'm ahead of you there. I can see that coming for sure. Look, do you figure you can use the radar?"

Phillip had never sat in the rear seat of a Starfighter and wasn't trained in radar intercept. We were pilots not radar navigators.

"I don't know. Why bother asking anyway? What's the point?"

"Just this. I don't know how she figures to vector us to the target or how far away from here the hit will be. I'll bet they'll give a long course and leave it to us to make the intercept contact with the 104's equipment."

"So?"

"There's a possibility you haven't thought of." I was just thinking of it myself for the first time.

"What possibility? We have none. This is a one-way trip in a bloody rocket and you're pretending we can survive. Get off it Jack!"

"No listen. The plane we're supposed to hit is carrying someone pretty important right? I think it's the Russian president returning from the summit in Los Angeles. Horst hasn't said any different although I can't figure out why they want to do away with their own man. It doesn't matter anyway. The point is this. There's gotta be an escort with that plane."

"Nah Jack. No way. Fighters can't fly escort on an airliner across the ocean."

"Super Hornets can." I saw the agreement in his eyes. The Boeing F-18E/F Super Hornet has an extraordinary ability to loiter at slow, slow for interceptors that is, speeds and cover vast distances.

"They'd send up tankers from Thule."

"And Gander, Iceland and Scotland." I added.

"There'd be Sukhoi Flankers or something like them when they got within Russian range." He was getting excited. "Those things will have live ammunition. The minute we show up on their scopes we're going to get hit."

"No not in peacetime. We'd have a couple of minutes while they try to figure out whether we're in their airspace by mistake. They'll waste time trying to get us on the radio. Of course, then they'll nail us to the sky."

"Well so what? What the hell difference is it going to make? We're dead meat if we go near them and just as dead if we try to get away"

I didn't answer because something was starting to bubble in the bottom of my brain and it needed time before I could make use of the idea. I turned back to the manual and looked up the takeoff and cruise data. I spent time trying to remember the feel of the beast, trying to remember how natural and comfortable it had once been to ride the rocket with a man in it as the reporters had once called it. But it was a wild and tricky beast that liked to eat pilots, so then they started calling it the widow-maker.

Some of the labels eluded me. RWR came back easily; Radar Warning Receiver, a device to let the pilot know when someone's radar is tracking. For sure that would be lit all the time Horst was painting me. PPI and AAA eluded me and after a while I gave it up and concentrated on engine settings and speeds. There did not seem to be any way of reabsorbing in one hour what had taken months of lectures and courses and hours in the simulator to learn.

That faint idea I'd had was starting to form, yet I still had no words to put to it. I had the feeling I would have to get close to that airliner by being a ghost. More, I thought, like trying to sneak blindfolded onto a stage and steal Yorrick's skull from Hamlet's hand without anyone seeing. You'd have to be either a ghost or, you had to find a way to cut the theater's house lights.

It all depended on Horst giving me the information I needed without suspecting. "Teller," I shouted across the room. "I need to talk to your boss right away. Tell her she's forgotten the escorts."

He looked at me for a moment then left the dais chair and walked out. Phillip grabbed my arm. "What the hell Jack?"

I didn't look at him. Instead I tapped the table of figures on the page of the manual headed, "ECM, Effective Distances." He didn't understand and I didn't want to say anything in case we were overheard. I lit the last cigarette and waited for Horst.

"All right what is this about?" Horst said the moment she entered the room.

"That plane will be escorted all the way across the continent and the Atlantic, first by American fighters then Russian."

"Yes I am aware of that."

"Well it will be impossible to intercept without detection. We'll be shot out of the sky before we get within thirty miles."

"Oh don't concern yourself with that."

"Why shouldn't I? I'm the one who'll get shot down. What's the point of sending me up if there's no way of getting at your precious airliner?" I put as much puzzlement as possible into my voice. "You've given me no choice but to fly the plane and now there's no way getting within shooting distance."

"The flight track comes within 150 nautical miles of here, south of the island. You have experienced our jamming capabilities. We have installed a much stronger version on Resolution Island. The airliner and its escort will fly into a circle of electronic darkness where their radar will work only poorly and over short distances. Their radios will not work at all. That will give you the chance you need. We'll vector you to their estimated position and you will track them visually."

"You could have told me this earlier you know."

"You would have been told before takeoff. Now I suggest you get ready. It's time to go."

On cue, far off down the hill, I heard the rising whine of a J79 engine. It rose into that hellish Banshee scream unique to Starfighters. It is a sound that never failed to chill the blood of any who heard it.

I could almost feel the slick polished yellow skull of poor Yorrick.

DOING THE CHECKLISTS

*T*he Bell 412 carried us down to the shore.

The newly made ice thickening the airstrip glowed deep blue against the white of the uncleared sea ice. The ice runway had been cleared for something like fifteen thousand feet; an incredible distance, even for a Starfighter. Horst had made sure it was well long enough for the Starfighter, and for some reason I couldn't work out, she'd also had it made wide enough for a 747. A yellow, tracked bulldozer rolled down the strip from the far end, its diesel exhaust leaving basketball sized puffs of black against the clear sky.

Once the helicopter's rotors stopped their keening and ran down to a stop, I heard the tractor's engine thud, thud, thud transmitted across the mile separating us. The light wind of the early afternoon was gone now. The sun was passing the western end of the strip where we stood. I looked down at my feet on the new-ice at the inch deep ruts scored by the bulldozer and understood about the braking.

The Starfighter crouched at the end of the runway, needle nose down and T-tail high. "Must have been a hell of job to get that down the island and assembled." Phillip said.

I didn't say anything. I walked to the fighter. The whiteout that had hit Iqaluit hadn't come this way. The snowbanks on the side of the strip were sun eroded. There was no sign of drifting. "I hope," I said as I reached the plane, "that they got it put together the right way round."

Phillip put out his hand to the leading edge of the port wing. He did it carefully because the guards were off and the edge was sharp enough to draw blood. The Starfighter has very little wing. Its maximum weight of almost twenty-nine thousand pounds is kept in the air by only twenty-one feet of wingspan and about a third of that is taken up by the width of the fuselage. The tiny wingspan is what gives the 104 its exceptional ability to accelerate and fly faster than anything else with the same power, even today decades after its front-line days.

That ridiculously short wingspan also makes it a dangerous plane to fly. It will lose altitude in an instant with too incautious a flight attitude.

I walked around the nose and along the wing giving close attention to the way the plane had been assembled by Horst's team.

But the team was much much larger than I thought. A white camouflaged tent had been erected as a hangar on the ice. There were at least two dozen technicians standing at its entrace watching us circle the Starfighter. They had been the ones to assemble and test the plane. I hoped they knew their jobs.

I didn't see any buckled metal or scars where wrenches and screwdrivers had been forced to make things fit instead of doing the job properly and safely, so I assumed that they did know what they were doing.

It had wing tanks of course. The internal tanks don't hold much and the J79 is a thirsty brute for kerosene. This one was fitted with under wing drop tanks as well. They slanted nose down in a way that always made me think a bolt had broken somewhere and the the tanks were about to fall off. Four slim sidewinders were racked under the wing, locks out. I reached out and idly spun one of the tailfin ratchet wheels thinking things through.

I came alongside the side and reached the orange painted ladder hooked on the canopy rail. I called to Phillip who was peering at the angle of attack sensor. "Coming up for a look?" I climbed the five or six steps and lowered myself into the front seat. After all the years it still had that Lockheed smell of plastic, grease, leather and fine machine oil. I breathed it in, trying to use it as some sort of time machine that would take me back to when I actually knew how to fly the thing.

The panel was different from the Starfighters I was used to. It had been heavily upgraded by NASA for its research program. I suspected that there had been a lot of changes to the engine and controls as well but I had no idea what they might have been. The Starfighter had always been a touchy beast to fly and the changes might well have turned it from a surly, aggressive bar drunk spoiling for a fight, into an out and out psychotic killer.

Some of the gauges were unknown to me. NASA had built so much sophistication into the instrument panel and around the sides of the cockpit that it made me think the thing could fly to the moon. Maybe that's what NASA had in mind.

The radar screen was smaller and the toggle boards were laid out differently but the stick was the same and the feel was the same. "What are your private vices lady?" I asked softly at the dead instruments. "How will you try to kill me, how do you like to be flown, where are your ticklish points lady?"

Every plane is different and I was vitally interested in how different this one might be. "If I roll too fast how nasty do you get? Are you a healthy lady or when one of your systems fail do others drop as well? Tell me Lady, tell me how you fly now before we find we cannot live together." Nothing, and nothing expected, yet the ritual satisfied. I had the feel of the seat and the stick and the view out of the canopy and it all felt good.

A light layer of frost dusted the cockpit. I was wearing a cotton flight suit, light gloves, a visor helmet, and flight boots that were a size slightly too large. I started to shiver and chatter with the cold.

Phillip climbed in behind me.

I closed my eyes and sought the feel of the plane. I needed the unconscious spread of my body through all fifty-nine feet of the beast so the plane became me and I became the plane. It wouldn't all come, but there was a nostalgia for the days at Baden Baden and the cold of early morning sorties in the fog of November over the industrial sprawl of West Germany.

The fuselage rocked. Horst came up the crew ladder. "All set Captain?" She slapped the top of my helmet.

"Are you going to tell me what we're up to now or do I just figure it out by myself?"

"We will vector as I have said to the target. There is an escort of three F-15's of the United States Airforce and an Aurora of the Canadian Air Force. The Aurora will turn south at Resolution Island. It may stay with the flight when they start having trouble with the radar, in any case it is not a threat to you. Your target is Air Force One."

"What! You said it was the Russian President!" And then the world turned in my head and things were quite different. "You want me to shoot down the President of the United States?"

"No, I did not say that and in any case it is not the president you are shooting down. The Presidents."

"They both on board? Are you trying to start a nuclear war?"

"We estimate there may be a limited exchange although that is doubtful. The real point is that by cutting down the leadership of both countries we will be creating a period of confusion.

In that confusion the people behind this operation will exert control to bring stability to the superpowers."

I was stunned. I took off my helmet to hear her better. "You telling me that there's a coup in the works here. That you are taking over both countries?"

"Don't look so surprised Mr. Standish. Military men on both sides have the same fear of death and look at problems in the same way. It became obvious some years ago on both sides that the politicians are out of control and the only safe way to rule the nuclear arsenal is to put it in the hands of people who would be the ones to use it. We won't be interfering with the internal governments. The replacements for the dead men will be allowed to govern as they see fit but never again will the politicians have control of the button."

"This is insane," Phillip shouted, "You'll have a nuclear war before the day is over. The whole world could be dead in two hours."

"Your concern is more immediate. You either shoot down the jet, believing my assurance that we control the bombs and at the very most there'll only be half a dozen loosed by commanders not in our control, or you die when I set off the bomb in this plane."

"But for God's sake Horst," I said, "Even if you succeed how long will it be before one part of your group thinks it can get total control. How long before there's another coup? Dammit, you military types only understand military power."

She was silent. We stared at each other for a moment before I added, "Just how did you know so far in advance that both presidents were going to be on the same plane? You've been planning this for months, obviously."

"It wasn't so much a matter of knowing as making. Who else has as much knowledge of what the leaders are up to than the advisers who tell them what to do? We engineered the summit in Los Angeles and our people on both sides steered things in the same direction. So it became inescapable to the two presidents at the end of their talks that they had an arms agreement. What more natural thing to do than to fly in harmony together to Geneva to announce it to the world?"

"If you have that much access then why couldn't you have poisoned their soup or something?" I asked wildly.

"Because Captain, it must happen in such a way that both sides blame each other for a period of time to allow our people to take total control. There are a great many people on both sides who are not part of our organization and they must be thrown into disarray for a time."

"I've got it." Phillip said. "That's why we're flying an American jet, but all of you are acting like Russians. That's why a Russian sub was at the island so there'd be a satellite surveillance record of it."

"And," I added, "That's why the cleanup of American material in your control room but the use of so much American technology. You probably laid a trail a mile wide of American and Russian clues so no one will know for sure which side was behind it."

"Exactly Standish. No one will be sure of who was behind the killing and because they can't be sure there will be no military action until it is too late and we will be in control."

"But it's all screwed-up isn't it? You had to kidnap us because you lost your own pilot and you almost lost us."

Her sunglasses slipped slightly. She pushed them back with a sharp jab on the bridge. "Yes there were major problems I'll admit. Fortunately the delays you caused me could be made up for by arranging delays in the talks. Had you escaped I would have had to fly this myself, and quite honestly I am not sure I could even get it off the ice. I am glad I don't have to fly it."

"Now. Gentlemen. I want you to start flying. Remember that if you disrupt this operation in any way that bomb will go off. Remember this too that if you carry out your orders you will be making the world safer than it has been since the invention of the first atomic bomb." She jumped down from the ladder and the ground power unit deepened its roar. The ammeter flicked over on the panel and the Starfighter came to life.

Phillip opened his microphone. "Jack we can't do it. I don't particularly want to die, but I also don't want to be responsible for a so-called limited exchange. God, that could mean a couple of million dead." There was fear in his voice.

There was just as much in mine. "Phillip there's no choice. I don't want to die either."

Then I told him about Yorrick's skull and the ghost.

JET BLACK OCEAN

*T*he power needles all came up.

Slowly, for it had been a long time, we went through the checklist. Out of remembered habit I pulled the red flagged pin and held it above my head to show that my ejection seat was armed.

With a whomp and a slight push in my back, the turbine started and began to whine. Exhaust temperature started rising and the power went to sixty percent. We were live. I closed the canopy.

Phillip's voice, stripped of all the low tones, came through my headset. "You know, I've never been in the backseat before. You wouldn't want to trade would you?"

I shook my head. "It's been a long time, but if I keep remembering that this is not a Twin Otter, we just might get off the ground."

"Ah, but do you have any idea how we're going to get back down?"

I didn't answer, because I had no answer.

We had a full fuel load with the wing tanks, perhaps, in theory, enough for about 900 nautical miles. One way. Of course, if we ran on full afterburner for any time at all, particularly at low level, the fuel consumption would skyrocket and we'd go nowhere. It would feel as though the bottoms of the fuel tanks had rusted away.

"Checks done. If you're ready we'll roll." I said.

"Roger. Jenness base just checked in." Phillip was handling the contact with the control room.

I pushed forward, and then to the side to open the throttle against the brakes. Full military power bellowed behind me. I wanted that roaring power because I didn't want to stay on the ice a second longer than necessary. I had more faith in my ability to fly than in keeping the beast rolling straight on the icestrip.

Brakes off. The nose dipped slightly. We moved forward with a shove in the back.

Everything green. The noise building, ground moving faster and faster, then "Whooom," a violent kick as the afterburner lights and the speed on the ASI jumped. Vibration from the ice surface and a tremor on the rudder pedals.

I see the red flags planted to the side of the ice. No problem with handling and thank you God for no winds. The blast from the tail pipe melting the ice in our passage.

All five engine gauges still green although the speed is building so quickly I am having trouble keeping ahead of the plane. I must remember what to do. No line speed indicator at the side of the airstrip to tell me. I glance at the ASI. 168 knots! And as I am looking at it, the needle goes to 170. "Rotate!" That's Phillip in my ear. I have a great desire to snarl at him yet his call triggers my hand and I gently pull back on the stick using only my fingertips. The nose rises and I lose forward visibility. The Starfighter is on her mains now and the airflow is tightening between the slab wings and the ground. A final bump from the ice and the ground disappears. I keep pulling the stick back in a losing race to control the speed and we're shooting up. Full afterburner is running away with the plane and I can't catch up.

God the gear! 270 knots and it's still down. My hand flashes and the gear tucks away. The speed screams higher still.

I feel like I'm on my back in a rocket. Do the astronauts feel this out of control rush to the sky when they blast off? The shock wave diamonds of the AB must be thudding into the ice far below. How far? My Lord, 14 thousand feet and climbing at, what? How fast am I climbing? I can't read the VSI properly; either it's not working or I am looking at something else.

Keeping back on the stick and staying subsonic, passing thirty-thousand feet and now time to ease out of the afterburner.

I feel the difference as my body eases forward into the seat harness straps.

The fuel flow gauges show the difference. The gauge needles slump to calmer levels. The acceleration ends and I aim to level out of 35 thousand but it passes and I settle for 38 thousand.

Then the world quiets and I hear the harsh rush of oxygen through my mask and feel the sweat down my back. "What's the course?" I asked Phillip as I tried to bring some order to the cockpit.

He came back instantly. "183 degrees, present heading 97 degrees."

Somehow I had wandered ninety degrees from the takeoff heading and it did not surprise me. It had seemed as though my flying had amounted to little more than just hanging on while the rocket took me into near earth orbit. I looked at the gyrocompass and turned to the heading marked by the little white bug I'd set earlier on the dial.

"Not a bad takeoff for someone over the hill." Phillip sounded relieved.

"You forget how wild these things are." I said.

I tried to recall how the 104 handled at this altitude and failed. I thought I'd try a steep bank s-turn to get her feel.

Blam! The world exploded and came back together again.

"Christ Jack warn me next time."

"Sorry." I gasped for breath. "I just wanted to try a turn or two. This horror is really sensitive." All I'd done was push the stick to what in a normal plane would be a steep bank and this one just snapped right around inverted.

I tried the turns again, but this time only tickling the stick and getting the feel back. The next turns were civilized but I could feel how close this plane always was to killing me.

"Coming up to 183 again. Now!"

"Thanks." I locked on and tried to get a sense of where we were. The world below was flat white except the ocean which was jet black. We shot on at Mach 0.8. "Are they vectoring us?"

"Yeah and I've got the target on the scope. Four blips. Thirty nautical miles. Scopes clear."

"Four eh? The Aurora must have gone home. Just us, the Strike Eagles, and Air Force One. You know, I really do not like the idea of taking on those fighters."

"You and me both but how far do you think we'll get before she blows us up?"

"We're thirty miles from the coast."

"Thirty feet would be too far if we landed in the water."

Then I saw them. "Contrails 12 o'clock high." The furry white threads traced across the blackening blue of the sky in front of us.

"I have a challenge IFFI," then, "No, no it's gone. I guess that jamming of Horst's is doing its work."

I reached over to the breaker panels and shut down the power to the radios. I left the attack radar and intercom alone. I couldn't see how they would hurt.

The fuel was holding well so I went to afterburner and climbed to 40 thousand feet up-sun of the 747 and the escort. "I have them visual." I called. I was about to add more when the picture changed in my mind. It didn't look right to me.

The green mottle of the F-15 camouflage leaped toward us as we came in on the intercept.

The big transport sat fat and slow below us against the black of the sea. And then my mind finally shifted and I stopped seeing what I had been expecting to see and instead saw what was really there.

"Phillip that's not a 747. For God's sake, it's a B-52." It was the H model with the streamlined housings under the nose that looked like witch's warts.

"That's not Air Force One," he said. "It's a bomber. What the hell's it doing here?"

"I don't know but we're in deep trouble now. That thing is as deadly as the F-15's." It bristled with guns and slim white air-to-air missiles. The Strike Eagles were racked to the full war load.

I pushed the nose down and started a turn to get away from the high cover Strike Eagle that had picked us up and was now turning like a shark to feed. Our model of Starfighter was limited to Mach 1.8 because of the twin canopy. At that speed the fuselage and the airfoil shape of the canopy provides too much lift. You compensate with a negative angle of attack and that would be all right except the fuel tanks can't take that kind of stress. I remembered the limitation as we dived, but forgot how quickly the Starfighter picks up speed. Before I could react, we were way out beyond the flight envelope.

We dropped almost straight down and I pulled six and a half G's before I got her out. The 104 slashed back up to the B-52 in a zoom climb. I didn't plan that either. The fighters were far away at the bottom of their dives. The first one was just coming up and casting about for me. Someone was going to get hell, I thought, for being suckered away from the bomber instead of staying close. One of the fighters should have stayed behind instead of joining the other two in the chase.

The Stratofortress filled the sky above us and we shot up at its belly, a perfect gun target.

It covered the sky. Eight Pratt and Whitney jet engines dangling under 185 feet of wing. Four-thousand square feet of wing and we were looking up at it through the canopy less than fifteen feet away. I levelled the Starfighter and sat there under the wing looking at the white nuclear blast paint and watching the aluminum ripple as the spars flexed to the flight load. The pilots either hadn't seen us come up under them or they were scared of making a move and colliding with us. One twitch and we'd mate in fire.

"Jack. I think we're a ghost. This is a two-blip spot."

"Well it's what we wanted isn't it? Mind you I didn't plan to do it this way. These guys are mad as hell at us. But, they can't get at us without hitting the bomber."

We were where I wanted to be, in a two-blip spot. On Horst's screens all she'd see would be one target instead of two. I didn't fear the bomb anymore. When she'd told me about the jamming equipment on Resolution Island, she had all but admitted to me that she had no control over the bomb either.

The jamming stopped all radio transmissions including the one that would set-off the bomb. But now, I had three war armed Strike Eagles after me and I was sitting under a bomber that could disintegrate the Starfighter with just one of its rapid fire guns. But we were tucked in so close to the B-52 that they couldn't fire without hitting it.

The long box fuselage seemed to stretch and taper the same way that railroad tracks on a prairie disappear in the distance. I crept up the port side, feeling carefully for the buffet that would be sliding down from the mainplane. If it hit my T-tail, we could pitch up uncontrollably and spear the wing. Ahead, the ugly sprouting of ECM antennas and sensors marred the easy sweep of the nose up and around. Eight, hand long, stub antennas stuck out from under the chin of the bulb nose like the start of a beard. The twin boat-shaped pods, one holding the LLTV camera and the other containing the FLIR infra-red detector, swelled out in heavy, smooth mounds.

They really did look like witches warts.

I watched the nacelle containing both the number-three and number-four engines, judging just where we were. When I was sure, I eased down a bit and slid our tailplane back into its shelter. There was a regular chopping thud as we rode in the turbulent air shoved aside by the massive fuselage. I concentrated on holding my spot under the wing exactly. Sometimes the airframe buffet got rougher and a slight trembling would work through the 104, letting me know we were verging on stall speed. The Starfighter is very sensitive to attitude changes and the B-52 pilots could drop us straight out of the sky by any sharp movement, or even slowing just five knots. A stall in the Starfighter, when all the lift has gone from the wings, could take six miles of height to recover from, and that would about put us into the ocean.

I counted on the fact that the pilots were far too young to know anything about the Starfighter and wouldn't know just how sensitive it was to speed upset.

"Now what are you going to do?" Phillip either chuckled or gasped into his mask, I couldn't tell.

"I'm not too sure. But for a while anyway we're safe from those fighters." I watched one of them riding off the port wing and about a hundred feet below us. Another I could see off on the starboard wing of the 52. The third would be sitting high over the tail and ready to drop down on us if we tried to dive out from under. I could imagine every gun and rocket armed and set to fire. They couldn't fire as long as we stayed tucked under the wing.

The bomber's pilots must have been going crazy trying to see us. There were no ports in the belly. The cockpit windows were too far around the curve of the hull to allow the pilot to do more than catch a glimpse from time to time of a wing tip or the pitot probe sticking out of the Starfighter's nose.

"What the hell is a 52 doing here?" Phillip said.

I didn't know. "Phillip I'm getting a little anxious about things.

Something has gone wrong and I don't know how much longer we can keep this up. These things weren't supposed to be here. They'll either get us out of here or we'll run out of fuel," I looked at the fuel load and did sums in my head. Less than half an hour left in the air at the present rate of flow. "Look we don't have any choice. Drop the sidewinders. It'll save fuel."

"Uh no Jack. Not unless you want to back away a bit first." He was right. I looked at the wing above us. The loss of drag and weight would send the Starfighter bouncing up into the Stratofortress.

"Then we really are in trouble because we're getting low on fuel and if I back away those guys are going to cut loose."

He didn't answer.

The west coast of Greenland was well in sight as the B-52 continued its course. I estimated the mountains were just a hundred miles away and closing. We'd been in the air slightly more than 35 minutes and already the world was darkening. The sky past the mountains shaded down from light blue to black and then the shocking white glare from the Greenland ice cap that would show even in full night.

Phillip said, "Jack we have to try to get them on the radio."

"No, no way. I don't want to turn that radio on."

"Why not for God's Sake? We can't stay under here forever you know." He was shouting at me.

I pulled hard on the oxygen, held it in for ten seconds and let it out. I thought my voice quivered. "All right. Try to find their frequency." I punched the radio's circuit breakers back into their slots and prayed hard.

Two minutes passed while I played the balancing act to keep us under the flexing wing of the giant. All the time, my left hand was going forward and back on the throttle to keep station. The 104 is such a clean airplane that the slightest change in attitude sends the airspeed climbing or falling and formation flying needs gross amounts of throttle. It wasn't helping the fuel flow problem at all. My hamfisted attempts at formation flying made things worse too. The Starfighter's bobs and weaves must have been giving the F-15 pilots palpitations. Sweat dripped into my eyes stinging them until tears began to run. The cockpit was too hot but I couldn't take my eyes off the B-52 long enough to find the air-conditioning controls. I sweated more.

At last, a click in my ear as he opened his mike. "No. I can't find their frequency over the hash from the ECM."

I was startled. "Theirs, or do you mean Horst's?"

"I don't know. It's been so long since I've touched this stuff I barely can make it work at all. I'd guess we're sitting in both, with theirs blasting everything away. In fact, I'm not so sure we should be this close to all that microwave. The stuff from the island is blanked right out. Must be because of that they have their stuff going so strong. They must be more worried about a missile from there than trying to talk to us. Can't do both anyway."

Greenland came closer. The icecap yellowed with the fading sun. The sea had disappeared and we were over a depthless nothing. I counted on two things; that the B-52' s electronic counter measures had enough range to cover me, and that the Starfighter still had the edge on any other plane when in full panic afterburner dive.

"If you ever wanted to see Greenland again here's your chance," I shouted and I shoved the throttle and the stick forward together.

"Phillip drop the rockets!" And they tumbled free to fall to the sea.

We were supersonic in seconds under the combined effects of gravity and the afterburner. I was pressed hard back into the seat.

I pulled straight back on the throttle with a fast slam before our speed got too dangerous. I had no idea whether the Strike Eagles were close or not. The coast shot toward us and I started a five G pullout that didn't end until we were three-hundred feet off the water. I sweated yet more from the fear of a shock stall that would send us instantly into the water.

An F-15 caught up and passed us in a tight pull up, wings streaming with condensation fog. He got so close to the water that his slipstream left a streak of torn foam.

I dropped lower in an attempt to hide in the murk. No missiles fired—yet.

I punched afterburner again and the flow rate went back up to thousands of pounds an hour. Then the coast and another hard pull up to clear the rocks and finally the hills of coastal Greenland, black in the full night.

"Sondrestrom 11 o'clock." Phillip called.

I swung the nose between two hills and headed for the lights of the town. "We're going to have to jump." I couldn't have landed even if there had been a decent landing strip. The Starfighter was about out of fuel, too low for an approach, and I couldn't have made a night landing in that missile anyway after all the years away from flying it.

The Sondrestrom Air Base was built during the Second World War to accommodate the vast fleets of bombers and transports that were flown from North America to the war front. It was long enough for the Starfighter but it is a one way strip and it is surrounded by hugely high mountains, hills and cliffs. Nasty at the best of times for a modern and slower aircraft, instant suicide in a plunging dart of plane like the Starfighter.

"Get ready." As I said that, there was a surge of deceleration and the power dropped back through 80, 60 then 50 percent as the turbine ran down. Eight tons of very poor glider started to fall toward the ground.

In theory, a Starfighter has a three to one glide ratio although you'd be hard pressed to ever meet a 104 pilot who's tested the theory. For every thousand feet of altitude it loses in a glide the plane is supposed to travel forward three thousand, if everything is set properly. We weren't set at all. The flaps were in and we went down like a waxed brick, a very well waxed brick.

I heard the blast of Phillip's seat going up. I pulled my ejection lever an instant later.

We came down a hundred yards apart in the same ravine. The screams of Strike Eagles tight turning over our heads smashed out at the rocks and built massively in the ravine. It hurt my ears and I feared for my eardrums.

I saw wing flashes for a moment then they were gone.

A far overhead and thin roar came down on us as the B-52 went overhead unseen in the dark. A faint smell of hot jet fuel drifted down the ravine. I supposed it was from the wrecked Starfighter.

Phillip dropped his chute harness from his shoulders, the steel buckles ringing against the rock. Our dragging chutes shined faintly in the night like two huge rotting mushrooms. "There's no snow here." He said.

I didn't know what to say. The peace of the night after the events of the past hour, and of the past days filled me like a fine wine. I wished for a cigarette.

"You took a hell of a chance," he continued. "They could have shot us down or the bomb could have gone up."

"Yeah, I suppose it was a hell of a chance. The bomb didn't worry me as much as those fighters though. As soon as you mentioned their ECM was so powerful that it blanked everything, I figured it might have enough range to cover us from Horst's bomb signal while we came down.

And I guess I was right.

But still, those buggers could have shot us down with a missile and I don't understand why they didn't."

SOMETHING ELSE ALTOGETHER

e found out the next morning when the US Air Force Helicopter landed at the local police lockup where we'd spent the night under guard on military orders.

Two men in civilian parkas got out followed by three other civilians carrying weapons, not so much at the ready as just in that negligent half carry way that combat seasoned troops develop.

The two civilians spoke briefly with the police superintendent at the foot of the wooden steps to the police station. We watched through the glass front doors. A constable, or its equivalent in the Greenlandic constabulary, watched us. We'd been well treated. While we weren't under arrest, the superintendent had made it clear when we had been brought into the station that we shouldn't think about going anywhere until there were some answers.

The superintendent gave the new arrivals his office and left us with them.

"Mr. Standish and Mr. Tonquay," the taller of the two said, opening a canvas shoulder bag and removing an Olympus hand-held voice recorder. "What I want to talk to you about will remain secret. You will not be allowed to repeat this conversation as long as the general order remains in effect." He turned on the voice recorder.

I glanced at it. "And how can you make me?"

"We can't. But only if you agree to keep this quiet can we fill you in on what happened and give you proper thanks. Thanks from the President I add."

Phillip and I looked at each other.

There was no expression in the agent's face. I think they practice that.

"Okay. We agree."

"Fine. Excellent," he smiled and waved us to the two folding metal chairs in front of the superintendent's desk. His partner moved to the door, stood quiet for a moment as if trying to listen through it, then stood with his back to it. "First thing is, my name is George Palas and as you might suspect I work with the Central Intelligence Agency."

I thought of asking to see his badge out of sheer bloody mindedness then decided that I'd had enough sparring for a while. "Got a cigarette George?"

He shook his head. I turned around to his partner and got the same answer. I sighed. It was getting harder and harder to stay a smoker in a non-smoking world. It really was becoming clear to me that life would become a lot less stressful by tossing the cigarettes.

"Mr. Standish, the President of the United States asked me personally to pass on his deepest thanks for what you and Mr. Tonquay have accomplished. It is no exaggeration that you two are solely responsible for averting a horrible crisis that would have left millions dead.

We have known for some time of the existence of a plot to take over both governments. But we and our Russian colleagues were unable to uncover its leaders. Neither did we suspect the attempt on the lives of the two leaders. We were aware of the woman you know as Aeva Horst and that she had lately dropped from sight. We did not know that she was heading an operation in the Canadian Arctic."

"So what made you switch Air Force One for the B-52?"

"Your video message. It was sent by your friend. After a delay while we and the Canadians tried to confirm it, things began to happen. Once we knew that Iqaluit was cut off, we could believe it. And once the contents of the message got to the right level where there were people who knew of the military plot, things happened quickly."

Phillip asked, "Why send the planes at all?"

"Because, we needed time to get a strike force into the Arctic to hit their island base. If we had postponed the supposed presidential flight there would have been suspicions and Horst's people might have pulled out." He looked at me without blinking for a long moment. "And if they had suspicions they would have killed the two of you."

"We damn near got killed anyway." I said. "Those F-15's were war-loaded."

"No Mr. Standish. They were there to protect you. If there hadn't been so much electronic interference you would have been able to talk to the crews and find that out. I understand by the way from the flight leader that you did a remarkable job of outrunning his planes. You must be quite a pilot."

"Quite an idiot you mean!" Phillip's barking laugh seemed to fill the building. "It wasn't interference that stopped your guys talking to us. Quite a pilot here had the radios off."

I felt hot blood flood into my face. "I thought maybe Horst had used the radio circuitry as part of the bomb trigger," I said. "I figured that maybe she didn't have enough time to build a separate radio receiver into the plane for the bomb and had simply hooked it into the radio."

Phillip smirked, "And when he did turn it on we were too close to the bomber and its electronics were blanketing us."

"So what about after you got away to the coast?" George Palas had a puzzled look on his face.

I cleared my throat, shifted in the chair to half turn away and wished helplessly for a cigarette. "I turned them off again. I thought we'd be exposed to Horst's triggering transmission."

Palas snapped the recorder off. "Well, I don't think we need to second guess." He got to his feet. "If you two would care for a ride, I'm headed to the island. If she hasn't disappeared I'd imagine you'd like to see Horst and her fellows in different circumstances."

"Wait a minute," I said.

"What about Bylot Island? Isn't that part of this story? Were those game wardens and guards more of Horst's people?"

"No," Palas said, "Bylot Island is something else altogether different, and as dangerous as this affair."

"Like what?" Phillip said.

Palas waited a few long moments, then seemed to make up his mind. "It is something we are hoping that you and Mr. Standish can take a quiet look at for us."

"Flying spies huh?" I grinned. "A boy's adventure."

I caught Phillip's eye. "Sure, we can do that, but we are going to need a plane and new jobs because I think ours have disappeared."

Palas nodded, and we were done.

ABOUT THE AUTHOR

Rick Grant is a pilot, as well as journalist and consultant, with years of experience throughout the Circumpolar Arctic.

He is a British and Canadian citizen with many years of experience as a correspondent and producer in Television and Radio

For the past several years he has worked as a consultant to international aid groups and military commands, such as the U.N. and NATO, in most of the world's war zones and humanitarian disasters.

Rick Grant can be contacted through
www.rickgrantwriter.com

THERE'S MORE . . .

There is an occasional newsletter (never more than once a month and frequently more rarely) that will let you know what Rick Grant is working on.

Subscribers will get access to early editions of new books in advance of publication.

You can also opt to become an early reader for novels that are still in progress.

You can sign up for the newsletter here

www.rickgrantwriter.com

DEDICATION

For Catherine McClelland, my closest and dearest companion. She tethers me to her reality and I deeply appreciate the love.

To Major James Bigglesworth, and Captain W E Johns, who opened the skies for me as a pilot, writer, and adventurer

www.ingramcontent.com/pod-product-compliance
Lightning Source LLC
Chambersburg PA
CBHW050026180626
46810CB00002B/590